Too Darn Hot

**Center Point
Large Print**

**This Large Print Book carries the
Seal of Approval of N.A.V.H.**

Too Darn Hot

SANDRA SCOPPETTONE

CENTER POINT PUBLISHING
THORNDIKE, MAINE

This Center Point Large Print edition
is published in the year 2006 by arrangement with
Ballantine Books, an imprint of The Random House
Publishing Group, a division of Random House, Inc.

The text of this Large Print edition is unabridged. In other
aspects, this book may vary from the original edition.
Printed in the United States of America.
Set in 16-point Times New Roman type.

ISBN 1-58547-789-3

Library of Congress Cataloging-in-Publication Data

Scoppettone, Sandra.
    Too darn hot / Sandra Scoppettone.--Center Point large print ed.
       p. cm.
    ISBN 1-58547-789-3 (lib. bdg. : alk. paper)
    1. Women private investigators--New York (State)--New York--Fiction. 2. World War,
1939-1945--New York (State)--New York--Fiction. 3. Missing persons--Fiction. 4. New York
(N.Y.)--Fiction. 5. Large type books. I. Title.

PS3569.C586T66 2006b
813'.54--dc22

                                                                    2006003310

For Linda

"If there's anything I don't like,
it's a smart-cracking dame."

—JACK PALANCE, in *Panic in the Streets*

Too Darn Hot

ONE

*Y*eah, it was hot enough to fry an egg on the sidewalk. I never could understand why people said that. Did somebody fry one then eat it? Who'd wanna eat a fried egg from the sidewalk? Especially in a city like New York. Maybe I'd try it. Not the eating part, the frying. But then people would think I was more of a screwball than they did already.

Nah. That wasn't true. Nobody thought I was loose in the upper story. It's just that most people didn't understand why a dame like me would wanna be a PI. And it wasn't that I set out to be. It's just the way it turned out.

In 1940 Woody Mason hired me as a secretary for his A Detective Agency. He was a PI. But then in '41, when the Nips hit Pearl Harbor, Woody felt he should do his duty for his country and left me to run the agency. That was two years ago and the war still wasn't over.

The office is on Forty-third Street between Seventh and Eighth. A few months ago the agency moved one flight up so now I had my own office and a proper waiting room where my secretary, Birdie Ritter, sat.

I'd had two murders since last spring, solved them both. The first one was prime and it got a lotta attention in the fish wrappers, so I had a bunch of clients for a while. Just cause people saw my name in the paper they figured I was the best (which I might be) and they hired me for everything from finding a dog to solving another murder. Not bad for a twenty-six-year-old gal from Newark, New Jersey.

Even though the rush was over my dance card was full at the moment, so when Birdie knocked on my door and said I had a possible client in the outer office, I wasn't overjoyed.

"Guy or gal?"

"Gal. She's cryin, Faye."

"They're always cryin."

"Ah, don't be a tough tootsie with me. I got yer number, ya know."

And she did. Always. Birdie kept me honest, like they say. She was the cat's whiskers, far as I was concerned. And she was also whistle bait, a tall blonde with brown eyes that screamed *Come get me,* even though she wasn't that kinda girl.

"So what's her can a peas?" I asked.

"She didn't gimme particulars. I could hardly make out what she was sayin through the waterworks. Somethin about a guy."

"What else would it be?"

"Yeah. So will ya see her?"

"Ya know I will. What's her moniker?"

"Claire Turner. Least I think that's what she said."

"Okay, bring her in."

"Will do."

"Bird?"

"Yeah?"

12

"That dress yer wearin is easy on the eyes. New?"

She smiled. "Yeah. Pete bought it for me."

Pete. "I thought ya were gonna dump the bum."

"I tried, Faye. We had a lollapalooza the other night and when we made up, Pete came round with this getup. What could a girl do?"

"Well, it suits ya to a *T*." And it did, with the colorful butterflies on white cotton and a diamond cutout below the neck.

"Thanks. I better get the jane waitin out there before she floods the office."

Birdie and Pete'd been on and off since I'd known her, which wasn't that long, come to think of it. But she'd told me they'd been seeing each other for a few years and it was always a battle. Pete wanted to get married and Birdie didn't, which was the source of most of their rhubarbs.

In a mo she was back with Claire Turner.

You got yer lookers and you got yer lookers. This Turner broad was the real thing. She was a long drink of water, maybe five feet nine inches. I knew being just shy of five four sometimes gave me a skewed slant on height, but this was one tall cookie.

Her hair was black and wavy, flowing down to her shoulders, and the ends blew a little from the standing fan I had going. She had a body that looked to have perfect measurements and it was wrapped in a white suit, short padded jacket with a pink blouse underneath.

Her eyes were almond-shaped and that shade of blue

close to lavender. Also they were slightly pink from crying. She had full lips painted ruby red. And when she spoke one dimple creased her right cheek. I pegged her to be about twenty-two or -three.

"Miss Quick?"

"Yeah." I stood up and held out my hand.

She took it and gave it a fast squeeze like she might get typhoid if she held it too long. Broads didn't go in much for handshaking. But I did it anyway cause it always got them a little off kilter.

"Miss Turner, is it?"

"Yes. Claire Turner." Her voice was husky.

"Please have a seat, Miss Turner."

She took the green leather chair in front of my desk. Since my fortunes had risen and we'd moved, I'd done some decorating to make the agency look more like a real office instead of a toy to go with the trains under a Christmas tree.

She opened her white pocketbook and took out a pack of white Lucky Strikes, cause Lucky Strike green had gone to war. I didn't know what the green was doing over there, but that was the deal. While she fussed with them I got a Camel from my pack and was ready with a match when she put the cig between her lips.

"What can I do for ya, Miss Turner?"

"I'm not sure anyone can do anything for me," she said.

If I had a nickel for every potential client who said something like that I'd be one rich girl. Why did they

14

come here if that's what they thought? "Tell me what's on yer mind and we'll see what I can do."

"It's my boyfriend. He's disappeared."

How unusual, I thought. Then I told myself I was getting much too cynical.

"Go on."

"I've been to the police, but they don't pay any attention to what I have to say."

"Well, I'm gonna pay attention so tell me every-thing. Let's start with his name."

"Charlie Ladd. Private Charlie Ladd."

"He's in the army?"

"Yeah."

I put my finger inside the roll at the bottom of my hair and gave it a little flip. "So when ya say *disap-peared,* ya don't mean he's missin in action, do ya?"

"Oh, no. He was here on leave for a week. He arrived on Saturday. We saw each other the first three nights."

"What happened on the fourth night?"

"He didn't show up."

"Show up where?"

"At my apartment."

"You live alone?"

"Yeah."

"And where's that?"

"West Sixty-first Street."

"You work, Miss Turner?"

"I should be at work now but the boss gave me an hour."

"Whaddya do?"

"I'm a salesgirl at Wanamaker's."

There wouldn't be a lotta money coming my way, but sometimes that didn't matter.

"So ya had a date for Tuesday night and he was supposed to pick ya up at yer place and didn't call. Just didn't show. Right?"

"Right."

"What'd ya do about it?"

"I phoned his hotel but he wasn't in."

"What hotel's that?"

"The Commodore."

I knew that lotsa the soldiers and sailors stayed there. You couldn't beat six clams a night to be right on Forty-second Street. I made a note of the hotel.

"He ever stand ya up before?"

She sat straighter in the chair. "He didn't stand me up, Miss Quick. And no, he's *never* stood me up."

"What'd ya do yesterday?"

"Same thing. I kept phonin and he kept not bein there."

"So what happened to him?"

"That's what I wanna know. That's what I want you to find out. Why do you think I'm here?"

"I gotta ask a lotta questions that sound dumb, Miss Turner. Bear with me, okay?"

"Sorry. I didn't mean to get on my high horse."

"So ya haven't heard from him since Monday night, right?"

"That's right."

16

"Did ya call anybody? Any of his friends?"

"He's from Rhode Island. He doesn't have friends here."

"Not even buddies he was on leave with?"

"Well, yes. I thought you meant civilian friends."

"So who's he on leave with?"

"I can't remember his name."

"Just one?"

"Lemme think. David. Yeah. He was named David."

"David who?"

"I didn't pay attention to the name."

"Do ya know Charlie's family?"

"No. He said he'd introduce me when the war was over." She looked like someone had taken the shine off her.

"Where'd ya say he's from?"

"Rhode Island."

"Did ya think he mighta gone home to his family?"

"Why would he do that without tellin me?"

"Have ya called his parents?"

"No. I couldn't do that. I told you, I don't know em. Besides, it'd look desperate, if you know what I mean." She killed her cigarette in the glass ashtray on her side of the desk.

"And he's got no friends in this area."

"Well, one."

I gave her a look and she knew what it meant.

"I forgot about him before. I never met him."

"And?"

"Charlie told me they'd gone to Franklin and Marshall College together. Best friends in school."

"What's his name?"

"George Cummings."

"He in the service?"

"No."

"Why not?"

"I don't know."

"Did ya call him?"

"No."

"Ya got a problem usin the Ameche, Miss Turner?"

"The what?"

"The phone. Don Ameche played Alexander Graham Bell as in *The Story Of.*"

"I never heard that one."

"Wanna give me his phone number?"

"Don't you mean his Ameche number?" She giggled and put her hand over her ruby lips.

I decided to play. "Okay. Wanna give me his Ameche number?"

"I can't. I don't have it."

I made a note to get the number. "Where's he live?"

"I don't know."

"He live in the city?"

"I don't think so. I mean, I would've met him if he did. On the other hand, Charlie always wanted to be alone with me."

"And Charlie never said where his best friend lives?"

"No. Why would he? We didn't spend a lotta time talkin about his pals, Miss Quick."

"Right. How about his parents' address and phone number? I guess ya don't have them, either."

"That's right. I don't. There was never a reason for me to have their Ameche number." She smiled like a little girl, proud she'd learned a new word.

"What about *your* Ameche number. Ya know that, don't ya? And yer address." I wrote it all down.

"How'd ya meet him?"

She lit another cigarette, tilted back her head, and blew out a smoke stream. "It's gonna sound bad and I'm sure you'll think I'm awful." She blushed.

"Try me."

"I had a date with another fella, Van Widmark, and we were meetin at the Biltmore, under the clock. Van was late. I was standin there and I guess I looked put out. At least that's what Charlie said." Her eyes flashed at the mention of this memory. "Charlie came over to me. He was very polite. He asked me if I needed any assistance."

"Assistance?" I squashed my cig.

"He thought I might be stranded. I told him I was waitin for my date who was a captain in the marines. And then I asked him what his rank was. I've never been good at learnin those. He told me he was a private. One thing led to another and before I knew it we were laughin and havin a good time. Van still hadn't shown up when Charlie asked if he could call me. Well, I'd never done anything like that, but it's different now, isn't it?"

"What is?"

"I mean it's wartime and it feels like all the rules are off."

"Yeah. I guess ya could say that. So ya gave him yer number?"

"Yeah."

"Did Captain Widmark ever show up?"

"Sure."

"Did the two guys meet?"

"Yeah. Charlie pretended we were old friends."

"So ya dumped the captain for the private?"

"It wasn't like that."

"How was it?"

"Charlie called me the next night and we went out. I guess ya could say it was love at second sight."

"What about Widmark?"

"I told him the next day."

Yeah, that was a lot different from what I'd said.

"Where's Widmark now?"

"He's no longer in the marines."

"Why not?"

She looked down at her skirt and smoothed out nothing. "He was discharged after he was wounded."

"So where is he?"

"He's here in the city."

"Address and phone, please."

"There's no reason to talk to Van."

"Ya want me to take this case, Miss Turner, ya hafta let me decide who to talk to and what I think is important." If clients knew who to talk to and what to look for, why in the Sam Hill did they come to me?

"Van doesn't have anything to do with this."

"That's exactly what I mean. Ya hafta let me decide that. So, address and phone number."

She opened her purse and took out an address book, ran a pointed polished nail down the alphabetized side to the *W*'s, I guessed, opened the book, and read me Widmark's info.

"Ya went to the police, ya said."

"After work yesterday."

"What'd they tell ya?"

"They told me they'd look into it and that I should come back in a week."

"Real helpful."

"I think they thought I was jilted or somethin the way they looked at me."

"They look at everybody that way." I had no idea what I meant by that, but it cut off the jilting avenue. "Anything else ya can tell me?"

"I don't think so." She went into her pocketbook, brought out a tortoiseshell compact, opened it, and took a gander at herself.

I thought this was a strange time to be checking her makeup. But I didn't want to judge her just cause I wouldn't do it. Then again, I wasn't the raving beauty Miss Turner was. Although *pretty* had been used to tag me.

After putting a dab of powder on her unshiny nose she snapped shut the compact, and the powder made a little puff in the air.

"So ya wanna hire me, Miss Turner?"

"Well, yeah. Sure." She returned the compact to her pocketbook.

I hated this part. "My rates are . . ."

She shook her head.

"What's that mean?"

"It means I don't care what your rates are. I gotta do this. I've been savin up."

"For what?"

"My trousseau."

"You and Ladd are gonna tie the knot?"

"I hope so."

"But he hasn't popped the question yet?"

"No. But I know he will."

Not if he's dead, I thought. Instead, I said, "So about my rates."

"That's okay."

"Ya sure?"

"I said it was okay."

"If it gets too tough on yer piggy bank tell me and we'll work somethin out."

She let out a big sigh of relief.

"You have a picture of Private Ladd?"

"Sure."

"Could I have it?"

"Forever?" She stuck out her lower lip and looked like a big baby.

"Forever what?"

"Will you keep the picture forever?"

It seemed a cockeyed kind of question to me. "Nah. I'll give it back when the case is over."

"That means when you find him?"

"Yeah."

"Dead or alive?"

I was beginning to think this was one wacky tomato. "Ya think he's dead, Miss Turner?"

"No. At least, I hope not."

"Ya have any reason to believe someone mighta killed him?"

"No. Why would I?"

"You're the one said *dead or alive*?"

"I'm tryin to be realistic, that's all. I'm not a babe in the woods, you know."

"Course not. So could I have the photo?"

She went digging in her handbag again and came out with a wallet. She unsnapped it and took a photo from the group of picture holders, stared at it like she wanted to burn the image into her brain, then handed it to me.

The picture looked like it was taken from a mile away. I could make out a guy in uniform, but that was it.

"Miss Turner, ya can't expect me to know what he looks like from this, can ya?"

"You didn't ask me if it was a *good* picture or not."

"That's true. I didn't. Wanna tell me what color his eyes and hair are?"

"Brown. They're both brown. And he's six feet tall."

"Any distinguishin marks on his body?"

"I wouldn't know." She sounded insulted.

"Yeah. Well, I'll ask his mother."

"That would make more sense."

I was getting the impression Claire Turner was trying to make me think she was as innocent as Shirley Temple. I wasn't buying.

"How about a better picture? Ya got one?"

"At my apartment. It's too big to fit in my wallet."

"Think ya could let me have it for a while?"

"Okay. Should I bring it here?"

"You gonna be home tonight, I'll swing by and get it, that's okay with you."

"I'll be home waitin for Charlie to call. Sure, you can come over."

"Swell."

"What happens now?" she asked.

"I have to interview people, see what they know or don't know. Usually one person leads to the next." I stood up to show her we were done.

"Is that it then?"

"For now."

"Shouldn't I give you some money?"

Funny, I always forgot that part. "Yeah. That'd be good. For the first week. If I find him sooner, I'll refund whatever's left over."

She dove into that pocketbook again and took out a yellow envelope. "Take this."

"But—"

She interrupted to tell me how much was in the envelope and ask if it was enough. I told her it was far too much and tried to give some back, but she said she trusted me and we'd work it out when the case was over.

"I'll call you later about gettin that photo."

"All right. Thanks."

"By the way, can I call ya at work?"

"I guess so."

"Wanna gimme that number?" She did. "What department are ya in?"

"Shoes." She shrugged. "Usually they have a man doing shoes, but, well, you know."

"Yeah. I guess we're all doin things we wouldn't be doin if there wasn't a war goin on."

"I guess."

I wanted to track down Ladd's army buddy at the hotel so I asked her one more question. "By the way, where was Charlie on leave from? Where's his base?"

"In Georgia. Fort Benning."

"And you're sure there's no other friend of Charlie's in the area besides George Cummings, who ya never met?"

"I'm sure."

We didn't shake hands again and she left.

Why did they always tell at least one lie?

TWO

*a*fter Claire Turner left I shouted for Birdie to come into my office. I kept meaning to get one of those things two people can talk through, but I kept forgetting.

25

"Yeah, Faye?"

"I need some addresses and phone numbers." I lit a cig and looked at my notes. "Ladd in Rhode Island, don't know what city."

"Lad? Is that like Lassie's boyfriend or somethin?"

"What's that supposed to mean?"

"Yer not givin me much to go on here, Faye. Lad. Is that a name?"

"Whaddya mean, is that a name?"

"So I call information in Rhode Island and say, *I'd like the phone number of a lad, please*?"

"Wait a minute. How're ya spellin that?"

"I'm not spellin it. I'm sayin it."

"You said *a* lad. You mean l-a-d?"

"Yeah. L-a-d. Ain't that how ya spell *lad*?"

"That's not the kinda lad it is. It's L-a-d-d."

"Ohhh. A double *D*. Makes all the difference. Hello, operator, will ya give me the phone number of Ladd, L-a-d-d? No first name, no city. Yer givin me a hard row to hoe here, Faye."

I shoulda asked Claire for Mr. Ladd's first name. Still, I had to defend myself. "That's what I pay ya for."

"You pay me to go crazy callin information with only a last name in every city in the whole state?"

"It's the smallest state in the Union."

"Oh, that makes all the difference. Why didn't ya say that to start with. I don't even know the names of the cities."

"Ya have to go out and buy a map."

26

"Now ycr gettin bonkers, Faye. Who'd have a map of Rhode Island?"

"Bird, I know you'll find a way. I have complete faith in ya."

"Well, ya may be whistlin Dixie on this one, Faye."

"Try Charles Ladd first. Then any other Ladd ya can find."

"Who elsc ya want me to find?"

"George Cummings. I don't know where he lives."

"Oh, this is dynamite info."

"He went to Franklin and Marshall College."

"Where's that?"

We stared at each other.

"You don't know that either, huh?"

I shook my head.

"You ever think of a different line a work, Faye?"

"Findin out where a college is won't be hard."

She mimed holding a phone. "Hello, operator, can ya gimme the number for College Central?"

"Call the main library."

"Big help. So you're takin her case?"

"Yeah."

"What's the situation?"

"A missin boyfriend."

"Jeez, Louise. If I hired a PI every time Pete went missin, I'd be broke."

"I think it's different, Birdie."

"So gimme the scoop."

I did.

"You think he's done an amscray or it's somethin else?"

"Unless Turner's lyin, and I wouldn't put it past her, then I think somethin bad has happened to this soldier."

"Bad like . . . bad?"

"Yeah."

"Whatcha gonna do now?"

"I'm goin to the Commodore."

"The soldiers' hotel. He's stayin there?"

"She told me that's where he was. So I'd better give it a once-over."

"Good thinkin, Faye."

I gave her a look but she missed it. "Thanks, Bird."

As she headed for the door, her back to me, she waved a hand in the air as if to say *Think nothing of it.* Birdie Ritter was a corker, all right.

The Commodore Hotel wasn't that far from my office, which was a good thing cause I hated going out in the heat. I grabbed my pocketbook, my summer hat, and left.

On the street I felt like I was melting. I was wearing the coolest dress I owned, but it still felt like I was swaddled in a snowsuit.

A few doors down from my building was a candy and cigar store where I got my cigs and papers when I didn't get em in Greenwich Village where I lived.

The owner was a mug who went by the moniker of Stork on account of his resemblance to one. And the regulars who hung out there were Blackshirt Bob, Fat

Freddy, and Larry the Loser, better known as Loser. A trio of upstanding gents who spent their time in the craps game Stork ran in the back room, and betting on anything that struck their fancy. They even had a bet on me.

When Woody went off to war and left me in charge, the bet was between whether I'd run the place into the ground before he came home or make a go of it. I knew this cause Stork spilled the beans to me one stormy afternoon when we were in the place alone. But I never let on I knew.

When my first murder case hit the front pages, the boys were heartbroken. All except Stork who was betting I'd make it work.

We said our hellos and Stork put a pack of Camels on the marble counter. I wasn't picking up my papers now cause I didn't want to carry them around. From the brown Bakelite radio on a shelf behind Stork came Rudy Vallee singing "As Time Goes By." I ordered a Royal Crown.

"So, Faye, any new cases?" Fat Freddy asked. Every day he was looking more like ten tons of flour in a five-pound bag.

"Matter of fact, I just got a new one this mornin."

Stork said, "I hope it ain't another big M." He poured my RC into a glass with ice.

"Don't know yet. Right now it's a missin person case." That first swallow was swell.

"Yeah? Who's missin?" Loser asked. He was famous for picking the also-ran bangtails. I didn't think he ever lost at that.

"Per usual, I'm not at liberty to divulge."

"There she goes," Blackshirt Bob said. "Like the FBI or somethin."

"Leave her alone," Stork said. He was always trying to protect me, which was why he didn't want my case to be a murder.

"We're just interested," Freddy said.

"Yeah, Faye's our gal."

"Give it a rest," Stork said. "Now, you be careful, Faye. No matter what kinda case it is, ya never know."

Bob said, "Ya never know what?"

"Remember when she was conked on the head?"

"Ah, Stork," I said. "That's not gonna happen again."

"How can ya be sure?"

"I can't. But I could walk outta this door right now and get beaned by a fallin flowerpot." I took a big swig of my RC.

"Yeah," Loser said. "Who wants to make a bet on that?"

"Shut yer trap, Loser. We ain't bettin on Faye's well-bein. Right now she's in fine whack and that's the way she's stayin."

"Thanks, Stork."

Freddy said, "Ya got a will, Faye?"

"Hey!"

"What's a matter wit you?"

"Can it."

"I was just wonderin."

Freddy was always trying to tap me for a fin or so but this was going too far. "You wonderin if yer in it, Freddy?"

"I'd never be so crude."

"Since when?" Blackshirt said.

"So whaddaya askin her that for?"

"I'm makin conversation is all."

"Lemme take ya outta yer misery, Freddy. I don't have a will. I have nothin to leave. But when I do, I'll be sure to put ya in it."

His round face lit up. "Yeah?"

"You bet." I finished my RC. "Gotta go now, fellas." I paid for my Camels and drink, waved to the boys, and went out into the Arabian desert.

The sun pounded on me with no letup right through my white hat. I went down a block to Forty-second Street and turned east. Everybody I passed looked beat down to the ankles and I knew it was the weather. Rich people got outta town for the summer, but us working stiffs didn't have that luxury.

The Commodore Hotel was connected by a walkway to Grand Central Station. The hotel was pretty tall, not high like the Empire State, but for where it was you could say it was impressive—if you felt the need.

The doorman opened up for me and I went into the huge lobby of gilt and marble. There were velvet club chairs located around the joint so people could sit and wait or read their newspapers. Potted plants were placed near columns, and bellhops flitted everywhere.

31

I went up to the main desk. Three women stood behind it. And a guy, maybe fifty, in a blue uniform with gold piping around his lapels who came over to me. He had a face as interesting as a piece of gefilte fish.

"May I help you, miss?"

"Could ya please ring Private Ladd's room?"

"Do you know the number?"

"No, I don't."

"That's quite all right. I'll look it up."

He turned to a large ledger and ran a thumbnail down a page. Then he smiled at me. "I'll ring him now."

I watched while he listened with an earpiece. After a bit he hung up, then looked in a cubbyhole on the back wall. Shaking his head, he came back to me.

"I'm afraid he doesn't answer and his key isn't here so he's probably out."

"But he could be in?"

"Well, it doesn't seem likely, does it?"

"I'm a private investigator and . . ."

He stifled a laugh, which I was used to when people heard my occupation.

". . . and the soldier is missin. I'd like to look at his room."

"Oh, no. No, no, no. We can't have that."

The three women turned to look at him because his voice had risen a pitch.

"Could I see the manager, please?"

"He'll tell you the same thing. We don't allow

anyone in our patrons' rooms." He pulled at his jacket lapels, then flattened them.

I could see this guy was in a flusteration.

"Manager."

"Miss, I don't think you understand. It's a matter of our guests' privacy."

"Manager."

His brown eyes grew wider, and the gefilte complexion was turning red. I thought I saw some white foam at the corners of his mouth.

One of the clerks came over to him. She was tall and had crossed eyes. "What's the matter, Mr. Stanwyck?"

"This girl, who claims to be some kind of investigator, wants to go into a guest's room when the guest is out."

"You can't do that, miss," she said.

"I'd like to see the manager."

"Mr. Duff is very busy."

"So am I. If ya don't get him for me, I'll have to get the police in here and I don't think ya'd like that."

"All right. Mr. Stanwyck, buzz Mr. Duff."

"Why don't you do it, Miss Hayden?"

"One, I'm your boss, and two, this is your pickle," she said, and walked away.

Stanwyck, looking embarrassed, turned on his heel and went to a phone. He kept his back to me so I couldn't hear what he was saying. Then he replaced the receiver and returned.

"Mr. Duff will be out in a moment."

"Thank you, Mr. Stanwyck."

He pressed his lips together so hard a white halo formed around them. "You're welcome." He left me there waiting for Duff while he swanned off, as far from me as he could get.

A bellhop called over and over for a Mrs. Massey. Either she wasn't there or she didn't want to be discovered.

I spotted Duff before he looked my way. *Stuffed shirt* didn't begin to describe him. He held his head tilted back so that he led with his pointed chin. Maybe that was so his pince-nez didn't fall off. His eyes seemed to be looking down his cheeks. He had ears like croquettes, and a fringe of hair ringed his head. He wore a black suit and tie. I guessed he was in his sixties.

"May I be of service to you?"

I explained what I wanted.

"But I can't possibly let you into a guest's room when the guest isn't there. Surely you see my point."

"I do." I took out my PI license and showed it to him.

"That won't change my mind, Miss . . ." He looked down at my license again. "Miss Quick."

"Should I get the police here with a warrant?" I couldn't really do this but he didn't hafta know that.

Duff frantically looked around as though he might find the answer from one of the old gents sitting in the lobby. "If only our house detective were here, it would be different. But he's out sick."

34

"Sorry to hear it. Now I'd like to go to Private Ladd's room."

"So the guest is one of our brave boys in the service?"

"That's right, and he's been missin for two days."

He leaned toward me and in a whisper laced with garlic he said, "These boys are full of fun and games when they get to New York, dear girl. And you can't blame them after what they've been through. But on leave they have a high old time. Your private could be almost anywhere." He wiggled his eyebrows like Groucho Marx.

"First off, Mr. Duff, he's not *my* private. I'm workin on a case and I've been hired to find the soldier."

"Yes, I understand."

"I don't think ya do." I started to move away. "I guess I'll get that warrant."

"No need for that, Miss Quick. We'll go to his room together. This is highly unusual and I'd appreciate it if you'd keep it to yourself."

"Absolutely, Mr. Duff."

"I have to get the passkey. I'll meet you at the elevators."

"Thank you."

As I left the desk Stanwyck and Miss Hayden shot me looks that were meant to chop up my heart. I smiled at them, then crossed the lobby to the elevators. They were gold-colored and framed by rococo leaves and flowers.

Doors opened and closed while people got on and off. Finally Duff appeared, his face mottled now like red polka dots on a dress. We took the next elevator when it emptied.

"Good afternoon, Mr. Duff," the operator said.

Duff nodded. "Four."

The elevator stopped and we got off.

"This way," Duff said.

I followed him down the red-carpeted hall. We stopped at Room 405. The DO NOT DISTURB sign was around the doorknob and it gave me the jimjams.

"I really object to entering a room under these conditions." He flipped the card with a finger.

"He doesn't answer his phone, Mr. Duff. And his key's not downstairs."

He knocked. "Private Ladd? Are you in there?"

He knocked and called out Ladd's name three more times. No response. Then he put the key in the door.

Inside, the room was dark and had a bad smell. All the drapes were closed so Duff switched on a light.

"Do all yer rooms smell like this?" I said.

"Certainly not." He took a handkerchief from his breast pocket and swiped at his nose as though that would make a difference.

The bed was unmade but there wasn't anyone in it.

"I think you can see that he's not here," Duff said.

"I can see he's not in *this* room. Let's look in the bathroom." Though I knew we had to look in there, I wasn't thrilled about it, remembering the last time I'd done that.

We made our way around the bed and Duff switched on the light. The bathroom was empty. Back in the

36

bedroom I saw a canvas duffel bag on the floor. It was open but all I could see was a khaki shirt, the piece of clothing on top.

"I'll hafta go through this," I said.

He removed his pince-nez, closed his eyes, and pinched the bridge of his nose. "I *really* can't let you do that, Miss Quick."

I decided not to push the point right then.

"May we abandon this search now?"

"No," I said. "I need to check drawers, closets, any-place that could give a clue to where he might be."

"Well, hurry up. Clearly this room hasn't been seen to for days."

I looked in the drawer of the night table and found only the Gideon Bible. In the small desk drawer was Commodore stationery. I went to the wardrobe to open its doors.

"Why is this locked?"

"How would I know? However, it's obviously locked for a reason."

"Exactly. Can ya open it?"

"Miss Quick, I must insist that we leave here."

"Mr. Duff, we're not leavin till I open this wardrobe."

"What do you think you'll find in there?"

"I don't know, but I gotta look."

"Oh, all right. Here." He reached in front of me, put a key in the lock, and with a flourish opened the double doors.

That's when the naked man fell out.

THREE

*D*uff gave a yelp like a bleating goat and jumped backward.

"Who's that?" he asked.

"Goin out on a limb, I'd say Charlie Ladd." The body had no dog tags, though, so I couldn't ID him. He mighta been anybody. But since this was his room, you didn't have to be Einstein to figure that one out.

"What was he doing in there?"

"My best guess is that someone bumped him off, then stuffed him in the wardrobe."

"Why is he . . . naked?"

You woulda thought it was Mae West in her birthday suit the way Duff was acting.

"I don't know why he's naked. But I bet we'll find out. I think we'd better call the cops."

"Can't you handle this?"

Was he crazy? "Mr. Duff, I'm a PI—not a cop. When ya got a corpse, ya call the cops."

I could see that the guy on the floor was young and in good shape. His hair was brown, which tallied with the description of Charlie that Claire gave me, but since he'd landed front-down I couldn't see his face. I pulled the spread off the bed and covered the body. Then I went over to the phone on the desk.

"No. Wait, Miss Quick."

"Yeah?"

"I have to think."

Seemed chances of that were slim. "There's nothin to think about. We have no choice. The police gotta be called."

"Can they be discreet? I don't want to alarm the other patrons."

"They'll send a couple a uniformed cops and some plainclothes guys. I don't know how discreet they'll be."

"This is terrible for me."

I wanted to point out that it was more terrible for the guy on the rug, but I didn't think he'd get my meaning. I picked up the phone and asked the operator to call the local precinct. Once I got connected I gave the cop on the other end the info.

"I think we'd better go downstairs and wait for them," he said.

"Somebody has to stay with the body." I was pretty sure Duff wouldn't want that job.

"Oh. Yes. I see. Will you do that?"

"Glad to help out, Mr. Duff." I had to stifle a chuckle.

"All right. I'll go downstairs. Do you think they'll come in the front door?"

"I'm sure they will."

"Of all the days for Detective Arden to be sick."

"Don't worry about it. I'll stand guard."

"Yes, yes. I'd better go to the lobby. Maybe I can keep the police quiet, at least."

Fat chance. I watched as he headed to the door and

left. I could give the place a real look-see before the cops got there.

I poked my head into the open wardrobe. There was a khaki shirt, pants, and a dark brown jacket. I patted em down, but all the pockets were empty. I assumed these were Ladd's clothes. I couldn't give a real toss to the duffel bag cause the cops would know. So I took it slow and peeled back the clothes going as far down as I could. I swept my hand around inside, but there was nothing else.

I already knew there was nothing in the drawers. I felt kinda dumb doing it, but I got down on the rug and peered under the bed. Dumb or not, there were things under there—and I don't mean dust balls. I was pretty sure it was clothing and I was about to pull stuff out when I heard the thundering hooves of cops in the hall.

I got up in time to look innocent. Just as I'd thought, there were two plainclothes and two uniforms. One of the plainclothes told a uniform to stand guard in the hall. Duff was off to one side, wringing his hands and holding his handkerchief up to his nose.

The new arrivals were gagging and hurrying to pull out their own handkerchiefs. I had no idea why it didn't bother me that much, but I didn't wanna make the boys feel like sissies, so I took my sneezer outta my pocketbook and put it up to my nose. We all looked like idiots.

"You're the PI," a plainclothes said.

"Right. And who are you?"

"Detective Powell. This the body?"

What other lump would be under a bedspread on the floor? I nodded.

He pulled back the spread and saw that the body was naked. "This the way ya found him?"

Everybody was trying to break the IQ record. Did he think I'd undressed the guy? "Naked as a jaybird."

"You know who he is?"

"No." I told him why I was there and what had happened.

"So this could be Private Ladd then?"

"Could be." It occurred to me then that this could be Ladd's buddy, David. Why he'd be naked and dead in Ladd's room was another story.

"Don't nobody touch nothin. Ya touch anything in here?" he asked.

"Yeah, I did." I explained about the drawers, the wardrobe, the phone.

"You should know better."

I wanted to belt him. "I did all this, except for callin you guys, before I found the body."

"Even so."

"Even so?"

"Yeah."

"Listen, Detective, I came here lookin for Ladd, a missin person. I did what I needed to do."

The other plainclothes said, "We're wastin time with this broad. We'll get her prints so we can rule em out."

Powell nodded. "Where's the coroner?"

"I'm right here," a familiar voice said as he came

through the door. It was Glenn Madison, assistant to the coroner. "Hey, Quick, what're you doing here?"

"Too long to explain."

"Don't tell me you found a body again?"

"Whaddaya mean, *again?*" Powell asked.

Madison realized he'd put his foot in his mouth and looked at me like he was begging for mercy.

I had to answer. "Another case."

"And you found the body?"

"Yeah." I didn't wanna tell him it'd been two bodies.

Powell looked at me like I was Bonnie Parker. Then he said, "Do your stuff, Madison."

Glenn pulled the spread farther down and started to examine him.

"You see how he was knocked off?" Powell asked me.

"I didn't look." And I wondered why I hadn't. Maybe it was Duff's bleating got me off course.

Glenn said, "I think I know, but let me turn him over first."

"You'd better turn your back, miss," Powell said.

"Why?"

"Dincha hear? He's turnin him over."

"So what?"

"Don'tcha have no sense a decency?"

"Oh. Yeah." I thought the whole thing was stupid, but I'd already gotten off on the wrong foot with Powell, so I turned my back.

Glenn said, "He was strangled. See the thumbprints on his neck?"

"Can I turn around now?" Nobody answered.

"How long?" Powell said.

"He's been in and out of rigor, and the way he smells it could be as much as forty-eight."

"Can I turn around now?"

"Cover the body," Powell said. "Yeah, ya can turn around. But don't get in the way. You," he added.

"Me?" Duff was pointing to himself like he had no idea who he was.

"Can you identify this man?"

"Me?"

"Who d'ya think I'm talkin to?" Powell's face was taking on a reddish hue.

"I'd rather not."

"I don't care what you'd *rather*. Come over here and look at this guy's mug."

"I've never seen a dead person."

"Well, now's your chance," Powell said.

"Do I have to?" It looked like he might bust out crying.

"Look, mister—whatever your name is—ya gotta dead body in your hotel and we don't know who it is."

"Duff."

"What?"

"Wallace Duff. That's my name."

"I don't care what your name is. Get over here and look at this stiff."

"Why?"

"I wanna see if ya can identify him."

"I'm the manager. I don't check in guests."

43

"Who does?"

"Clerks at the reservation desk."

"First take a look-see yourself, then get those clerks up here pronto."

Duff took baby steps across the room like it might be easier to look if he got there later rather than sooner.

"C'mon. Get a move on," Powell said.

Duff stood above the body, his back to me. Powell was at the corpse's feet.

"Hey," Powell said, "open your eyes, Duff."

I guess he did cause a few secs later he shook his head, then quickly turned and scrambled to the doorway.

"I'll send the clerks up one by one," he said from there and beat it.

Powell turned to the other detective. "Stevens. Empty out that duffel."

Stevens pulled it open and dumped everything on the rug. There were clothes, but no personal items. No wallet. No ID.

Powell tapped a uniform. "Take this lady down to the precinct and get her fingerprinted."

"Yes, sir."

I didn't know if I should tell them about the clothes under the bed. I knew they'd find the stuff themselves, but there might be an ID there and I'd know now who he was.

"Let's go," the cop said to me.

"Wait a sec."

"Yeah?"

"There's somethin under the bed."

"Another body?" Powell asked with a wicked smile. I didn't take the bait. "Clothes."

"Look under the bed," Powell said to the uniform.

He got down on his knees, took off his cap, and shoved his head underneath. When he came up for air he said, "Yup. Clothes."

"Well, pull em out, you numbskull." Then to me, "Why'd you wait so long to tell us?"

I didn't like this Powell. I played it dumb. "I forgot."

"Forgot?"

"Yeah."

"Dippy dame."

Just what I wanted him to think. Sometimes I got more info that way.

The cop started dragging out one item after another. Pants, shirt, undershirt, underpants, shoes.

"These might belong to the victim," Powell said.

Or David, I thought. But let em find out about him themselves.

"There's nothin here to ID them," the uniform said.

Powell gave a big loud sigh. "Nothin's easy. Take this broad outta here."

"Now, listen, Powell . . . there's no reason I hafta go to the station."

"You gotta be fingerprinted and you gotta make a statement. What's wrong wit you? You don't know about procedure? What kinda shamus are you?"

I wasn't about to tell him I was the beginner kind.

At the precinct Detective Bendix gave me a pad and pencil and told me to write my statement. After that they took my prints and I was free to go. But Powell came back as I was making tracks outta there.

"Don't leave town or nothin," he said.

"Ah, too bad. I was plannin to go to Iceland."

"Don't crack wise wit me or I'll lock you up as a material witness," he said.

This I knew he couldn't do. I got the feeling Detective Powell didn't like me as much as I didn't like him. I left.

Stepping outside, I felt like a lobster being dropped in a pot of boiling water. It was still a sizzler. I walked west, back toward my office. I needed to talk to Marty Mitchum, my personal friend on the force.

My *most* personal friend, Detective John Lake, was my boyfriend, but I didn't like using him on my cases. He told me I could but I didn't wanna mix business with pleasure. I was seeing Johnny that night and I'd tell him about this cause we'd agreed we had to be able to yak about our work. But I wouldn't ask for his help even though I knew he'd offer.

Back at the office after I hung my limp hat on the rack I saw that Birdie was eating a sandwich at her desk, which made me realize I hadn't had anything since breakfast.

"What kind?" I asked.

"Pastrami on rye. Ya want half, Faye?"

"Nah."

"Ya want I should order ya somethin?"

"Okay. Same as you, Bird."

"Comin up."

"How ya doin with the Rhode Island kettle of fish?"

"So far I tried all the so-called big cities and there weren't any Ladds."

"Ya got more places to call?"

"Yeah."

"Keep on it."

"What happened at the Commodore? Ya find Private Ladd?"

"I mighta."

"Huh?"

I told her the story.

"So ya don't know who the lucky stiff is?"

"Not yet. I gotta track down Ladd's buddy who came on leave with him. Trouble is I only know his first name. Did ya get a number for George Cummings yet?"

"I called the college, like ya said. It's in Lancaster, Pennsylvania, in case ya ever wanna know. It took a little doin but I finally got a dame to tell me where Cummings is from."

"How'd ya do that?"

"I got my ways." She gave me a wink.

An annoying thing about Birdie was she wouldn't tell her sources. As her boss I coulda pressed her, but so far I hadn't really needed to know.

"So where's he from."

"Right here in good old New York City."

"Did yer *source* tell ya if he came back here after graduation?"

"She didn't know, but she said he wanted to be a stockbroker so he probably did."

"That makes sense. So have ya found him?"

"I'm gonna start on that after lunch."

I didn't wanna tell her to look in the phone book cause that'd be insulting and since I didn't need his number right away, I could wait until she finished her pastrami.

"Gotta make some calls," I said.

"Right."

I went into my office, put my pocketbook on the floor next to my chair, opened the drawer, took out my in-house Camels, lit one, and picked up the phone.

I tried Marty at his precinct but he wasn't there so I dialed Smitty's, his favorite gin mill. The day guy, Lupino, answered and I asked for Marty. I had to go through a rigmarole with some of the bartenders cause they protected Marty from Bridgett, his wife. But the main guys, Lupino and Coburn, knew me now.

"Hey, Faye," Marty said.

"I need yer help."

"Shoot."

I told him the story. He said soon as there was an ID on the John Doe, he'd give me a jingle. Or if I was out burning shoe leather, ring him.

Next I dialed Van Widmark's number. A man picked up on the first ring.

"Mr. Widmark?"

"Who's calling?"

"Ya don't know me. My name's Faye Quick. I got yer name and number from Claire Turner."

Silence.

"You there?"

"What is it you want?"

"I'd like to come over and talk to ya."

"Why? Who are you?"

"Sorry. I shoulda said right off. I'm a private investigator and I'm on a case."

"What kind of case could have anything to do with me?"

"Probably no kinda case, Mr. Widmark, but I hafta check out a few things with ya."

"Are you working for Claire? Miss Turner?"

"I can't tell ya that."

"Then I can't see you."

"Wait a minute, Mr. Widmark. I told ya I got yer number from Miss Turner. Isn't that enough for ya to know I'm legit?"

Silence.

"You there?"

"I'm thinking."

I waited.

"All right," he said. "When do you want to come?"

"Soon as possible."

"How about in an hour?"

"Fine. Thanks."

Right after I hung up Birdie came in with my sandwich. "I got ya an RC, too."

49

"Thanks. You been outside, Bird?"

"Not since I came to work."

"It's hell out there. Don't go if ya don't hafta."

"Me and Pete are goin to Coney tonight, sit on the boardwalk, take in the breeze."

I unwrapped my sandwich and took a bite. Delish.

"You seein Johnny tonight?"

"Yeah."

"Ya oughta go someplace cool."

"I think we're goin to the movies where they got air-conditionin."

"Whatcha seein?"

"*This Is the Army*, that new musical."

"I hear that's a good one." She started singing the title song.

"Can it, Bird."

"Ya don't like my singin?"

"I like it fine. I'm just not in the mood."

"Well, tell me when ya are and I'll do all of 'Yankee Doodle Dandy' for ya."

"I'll be sure to let ya know."

"You want anything else?"

"I'm just gonna eat my pastrami and read my book."

"Suit yerself." She left my office swinging her behind and singing "You're a Grand Old Flag."

FOUR

*V*an Widmark lived on the Upper West Side. There was almost nothing worse than going down into the subway on a hot, humid day. Beyond the smells that could turn a girl's stomach, it felt like walking into a public bathhouse. Steam seeped from the walls, the ceiling, the floor, and from the trains themselves.

The platform was crowded and I wondered where all these people were going in the middle of the day. Same thing I wondered when I went to daytime movies. Didn't anybody in New York City work? Course I worked and I was there.

The train and its load of steam came in. I got a bench seat next to the window. Not that I could see anything through it. I eyeballed the people around me and once again decided that the human race was a funny-looking bunch. Would somebody from Mars think that?

A guy down the line was reading the *Daily News*. The back page was hollering about the Yankees being Number One. Of course they were number one. With a roster like they had, who could beat em?

A woman sat down beside me and said, "I haven't slept in two years."

I turned and gave her the once-over. She didn't look crazy so I said, "How come?"

"I know if I close my eyes and sleep, I'll never wake up again."

An interesting theory. This gal had white hair and by the look of her pleated skin, I figured she was in her late seventies.

"How d'ya keep yerself awake?" I asked.

"Sew and pull."

That was a new one to me. "What's that mean?"

"I sit up sewing little squares together and then I pull out all the stitches. It does the trick."

"It's good ya found a way to stay awake."

"Yes." She smiled and I could see how pretty she once was.

I smiled back and turned away, then opened my book.

After a few moments she said, "What are you reading, dear?"

"*The Human Comedy.*"

"You'll like it. I read it when it was first published."

"I can't afford new books. Sometimes I get em from the library, but if I want to own em I gotta wait till they turn up in used-book stores."

"But that only came out in February."

"Well, that's six months ago. Anyway, I found it in my favorite store."

"And what's that?"

"The Bookman on Fourth Avenue."

"I love those stores down there."

"Me, too."

"I've probably been in The Bookman, but I never remember names."

No wonder if she hadn't slept in two years.

"This is my stop," she said. "It's time for me to walk. Nice talking to you, dear."

"You, too."

I watched her go to the doors, and she was pretty sprightly for somebody who hadn't had forty winks in two years. Crazy as a loon but a sweet old thing. When she got off and the train started moving again, I laughed in my head cause I figured I'd been had. Couldn't work out why she'd want to tell a whopper like that, but I had to admit it was a way to get someone to talk to you.

I opened my book again and read until we got to the Eighty-sixth Street stop, where I got off. As I headed for the stairs, I felt that something was different. It was my pocketbook. Lighter. Oh, no.

I stopped and opened it up. My wallet was gone. The sweet old thing! I'd had my purse between us and never noticed. I couldn't imagine when she'd done it. I thought I was looking at her the whole time. That was it. I was looking at *her*. Misdirection. It was something scam artists did all the time. Magicians, too. I didn't even hear the clasp of my purse open and shut. She was good. Well, this was some snafu.

I couldn't picture myself panhandling for a nickel to get back to Midtown so I knew I was gonna have to tap Widmark. What was the worst that could happen? He could chuck me out of his apartment. So what? I wasn't gonna hustle him for the five cents till the end of the interview. If he wouldn't dish out I might have to pass the hat on Broadway after all.

I had to put this dilemma on the back burner and concentrate on what I was gonna ask Widmark. I climbed the stairs to the street and headed for 145 West Eighty-sixth.

But I couldn't stop thinking about it. Me, clipped like any regular mark. My mind went right to the boys at Stork's. I could see them laughing, Fat Freddy holding his bellies. Well, they never had to know. I sure wasn't gonna wag the tongue to those mugs.

And Johnny? Did I have to spill to him? He'd think I was an easy target. Maybe not. He wasn't like that. He'd understand.

I wouldn't tell him.

The people on the street looked like limp linguini. It was getting hotter by the second. I picked up my pace so I could get into a building away from the sun. I turned on Eighty-sixth toward Amsterdam. Nice trees there.

Pretty soon I was at 145. Naturally there was a doorman but he wasn't quite as spiffy looking as the ones on Park Avenue. His gray uniform was slightly shabby. No gold braid. And the brim of the cap he wore had lost its sheen.

I said I was there to see Mr. Widmark. He rang him, then told me to go up to the tenth floor, Apartment 10B.

I knew when the elevator came down the operator would be as old as they all were—now that the young ones were in the army. So when the doors opened, I was knocked back on my heels.

There was a jane at the controls. I'd never seen a girl running one before, but why not? Girls were doing almost everything else. I guessed that the old men were getting too old to do a lot of things.

She was in full uniform: jacket, pants, the whole thing. Miss Operator gave me the fisheye.

"You gonna stare all day or get on?"

"Sorry." I stepped into the elevator.

"What floor?"

"Tenth."

"Who ya gonna see?"

I had a feeling she wasn't supposed to ask, but I told her anyway.

"Nice fella."

As long as she was gonna be personal about this I decided I would, too.

"He get a lotta visitors?"

"Not too many. I think his girlfriend threw him over. She came in the beginnin, but I ain't seen her lately."

I wondered if she meant Claire Turner.

"Tenth floor."

It was a smooth landing.

"He's right over there." She pointed across the hall.

"Thanks."

"Poor guy," she said.

I turned, but the doors had closed. Was she still talking about him being jilted? Or was it something else? I'd probably never know.

I rang Widmark's bell.

"Come in," he shouted.

55

Some gentleman. I opened the door. There was a small foyer, but I could see the living room—and Widmark. He was sitting there. In a wheelchair. Now I knew what the elevator operator meant.

"Come in, Miss Quick. Sit down." He pointed to the striped sofa.

I sat where he wanted me to. There was no question I was thrown off my game by him being in the wheelchair and I musta showed it.

"No one told you, I gather?"

"Told me?"

He sighed like he'd been through this a million times. "That I'd lost my legs at Guadalcanal."

"No. No one told me."

"Well, don't worry. I'm used to it."

Widmark was a handsome guy. He had a ginger crew cut and green eyes that looked like they'd seen more than they ever wanted to. It didn't seem likely that he could've had anything to do with either Ladd's disappearance or the murder of John Doe. He wasn't a person anyone would forget and, besides, it would be hard for him to get around. But you never knew, he might be helpful.

He was wearing a white dress shirt buttoned at the neck, no tie. The rest of him was covered with a maroon blanket that clashed with his hair.

He said, "Now that you know, do you still want to talk with me?"

"Sure."

"You said on the phone that you wanted to talk

about Claire. So what do you have on your mind, Miss Quick?" He took a pack of Old Golds and a lighter from his shirt pocket.

"Call me Faye." I went into my pocketbook, empty of my wallet, and took out my cigs. Widmark lit his with a Zippo.

"Sorry I can't light yours," he said. He meant he couldn't reach me from the chair.

"I'm doin fine," I said, and lit up. "I don't think I said I wanted to talk about Claire. I said she'd given me your number."

"So you did. What do you want to talk about then?"

"Miss Turner told me you two used to be an item." Oops.

He smiled. It was crooked and I liked it. "I guess you could say that. We'd been dating for about three months when Ladd came along. You know about him, don't you?"

"Know what?"

"That he stole her from me. Right in front of my eyes." He blew out a lotta smoke, like a boiling teakettle.

"You bitter about that?"

"I was at the time. But now that I'm like this none of it matters."

"Meanin?"

"What girl would want to be stuck with a cripple? Claire would've left me by now anyway."

In the movies girls always said things like, *I didn't fall in love with yer legs, Jim.* But this wasn't the movies and he was probably right. I wondered again if

57

Claire had been the girl the elevator operator had mentioned.

"Claire come to see ya much?"

"No."

"Not ever?"

"Not ever."

So she hadn't been the one.

"I think she's too ashamed," he said. "It's foolish of her, but that's the way it is."

"Ashamed she left ya?"

"It was the way she did it."

"How was that?"

"By Western Union."

"Really?" That seemed shabby. "What'd she say?"

"I know it by heart." He closed his eyes. "Van, please forgive me. Stop. I've met the man of my dreams. Stop. I'll always care for you, but I have to say goodbye. Stop. Love, Claire. Big Stop. Big End." He opened his eyes.

"That's lousy."

"Not how I would've done it," he said.

I couldn't figure out if she did it that way cause she was naïve or dumb. I guessed she wasn't trying to be mean, but I didn't really know her.

"What d'ya think of Charlie Ladd?" I said, and took a drag on my butt.

"I don't know him. I met him at the same time Claire did."

"At the Biltmore?"

"That's right."

"You never saw him again?"

"No. Why?"

"He's disappeared."

"From where?"

I explained.

"He's probably out on a binge."

"Is he a drunk?"

"Not that I know of. I didn't mean that. When soldiers are on leave, they often get soused. Hit all the gin mills they can."

"D'ya think Ladd would do that when he was supposed to meet Miss Turner?"

"I wouldn't do it. But I don't know what Ladd would do. I told you, I don't know him."

"Sorry."

"How long has he been missing?"

"A couple a days. But here's the thing, Mr. Widmark. A dead man was found in his hotel room. There was no identification."

"Was he a soldier?"

"Looks like it."

"And he didn't have his dog tags on?"

"No."

"So how do you know it's not Ladd?"

"We don't. Yet. When I left the scene, the cops were gonna get the hotel personnel to see if anyone knew him, any of them checked him in."

"I hope you don't expect me to identify him."

"Never entered my mind."

"I like that song," he said.

"What?"

" 'It Never Entered My Mind.' You know it, don't you?"

"Why are we talkin about songs?"

"Song. We're talking about *one* song. You know the words?"

"Yeah." It was one of the songs I wanted to sing in my act if I ever got to do one.

"I always think of Claire when I hear it."

At least we were back to Claire. I thought about the words. "I can see why ya would."

He smiled sadly and then he killed his cig in a heavy-looking ashtray. I figured it was so he couldn't accidentally knock it to the floor. "And you thought I'd know where Ladd was?"

"Anything's possible, Mr. Widmark."

"Is Claire all right?" He wheeled himself closer to me but he still wasn't within arm's reach.

"She's fine. Worried about Private Ladd."

"Can't she identify the man in Ladd's room?"

"She doesn't know about him yet. She'll have to view the body later if no one else can ID the corpse."

"Did she hire you?"

"Can't tell ya that, Mr. Widmark."

He nodded. "I'd do anything to help Claire. But I don't know what to tell you."

"Ya still in love with her?"

"I'll always be in love with her."

"Would ya do anything to get her back?"

"I'd . . . what does that mean?"

"It's not a trick question."

"If you mean would I kill Charlie Ladd or some man in his hotel room, I wouldn't. Not even if I could get there. And even if I could get there and wanted to kill this mystery man, I can't see how that would get Claire back."

"I just asked if you'd do anything to get her."

"In case you haven't noticed I'm no longer a man. There won't be Claire or any other woman knocking on my door."

"Speakin of that, I heard there was some girl who used to visit ya, but no more. Who was she?"

"Where did you hear that?"

I shrugged.

"I get it. I answer the questions but you don't."

"Somethin like that."

"And what if I don't answer."

"Nothin. Ya don't hafta talk to me."

"Maybe I won't."

"Ya don't wanna tell me who yer lady visitor was?"

"It wasn't Claire."

"Did she know Claire?"

"You could say that."

"Do ya?"

"What?"

"Say that. That she knew Claire."

"She did."

"Can't ya tell me her name?"

"I could, but I'm not going to. I'm not getting that girl in trouble."

"She wouldn't get in trouble."

"Then why do you want to know her name?"

"Can ya tell me why she stopped comin around?"

"I told her to stop."

"Why?"

He lit another cigarette.

"Why'd ya tell yer girlfriend to stop comin round?"

"She wasn't my girlfriend. I told her to stop because it . . . it wasn't good for her."

"Good for her? Why not?"

"Forget it, Miss Quick. I think it's time for you to go now."

The words I loved to hear. The words I'd heard too often. I stood up.

Widmark didn't say anything. Just sat there looking down at the blanket that covered his missing legs. I started to leave and then I remembered my stolen wallet.

"Mr. Widmark. I have one more question."

He looked up at me. "Yes?"

"Could ya lend me a nickel?"

"What?"

"My wallet was stolen on the subway up here and I don't have any money. I'm very embarrassed to ask ya for it, but I don't have any choice. I hope you'll understand."

"Who stole your wallet?"

"I don't know." I wasn't about to tell him that it was an old lady.

A grin grew on his kisser and then he broke out guffawing until I thought he was gonna hurt himself.

I waited.

"I'm sorry. It's just that . . . you're . . . well, you're not much of a detective, are you?"

What could I say to that?

"Can I have the nickel?"

"Sure. Take it from that jar over there."

He pointed to a small purple vase with a large opening. I dipped in and came up with some change, went through it, picked out the nickel, and threw the rest back.

"Thanks," I said.

"Think nothing of it." With that he started laughing all over again.

I was gonna thank him for seeing me but there was no way I could break through the laughing and I didn't feel like hanging around till he stopped. I went out the door and rang for the elevator.

I could still hear him while I waited. It was nice to know I could lay em in the aisles.

The elevator came and I got on. "I was wonderin somethin," I said.

"Yeah? You're not the first."

"Meanin?"

"What's a nice girl like me doin runnin an elevator?"

"That's not what I was gonna ask. A war's on and there's a man shortage. Everybody knows that."

"Come to think of it, it's only old geezers who ask

me." She gave me a knowing smile. "Whaddaya wanna know?"

"That girl who used to visit Mr. Widmark? The one you mentioned? You ever get her name?"

"Yeah. It was Lucille Turner."

FIVE

*W*hen I came through my office door, Birdie was holding up a bunch of pink message notes in one hand and, in the other, my wallet.

"Where'd ya get that?"

"A little boy delivered it."

"A little boy?"

"That's what I said."

I took it from her and opened it toot sweet. No filthy lucre. But everything else was there. I had nice pictures of Johnny and me from one of those machines that were four for two bits. He had the other two. And there was one of Woody in his uniform and some of me with my girlfriends, making faces and acting nutty. And my library card was there, which made me breathe easier. I kept my PI license in a separate folder so I hadn't worked myself into a lather about that.

"How'd ya lose it, Faye?"

To tell or not to tell. "I met up with a pickpocket."

"Yer kiddin."

"Nope."

"Where?"

64

"I don't have time to go into all the details, but suffice it to say my wallet got liberated on the subway."

"He musta been some smooth operator to get it outta yer bag."

Not in a million years was I gonna identify the thief who boosted my property. "*Smooth* is the right word. I never felt a thing."

"How'd ya get back here?"

"I had to tap the guy I was interviewin."

"I bet that put a crimp in your tail."

"It wasn't fun. This boy just knocked on the door and gave ya the wallet?"

"He didn't knock and he didn't give. He banged and threw. I'm happy to say it didn't hit me."

"Did ya get a look at him?"

"Ya don't care that it didn't hit me?"

"Bird, what's to care? If it'd hit ya, I'd care."

"It's gettin dangerous to work around here."

"Meanin what?"

"Nothin. I'm just sayin."

"Anything more on the Rhode Island Ladds?"

"I got a few more places to try, but nothin yet."

"What's takin so long?"

"*You* wanna try?"

"Hold yer water. Any important messages?"

"Some new people, some old, and . . . oh, yeah, somebody named Johnny Lake."

"Hilarious."

I took the memos from her, went into my office, turned on the fan, and stood in front of it.

All the way back from Eighty-sixth, I'd been thinking about this Lucille Turner. Could the elevator dame have made a mistake with the name? I didn't think so. I don't believe in coincidences. Lucille hadda be related to Claire.

Having the name I coulda gone back to Widmark's apartment and asked him who she was, but I wanted to talk to Claire first.

If Lucille was connected to Claire, why hadn't she mentioned her? And why was Lucille visiting Widmark?

I flipped through the memos real quick to get to Johnny's cause he wasn't always at the same number. The one on the message was his precinct. I dialed him there but he wasn't at his desk. So I buzzed him at Joe's Chili Parlor. Joe got him to the phone.

"Hi, Faye. What's up?"

I knew he couldn't be lovey-dovey in front of his cronies. Still. "*You* called *me,* Johnny."

He laughed and my heart did a tango. "We still going to the movies tonight?"

"Yeah, why not?"

"I wasn't sure since you found another body. You're really something, Faye."

"I guess I'm just lucky." I didn't bother asking him how he knew. The New York City Police Department was like a small town. "We're gonna see *This Is the Army*, right?"

"Right. I hear it's real good."

"Swell."

"I'll pick you up at seven. We can have a bite to eat, then hit a nine o'clock show."

"Sounds good."

"Okay. See you at seven."

"Bye, Johnny."

"Faye?"

"Yeah?"

"Watch your step, okay?"

"Would ya say that to a man?"

"No, but I wouldn't be having this conversation with a man."

"Very funny. See ya later." I could hear him chuckling as we hung up.

We'd been dating for about four months. We met on another murder case of mine. That second body I'd found was in his precinct. One thing led to another and before I knew it we were dating. Neither of us had said the three little words yet, but I had the feelings and I thought he did, too.

I'd been lucky to find Johnny. If you were a cop, you got a permanent deferment cause we needed the police on the home front. I'd been going solo for a while when I met him, but that wasn't why I picked him. He was everything I wanted in a guy. We even had our work in common. That, I had to admit, could get in the way sometimes. We'd had to break a lotta dates. But when we were together, we got along great.

I dialed Detective Powell's precinct. I wasn't sure he'd give me any info, but I had to try.

"Detective Powell," he said.

I told him who I was and then asked, "You identify the John Doe yet?"

"Why would I tell you?"

"I thought if ya hadn't, I might put ya on to somebody who could." I was thinking of Claire.

"You on the level?"

"I am."

"Cause if yer not I can make life pretty uncomfortable for ya."

"Meanin?"

"No help from the department, no way, never."

"I'm on the level. So did ya ID him?"

"So happens we didn't. None a those boneheads at the hotel knew nothin. Listen to them you'd think *nobody* ever checked in Private Ladd."

"Ya couldn't find his buddy?"

"Nobody knew about him neither."

"Gimme a little time and I'll call ya back with the name of somebody who at least can tell ya whether John Doe is Charlie Ladd or not."

"Why can't ya tell me now? Thought ya were on the level."

"I am. I just gotta make a phone call."

"You said . . ."

"Call ya back."

Next I dialed Claire at work. I got a lotta malarkey about who was I and why was I calling. And the clock kept ticking. Not that I was itching to tell Claire about the body in Ladd's room, but I hadda do it, and find out about Lucille Turner. Finally I heard

68

Claire's voice on the other end.

"It's Faye Quick," I said.

"Have you found Charlie?"

The first time I called a client, they were sure I'd solved their case. Fat chance.

"No. I need to clear up a few things."

"I can't stay on that long."

I heard her light a cig and it made me want to light my own, which I did. "Do you know anyone named Lucille Turner?"

Silence. I had my answer.

"Did ya hear me, Miss Turner?"

"Yeah, I heard."

"So who is she?"

"My sister."

"You never said ya had a sister."

"I didn't think it was important and you never asked."

Claire Turner could be a royal pain in the keister. "The more ya tell me the more I can help. May as well get your money's worth."

"That's the last thing on my mind. Why do you want to know about Lucille?"

"Her name came up. Can ya give me her phone number?"

"Why would you want to speak to her?"

"Have ya been listenin to me, Claire?"

"But what could Lucille have to do with Charlie?"

"One last time. Follow my ground rules, no exceptions, or I'm through. You wanna find yer soldier boy or ya wanna give me the runaround?"

"Lucille and me . . . we're estranged, like they say."

"Why's that?"

"Lucille's got nothin to do with this, and I'm not goin into family problems."

"You just don't get it, do ya? I'll put yer refund in the mail."

"No, wait. Please don't give up on me. All I want is to find Charlie."

"This is tough enough without you gettin in my way."

"You're the boss. Whatever you say goes."

I wondered how long this little honeymoon of ours would last. She was sincere enough now cause she was scared. All my instincts told me I should drop this, but I'm a stubborn girl.

"Okay. Tell me this, did Lucille know Van Widmark?"

"I think they met once."

"Before ya were estranged."

"Yeah."

"Do ya think she mighta seen him on her own?"

"Van? You mean, dated him?" She sounded miffed.

"Seen him."

"I doubt it."

"Why?"

"Have you met Van?"

"Yeah."

"Well, then."

"You mean cause he's in a wheelchair?"

70

"Yeah, I do."

"That wouldn't stop somebody from visitin him, would it?"

"Did Van tell you he'd seen her?"

"I haven't checked it out with him yet."

"Well, maybe you should."

This broad couldn't keep her yap shut. "Lucille's number."

"It's in my address book in my pocketbook, which is in my locker. I'll have to give it to you later."

They probably weren't too chummy if she had to look up her sister's number.

"What else did you want to clear up?" She could hardly wait to be cooperative.

"I went to Charlie's hotel room. Look, there's no good way to tell ya this. I found a dead man there."

She drew in her breath. "Was it Charlie?"

"We don't know." I told her what'd happened.

"So it could be anyone?"

"It could, sure." She didn't want to think it was Charlie and I didn't blame her. But more than likely it *was* Charlie and somewhere she knew that.

"Miss Turner, you're the only link we have to Charlie right now. We need this John Doe identified."

"I . . . I don't know. I've never seen a dead body. And if it's Charlie, I might go mad."

I didn't know why so many broads were so dramatic. I wondered if they got it from radio soap operas.

"They'll just pull back the sheet and show ya his face."

"But he'll still be dead."

I couldn't argue with that. "It would help a lot if you'd do it, Miss Turner."

"All right. Will you go with me?"

She was my client. What could I say? "Sure. Let me call and set up an appointment."

"Do you think it'll be today? I'll have to ask for time off."

"Call ya back soon as I know."

"No. I can't keep comin to the phone here. So when you call back, leave a message about the time and tell me now where to meet you."

"Across the street from Bellevue Hospital where the morgue is. There's a coffee shop there."

When we hung up, I dialed the morgue. It gave me the heebie-jeebies that I knew the number by heart. I asked for Glenn Madison. When he came on the line, we set up an appointment for later that day. I called Claire Turner's number and left a message to meet me at three-thirty.

Then I gave Powell a jingle and told him the arrangements.

"Ya made a morgue appointment without me?"

He sounded like a two-year-old. I said I'd see him later.

Next I tried Van Widmark's number to ask if Lucille Turner was his lady visitor, but there was no answer. I thought that was kinda strange, but maybe he had somebody who took him out now and then. Or maybe he didn't feel like answering the phone.

I bellowed for Birdie.

She came into my office. "Ya gotta get one a those thingamajigs. Ya want me to go shoppin for one?"

"No." I held out the pink message papers. "I want ya to call all these people back and tell em I'm goin outta town for a week. And if they want their money back we'll give it to em."

"We will?"

"Sure. Why should they have to wait?"

"Why will they?"

"I have a feelin this Turner case is gonna take up all my time."

"Anything ya say." She took the papers from me. "Your command is my word."

Claire Turner was waiting for me in the coffee shop when I got there. I wasn't crazy about that cause I always liked to be at a meeting first. She was sitting in a cherry-red leather booth at a Formica table, a Coke in front of her, the straw bent and unused, and a cigarette in the ashtray, the smoke rising in front of her kisser. I could see she was worried.

"You nervous?" I asked, sitting opposite her.

"Yeah." She took a tiny sip of her drink. "I just don't know what I'll do if it's Charlie."

"Let's cross that bridge later, okay?"

"I've been thinking."

Always a mistake.

"If it isn't Charlie, where is he? And if it isn't Charlie, why was a dead man in his closet?"

73

"Good questions."

"No answers?"

"Not yet. Another one of those bridges. Can I have yer sister's number and address now?"

"You mean you're gonna go see her?"

"I might hafta."

"Why?"

"Ya gotta let me do my job."

"Oh, all right."

I wrote down what she told me in my notepad. I didn't like it at all. Lucille Turner lived in New Jersey. Not that far away from my folks, in Newark. Plus, to get there I'd hafta get a car somehow. I'd worry about that later.

"Can we go soon?"

"Sure. Right now."

Her check was on the table. She put down some money and we left. Impossible, but outside felt hotter and stickier than when I'd gone into the coffee shop. At the corner of Twenty-seventh and First we waited for the light to change, then crossed.

The thing about Bellevue was it had a creepy rep. Everybody knew the squirrelly types landed there. They probably knew about the morgue. And even though the place was also a regular hospital, its look added to the sense of spookiness.

The redbrick building had big wrought-iron gates in front and bars on some of the windows. It loomed large, like a medieval dungeon.

The gates were open and we walked through to the

main entrance and directly to the elevators. I knew how to get to the morgue.

"I don't think I can do this, Miss Quick."

I gently put my hand on her arm. "Sure ya can."

"I wish Charlie was here."

Maybe he was, I thought. Had she forgotten?

"Claire . . . can I call ya Claire?"

"Sure."

"Claire, I know this is tough for ya, but I think yer made of strong stuff. I know ya can do this. And I'll be right by your side."

The elevator opened. The operator was one of those older guys and had a face like a turnip. We got on.

"Morgue, please."

He looked at me suspiciously. "You sure, girly?"

"Yeah, I'm sure."

"You two together?"

"That's right. What of it?"

"*You* I can see going down there, but not her." He pointed at Claire.

"Thanks, buster. Now get this thing rollin."

He grabbed the stick and the doors closed. Under his breath he grumbled, but I didn't try to hear him. I took Claire's hand and squeezed. She gave me a smile that came and went like payday.

The elevator stopped. "Morgue," the old guy said.

We got off to the grumbling of Handsome, and we turned right. I opened a big door and there was Powell, pacing in front of a girl sitting at a desk.

I introduced Claire and Powell, and I watched while

the grizzled detective turned to jelly just meeting this babe. What was wrong with men?

I took it upon myself to tell the girl that we were there to see Glenn Madison. She buzzed him on one of those things I hadda get and in a few minutes he came out in his white coat.

When I introduced him to Claire, it was easy to see he was also keen on her right away. This was ridiculous. I didn't think I wanted Johnny to meet this skirt. We all followed Madison back through a dark corridor and stopped at big steel double doors.

"It's going to be very cold inside, Miss Turner."

"That's fine. I could use some cold air."

Suddenly she was talking in a tiny voice, almost a whisper. I hated dames that did this. But both guys looked like what she said, and how she said it, was more important than Roosevelt's infamy speech.

We went inside. The room had metal gurneys all lined up with sheets covering bodies. Good thing. I didn't want Claire put off before we got to our John Doe.

Madison walked us down the right side of the room and stopped at a corpse with number 2831 on his toe tag.

"Are you ready, Miss Turner?"

He didn't bother asking the old shoe. Me.

"I don't know what it's like to be ready for this."

"You'll be just fine, Miss Turner. I won't let anything happen to you."

Oh, brother.

"Ya want I should hold yer hand, Miss Turner?" Powell asked.

"No, thank you," she said.

This was getting revolting.

"Okay," Glenn said. "Here we go. I'm going to pull this back enough for you to see his face. All right?"

Claire nodded.

He slowly peeled back the sheet and when the guy's face was fully exposed Claire gave a gasp and started to crumble. Powell caught her.

SIX

G lenn Madison had taken over and I watched while he carried Claire Turner out of the morgue room to his office, where he placed her in a chair and called for a gurney.

Powell picked up some papers from the desk and started fanning her with them.

"You think that's necessary?"

"The little girl passed out," Powell said.

"It could be her heart," Glenn said.

Claire opened her eyes. "Charlie."

"Would you like some water?" Glenn asked.

I always wondered what water was supposed to do in cases like this.

"No, thank you." She put her face in her hands and began to cry.

Helplessly, Powell looked at me. I shrugged.

"Glenn, ya better stop that gurney from comin down here."

"What gurney?" Claire asked.

"I thought maybe you should be admitted," he said.

"Admitted?" She eyed him like he was screwy. "I'm just so relieved. I expected it to be Charlie."

"You mean it wasn't?" I asked.

"I'd better cancel." Glenn picked up the phone and turned his back to us.

"Miss Turner," Powell said, "ya know who the stiff is?"

She looked shocked at his use of the word *stiff,* and he caught on real fast.

"I mean, the corpse, the body, the guy on the slab. Can ya ID him?"

"I've never seen him before in my life."

Powell and I looked at each other. We knew we were behind the eight ball again.

"I gotta get back to work," Claire said. She stood up and turned to me. "You'll keep looking for Charlie, won't you?"

"The police are on this case, Miss Turner," said Powell.

"Yeah, finally. Nobody paid any attention to me when I reported him missing."

"You didn't come to me. I'm on this case now." Powell shot her what was supposed to be a smile, but looked more like he was in rigor.

"Wait a minute. What case is that?" Claire said.

"This case. Who the . . . the gentleman is."

"I don't give a damn who he is. I just wanna find Charlie."

"Claire, if we can find out who this guy is, it might help us track down Charlie," I said.

"Did it ever occur to ya, Quick, that Ladd mighta bumped off our John Doe?" Powell said.

"Hey. What're you tryin to pull, you big lug?" Claire said. "Charlie wouldn't hurt a fly."

Powell didn't realize he'd put his hoof in his mouth because he came back with, "That's what they all say."

Course he was right but that wasn't the point.

"Claire, I'll stay on this thing as long as ya want."

"Thanks, Faye."

"Listen," Powell said. "You better stay outta my way, Quick. I find ya interferin with *my* case, I'm gonna lock ya up."

He marched out and didn't look back.

"Is that true, Faye?"

"Nah. He's just blowin smoke."

She looked at her wristwatch. "Oh, God, I gotta go."

"I'll walk you to a cab, Miss Turner."

What a turkey Madison was turning out to be.

"Ya don't have to do that, Glenn. I'm leavin, too."

"Oh. Sure."

"I gotta get crackin on the case of Miss Turner's missin boyfriend."

Glenn's face fell like a collapsible summer chair. I wondered where he'd been through all this. At least he got my drift and we left.

Outside, I said, "So, Claire. Yer parents speak to Lucille more than you do?"

"They don't speak to her, either."

"Why's that?"

"You'll have to ask them."

"Okay, I will." It was clear she was clamming up about this particular angle. I changed the subject.

"Does Lucille work?"

"Yeah. In a bookstore in Newark. She's the brainy one."

"I need the info on that. And for yer parents, too. You understand, don'tcha?"

"I guess. Yeah, sure."

She knew this stuff without looking in her little book. That figured for her parents, but Lucille's work number? She'd had to look up her sister's home phone.

"I really gotta go now."

I hailed a cab. She got in.

"You'll keep me posted, won't you? Oh, are you comin over to get the picture?"

It was late now and I had stuff to do before my date with Johnny. "I'll have to get it tomorrow."

"Okay. Bye."

I watched the cab drive away. What a mess. I'd been sure it was Private Ladd in the wardrobe. Open and shut, I'd thought. So who was the John Doe and why was he in Ladd's closet? Nothing was making a whole lotta sense.

I crossed the street and went back to the coffee shop.

The guy behind the counter was big and hairy. His sleeves were rolled up so I could see what might pass for a weaving experiment.

"Could I use yer phone?"

"You wuz in here before, wuzn't ya?"

"Yeah." I pointed to the booth where we'd sat.

"With the tomato, huh?"

"I was with another girl, yeah."

"She wuz somethin."

"She's taken."

"Too bad." As if he was God's gift and Claire would jump at the chance to do a two-step with him.

"Guess yer outta luck. So could I use yer phone? I'm only callin across town."

He motioned me behind the counter where the phone was. I dialed Birdie and asked if there were any important messages. There weren't.

"What about the Ladds?"

"I found em. Want the number?"

"You bet." I grabbed a napkin and wrote it down. "And George Cummings?"

"Got it."

I wrote that down, too. "Good work, Bird."

"Mercy bucow."

I told her I was going home and she could leave.

"Thanks," I said to the counter guy.

"Anytime. Hey, is that dame's boyfriend a soldier by any chance?"

"Yeah. Why?"

"I wuz wonderin if you'd put a word in for me."

I almost thought I heard wrong. "Listen, buster. I wouldn't put in a word for you with Whistler's mother."

"Who's she?"

"So long."

"Hey. Whazza matter wit you? I let ya use my phone and everything."

I didn't hang around to find out what *everything* was.

My crib was in Greenwich Village on Grove Street near Bleecker where carts lined a couple of blocks offering the freshest vegetables, fruits, and fish in town. I shopped there almost every day for my dinner, but tonight I was going out with Johnny.

Dolores, my neighbor across the hall, was sitting on the top step trying to cool herself with a hand fan.

"Oy, what a stinkin day, Faye. This must be what hell's like."

"Ya been sittin out here long?"

"I had my work to do, then I came out."

Dolores had a need to sweep the hall every day even though we had a janitor who did that. Course he didn't do it *every day*. She also wiped down the frame of her doorway and washed the two big windows in her apartment that looked out on the street.

And she wore a wig. It was different colors on different days, and always askew. Nobody in the neighborhood knew why she wore any of them and it wasn't something you could ask her about. She also went heavy on the makeup and wore mismatched clothes. Checks with stripes or polka dots, yellow with purple.

I took a closer look at her fan. "Where'd ya get that, Dolores?"

"World's Fair." She spread it out completely and held it open for me to see.

It said: 1904 WORLD'S FAIR. THE LOUISIANA PURCHASE EXPOSITION, ST. LOUIS, MISSOURI.

"I guess ya missed that one, didn't ya?" She gave me one of her big smiles, and a wink.

"I went to the one here in 1939."

"Yeah. That was a beauty, too. But for me, bubele, the one in St. Louis was the best. Oh, the lights on the water at night."

No one knew how old Dolores was but I figured she musta been somewhere in her thirties when she went to the fair. Who did she go with? I wanted to ask but I had to get ready for my date.

"I'd like to hear all about it sometime, but I need to get dressed."

"Ya got a date with that nice detective goy boy?"

"Yeah."

"When are ya gettin married?"

"Married?" Even the word gave me the jimjams.

"Ya heard a the institution, ain'tcha?"

"I'm not sure I'll ever get married."

"Ha. Ya say that now. But wait."

"For what?"

She nodded over and over like she had a special secret.

"I gotta go, Dolores." I hoped she wouldn't still be sitting out there when Johnny arrived. I was afraid she'd grill him about marriage.

"You go. Dress nice."

"I will." I went through the front door and into the vestibule. There wasn't much in my mailbox except a few bills. I opened the inside door and went to my apartment.

Zachary came sidling up to me, mewing. He was only a few months old. After Cedric died I waited over a year before getting Zach. He was a black cat with a white diamond on his forehead.

I leaned down and petted him. "Yer gonna eat in a minute."

My place was basically two big rooms with a small kitchen between them. The WC was off the kitchen. The apartment had been the parlor floor of a town house once upon a time. The living room had high ceilings with ornate moldings around them and carved cherubs in the corners. Two large windows looked over the street, and I'd hung red velvet draperies that I closed at night.

It was a big room. I'd put two sofas in there and three easy chairs, with a table folded up against a wall that I used for dinner company. Mahogany bookcases lined one wall and were beginning to strain at the seams. The right front corner was empty cause I was saving my pennies for the piano I was gonna put there. I could itch a mean ivory and I had pretty good pipes, too. You wouldn't say I rivaled

Billie Holiday, but who did?

I'd been nervous about telling Johnny what the empty space was waiting for, but he didn't laugh or think it was silly. Far from it. He was always trying to get me to sing. I told him I would when I got the piano. Well, maybe.

I put down Zachary's food.

Then I got the long-distance operator and gave her the Ladds' number. There was no answer. I was relieved. Telling parents their son was missing wasn't any can a corn. I'd try again the next day cause I knew I'd be getting home too late from my date to call then.

Now it was time to take a bath and change clothes.

Johnny and I didn't stay to see the second picture. We both loved *This Is the Army*. George Murphy was one of my favorites and I liked the way Frances Langford sang.

Holding hands, we walked from the Loews on Second Avenue. Johnny had a big hand and I had a small one. He was always saying he was afraid mine would get lost in his.

He was tall and lanky and had a long face with deep-set brown blinkers, a regular nose, and a full mouth— not one of those slits a lotta men have. All in all he was a good-looking guy. But that wasn't his main attraction for me. Not that I had anything against handsome men.

What I liked most about him was his kindness. Some detectives, like Powell, hafta put on a show about how tough they are, but Johnny never did that. I had no doubt that he *was* tough, but he didn't have the need to act that way. I also liked his sense of humor, his smarts, that he read novels, and the way he treated me.

We talked about the movie while we walked and before I knew it we were back at my apartment. He usually came in for a coffee or a nightcap, but he had an early-morning meeting with his captain.

He saw me to the vestibule and we kissed for a long time. When we broke apart he said, "Faye, there's something I want to say."

My heart did a jitterbug. After that kiss I didn't think he wanted to split up, but you never knew. Marriage passed through my brain and that was worse. I wanted to tell him to save it for a rainy day but I knew I couldn't do that.

"What's that, Johnny?"

"I'm not quite sure how to say this."

"Then don't say it." Lily-livered, that was me.

"But I want to."

"Okay." Behind my back I crossed my fingers on both hands.

"I think we should stop dating other people."

You coulda knocked me over with a cat's whisker. What other people? Maybe he was dating, but I wasn't.

I knew I had to say something so after a mo I said, "I didn't know you'd been datin a lot, Johnny." That was dumb.

"I haven't. I thought you might be."

"Me? Me?"

"You don't have to sound like it's an impossibility."

"It's just that it's so far from the truth. I never gave datin another guy a thought." I didn't add that they weren't lined up around the block, cause in my heart of hearts I knew if someone had asked me I wouldn't have gone anyway.

"So what do you think?" he asked.

Saying what he had out loud made our romance more serious. My knees knocking together told me I was scared, but I also knew this was what I wanted.

"I'd like that," I said.

"Good. Now you're mine."

Uh-oh. "And yer mine," I said.

"That's what I meant. We belong together. To each other."

I hoped that's what he meant.

"You've made me very happy, Faye."

I smiled up at him. He leaned down and kissed me. A sweet kiss.

"I'd better go now. I'll talk to you tomorrow."

"Okay."

We said our good nights and he waited while I opened and closed the inside door. Once in, I turned and we waved to each other. I watched him go down the steps.

When I got into my apartment, Zachary was there to greet me, mewing and winding himself around my ankles. I got rid of my pocketbook and picked him up.

"Guess what, Zach? We're goin steady."

The phone rang, Zach flew, and I went over to the telephone table and sat down before I answered. What if I picked it up to hear Johnny'd changed his mind? Then I realized there hadn't been enough time for him to get home. I reached for the horn.

It was Marty Mitchum.

"I didn't wake ya up, did I, Faye? I've been tryin ya all night."

"I just got in. What's up?"

"I heard ya didn't identify your John Doe."

"Right."

"Here's what I found out. All the clothes in the duffel fit Ladd. The stuff in the wardrobe, too."

"What about the clothes from under the bed?"

"They probably belonged to the dead guy cause he was five eight and Ladd's six feet."

"How d'ya know that?"

"Powell talked to Ladd's parents and they told him."

"So they know he's missin?"

"They're on their way to town."

I hated having Powell in on this but at least I was off the hook on telling the Ladds about their son.

"I think they gotta be upper crust cause they're gonna be stayin at the St. Moritz."

"Pretty swanky."

"Ya gonna go see em?"

"If I can. Who knows how hard Powell's gonna make it."

"Yeah. But I heard even though he buzzed the

Ladds, he's a lot more interested in John Doe."

"Ya know if he's gonna ask the Ladds to ID him?"

"Don't know that. But he probably will, don'tcha think?"

"Makes sense to me. Thanks for givin me the skinny, Marty."

"Ya betcha."

So most of the clothes were Ladd's. And only the stuff under the bed belonged to the stiff. I wondered what that meant. Did Charlie Ladd bump off John Doe, take off his clothes and shove em under the bed, then leave without taking anything but what was on his back? Or did John Doe check in as Private Ladd and get bumped off in Ladd's room? It didn't explain the clothes, but maybe there was something I wasn't putting together.

And did the killer want John Doe, or did he think he'd killed Ladd?

SEVEN

*T*he next morning at eight in the A.M. I got on the horn to George Cummings. I said his old-school chum was missing and that I'd like to talk to George. He said he'd meet me for coffee at the corner of Pine and Warren streets at O'Brien's Luncheonette, ten sharp. He'd be in a gray suit and sporting a striped tie. I told him I thought most men in there would be wearing the same thing. He allowed how that was true.

So I told him what I'd be wearing. A yellow short-sleeve number cinched at the waist. In my left-hand breast pocket there'd be a blue silk hankie. And on my feet I'd be wearing blue open-toed shoes with an ankle strap. He said it sounded cute and I almost hung up on him.

I didn't much like the Wall Street area, except maybe on weekends when it was quiet. Nobody lived there and the Stock Exchange was closed. So was everything else.

But this was a Friday and the place was jumping and the buildings were high. Summertime. I started singing that tune in my head. I knew it was wrong for my voice, but in my head I did a great job.

By the time I got to O'Brien's I felt like a dragon had been breathing on me. Inside wasn't much cooler.

Cummings stood up the minute I came through the door. Seemed like everybody was getting to meetings before me even though I got there early. He was a stocky guy with black hair parted on the left side. He was clean-shaven and as I got closer I could see that his specs were as thick as slabs of ham. He wore exactly what he'd said he would.

"Miss Quick, please sit down."

He did and I did. The place was full despite the hour.

"Would you care for some coffee?"

"Sure."

He signaled for a waitress.

I reached into my pocketbook and got out my Camels. Cummings was ready with a light before I

90

had the cigarette out of the pack. "Thanks."

He took his own from a leather-and-brass case and lit it with a matching lighter.

"So you're here to talk about Charlie, poor bastard. Oh, excuse me, Miss Quick."

"I've heard worse and call me Faye. Can I call ya George?"

"Of course."

"Yeah, I'm here to talk about Charlie. When's the last time ya saw him?"

"Let's see. Today is Friday so I guess a week ago."

I didn't let on that I was flabbergasted. "Ya mean last Friday?"

"We all met for drinks."

"Who's *we all?*"

"Me, Charlie, and the young soldier he had with him. Charlie and I went to college together."

"Yeah. I know." I took out my notepad. "What was the name of the other soldier?"

"Charlie's friend . . . give me a second and I'll think of it. Oh, yes. David Cooper. That was his name."

"Supposedly Charlie didn't arrive in town until Saturday," I said.

He chuckled. "He told Claire that because he wanted a night on the town with the boys."

"You know Claire?"

"Of course."

The waitress finally appeared. She was a bottle blonde with droopy dark eyes and an expression that said she didn't care what you wanted. "Yeah?"

"A cup of coffee for the lady, please."

"That all?"

"Faye?"

"Maybe I'll have a Danish. What kind ya got?"

"Cheese and prune."

I thought for a few seconds.

"This ain't like ya gotta decide between rubies or diamonds, ya know."

"Cheese," I said.

"Glad we got that one settled. Now life can go on. Anything for you," she asked.

"I'm fine with the coffee. Thanks."

She left.

"She's a little brusque," George said.

I smiled, thinking I'd like to give the broad one in the chops. "Have ya met Claire often?"

"Once or twice."

I'd been right. She lied about knowing him.

"Can ya think of any reason Claire would say she'd never met ya?"

"She said that?"

I nodded.

"No. I can't imagine why she would." He looked hurt.

"Maybe I misunderstood," I said.

He didn't say anything and looked down at his coffee.

"So where did you gents go on boys' night out?"

"Where *didn't* we go?" He was looking chipper again.

"Meanin ya hit all the spots?"

"That's right. From the Biltmore to Tony Pastor's and everything in between." He laughed then snorted.

"So ya musta been feelin no pain by the time ya went home."

"You could say that."

I saw that he was proud of that dubious accomplishment.

"What happened when the night ended?"

"I went home. I'm not sure where they went. I guess you can tell why I'm not in the service." He adjusted his cheaters.

"Your eyes?"

"Legally blind without these. Otherwise I'd be over there giving those Huns a run for their money."

Every guy who wasn't in the war wanted to be. And they all acted like they were Superman. If they only knew. I wished I could have Woody's letters printed in some paper. They wouldn't be so eager to get into it then.

"This David Cooper was in the service, too?"

"Army. A private like Charlie."

"And ya never saw or talked to either one of em again."

"No. I knew Charlie was planning to spend his time with Claire and I had no reason to be in touch with Cooper."

"Any ideas why Charlie would be missin?"

"None at all. To tell you the truth, I don't think he *is* missing."

"What's that mean?"

"I'm not sure I should tell you."

"George, if ya have any idea about where Charlie Ladd is, I think ya better tell me."

"Coffee and cheese Danish," the waitress said, and plunked it down in front of me, a slurp of java jumping the lip to the saucer. "Eat up."

"Brusque," I said.

"Very."

"So what about Charlie?" I squashed my cig in the ashtray.

"Well, we did have some female company that night."

"And?"

"Charlie seemed pretty taken with one of the girls."

"I don't suppose ya know her name?"

"I do. It was Ida Collier. She was some dish."

"And ya know where I can find her?"

"Well, not exactly."

I hated *not exactly*. "Ya mean ya don't have an address but ya know kinda?"

"That's right. She lives in town. I think she said Greenwich Village. You know those types."

"Yeah, sure. Real immoral." I took a bite of Danish. Very nice.

"Exactly."

"So what yer sayin is that Charlie mighta flown the coop for Ida?"

"Might. He was pretty damn interested in her."

"And what about Private Cooper? He interested in some babe, too?"

"I'd say he had a minimal interest in someone called Gloria Lane. She was pretty, too, but not like Ida."

"How about you, Georgie. Don't tell me you were left out of the activities."

"I'm married."

"And?"

"I don't cheat."

"No offense intended."

"None taken. Is there anything else? I need to get back to my office."

"This Cooper character. He act any special way toward Charlie?"

"I don't understand what you mean?"

"Was there any tension between them?"

He put his head back and stared at the ceiling like there was gonna be an answer up there.

"George?"

"I'm trying to recall."

"Lemme know when ya do." This guy was getting my goat.

He came back from mining the ceiling for info. "There was something odd about Cooper. Not odd, exactly. Quiet. He kept up with us drink for drink but he barely spoke at all. I thought he was a bit sulky."

Sulky. Who says sulky about a guy?

"Could ya describe him?"

"Look, Miss Quick. I didn't pay much attention to him. I didn't even know him. Charlie's my friend and I hadn't seen him in a while."

"So ya were more focused on him."

"That's right."

"Anything ya could tell me about Cooper would be helpful."

"Such as?"

"Color of hair, his eyes, anything?"

"I think he had dark hair. Yes, it was dark. But I can't remember anything else about him. The uniform tends to make everyone look alike."

"If ya saw him again, would ya recognize him?"

"Oh, yes. I'm sure I would."

"Then I'd like ya to do somethin, George. When ya get back to work, I'd like ya to call this number and ask for Detective Powell. Tell him ya might be able to identify the body found at the Commodore Hotel."

"Body?"

"Yeah. It's not Charlie, so don't worry. But the body was found in Charlie's room."

"This is incredible."

"Good word for it."

"And you don't know whose body it is?"

"That's right. Claire saw him and didn't know him."

"You think it might be Cooper?"

"I have no idea. Could be. But it might be somebody else altogether."

"I don't think I can do this. I can't tell them at work that I have to leave to identify a body."

"I said to call the detective. I didn't say ya had to go to the morgue during work hours."

"The *morgue?*"

"That's where they keep unidentified bodies,

George." I finished off my Danish.

"I have to go." He started to slide outta the booth.

I reached over and laid my hand on his. "Ya can be subpoenaed to do this, ya know." I didn't think that was true, but I didn't think he'd know, either.

"I've never done anything like this."

"Most people haven't. If ya can ID this guy, it'll be a big help."

"All right."

"You'll call Powell?"

"Yes. You have my word."

"You sure."

"Miss Quick, I've given you my word."

I caught the drift. Word and honor. "Okay. You have nothin to be afraid of, George. There's nothin gory to look at."

"I'm *not* afraid, Miss Quick. It's just damn inconvenient." He stood up and threw some money on the table.

The waitress watched him leave and made a beeline to our booth. When she saw he'd left money she settled down to her annoying self.

"Ya want anything else?"

"Now that ya ask, I think I'll have another Danish. And give me another cup a joe, too."

After my snack I went up to the Village to my apartment. Dolores was on the steps. Her wig was particularly cockeyed and it was hard not to say anything, but I kept my trap shut.

"Well, bubele, yer home early."

"Not stayin. I need to look somethin up."

"For yer case?"

"Yeah."

"I dunno how ya can stand rushing around in this heat."

"I can't stand it, but I don't have a choice. I'd love to stay and chew the fat with ya, Dolores, but I'm in an awful hurry."

"Sure, darling. You go."

"I'll see ya later."

"You'll see me when ya come out. I'll be here all day."

"Swell."

Inside, I went straight to the telephone table and took out the book. Zach was sleeping on the couch and couldna cared less about me cause it wasn't feeding time.

I opened the phone book to the *C*'s, turning pages until I finally came to the right name. There were all kinds of them. On the next page I found the *I*'s. Not too many of those. I found what I was looking for and wrote down the phone and address. She didn't live far from me. I wondered if I should call first. Better to take her off guard.

Then I talked to Marty and told him John Doe's possible name. Marty was gonna run a check in the hotel, see if he could find Cooper. I don't know why but I was getting a feeling more and more that Cooper was making the morgue home.

Outside, Dolores said, "See. Here I am. Here I stay."

"I'm off," I said.

I went down the steps and headed west. Ida Collier lived off Bleecker on Leroy Street.

For all I knew I'd find Charlie Ladd in her bed.

EIGHT

Collier's place was one in from the corner. The building was brick and looked slightly off kilter, like a broad with her slip showing.

I went up the steps to check the names and see what floor Collier was on. I found it. She was in the basement apartment so I hadda go down the steps and to the left, through a wrought-iron gate, and down three steps more. The shade was pulled on the window and why not? Open, anyone could see in.

I rang the bell. Waited. Rang it again. Waited. Once more.

"Hold your horses," a woman's voice said. The door opened a crack and a pair of sleepy eyes looked out at me.

"Are you Ida Collier?"

"Whaddaya want?"

"I wanna speak to Ida Collier."

"That's me. Who're you?"

I told her.

She laughed. "A private eye? C'mon."

I showed her my license. "I'd like to come in and talk to ya."

"About what?"

"Charlie Ladd."

"Who?"

Either she was a good actress or she didn't remember him.

"You were with him last Friday. A private in the army."

"I know lots of privates in the army."

I bet she did. "Look, can ya let me come in? It's hotter'n Hades out here."

"You think it's cooler in here?"

"You got a fan?"

"Yeah."

"I'll sit in front of it."

She let out a sigh the size of the Chrysler Building and opened the door wider so I could go in. The room was dark. I could barely make out what was what.

"Lemme put on a light," Ida said.

When she did, I saw she was in her bathrobe, which she wore over a long pink nightgown.

"Excuse my appearance. I had a late night." She gave me a knowing look.

There was an unmade bed in the corner and the rest of the room had a few chairs around a coffee table. There was a galley kitchen and a door that musta led to the bathroom. Unless Ladd was in there he wasn't with Ida Collier.

I looked around for the fan but didn't see one. The air was thick and hot.

"I need coffee," she said. "Want some?"

"Sure."

She went over to her little kitchen and lit the gas under the coffeepot.

Then she turned around to face me. She had wavy platinum hair like Jean Harlow, cool blue eyes the size of quarters, a straight nose, and full lips. The kinda girl a soldier on leave might wanna make hay with. After lighting up she put a hand on her hip.

"So, what can I do ya?"

I took out a Camel and lit it. "What about that fan?"

"It's broke."

"But ya said . . ."

"I said I had a fan and I do. You didn't ask me if it worked."

How'd I get so lucky playing games with a wiseacre in a room the size and temperature of a pizza oven?

"Can we sit down?" I said.

"Why not?"

We sat in chairs that weren't too steady.

"Miss Collier, I . . ."

"Ida. Call me Ida. What's your handle again?"

"Faye."

"Oh, yeah. So you were sayin, Faye?"

"Do ya remember meetin Private Charlie Ladd? It was Friday night."

She blew a smoke circle into the room. "A bell is ringin. He with a few other guys?"

"Yeah."

"A looker as I recall. Yeah, Charlie."

"Have ya seen him since then?"

"Nah. It was just one night."

"And where was that?"

"Jazz club. Village Vanguard on Seventh Avenue."

I knew it like I knew myself.

"So that was it then. In the club."

"And here. Later. I don't wantcha gettin the wrong idea about me. Me and Charlie was havin a deep discussion and when the others wanted to leave, well, me and Charlie wanted to go on with it. So that's what we did. I think the java's ready." She got up and swung her way to the stove.

So why did she pretend she didn't know who Ladd was?

"Meanin you left with Charlie and the other private?"

"Not quite. How d'ya take your coffee?"

I told her. "What's *not quite* mean?"

"The other guy left with my friend Gloria. A great gal."

She handed me my coffee.

I quashed my cig in a black ashtray. "Thanks. At first ya said ya didn't know who Charlie was. How come?"

"I didn't wanna be too agreeable, ya know?"

"No."

"Sometimes ya give with the info right off the bat and people take advantage."

"Like what?"

"You wouldn't wanna know."

I would, but some other time. "So ya remember the

other private? The one who went off with that great gal, Gloria?"

"Sure, I remember him."

"What about the third guy?"

"Kind of a stiff, ya ask me."

Maybe I'd pegged Ida wrong. She'd been straight with me for at least three minutes.

"You know where Gloria lives?"

"Sure. Say, what's this all about anyway?"

"Can ya give me Gloria's address?"

"I don't think I will."

"Why not?"

"Cause ya won't tell me what's goin on."

"If I tell ya, will ya give me Gloria's address."

"Yeah."

"Charlie Ladd's missin."

"Whaddaya mean missin?"

"He hasn't been seen since Monday night."

"You on the level?"

"Yeah."

"What about his friend?"

"David Cooper?"

"Was that his name? I never did get it. Glo probably did, though. Anyways, is he missin, too?"

"Not sure. But there's an unidentified dead guy in all this."

"You sayin somebody croaked?"

"Somebody was knocked off."

"Cooper?"

"Maybe."

"You've seen the stiff?"

"Yeah." I didn't think it would help anything if I told her I'd found him. "All we know is that it's not Charlie."

"That's good. I bet his girlfriend's tearin her hair out."

"Ladd told ya he had a girlfriend?"

"Sure. Showed me her picture, too. Nice-lookin babe. What's the matter? Why are ya lookin at me like that?"

"I'm surprised."

"At what?"

"That Ladd would tell ya about his girlfriend."

"Why? It's not like we was plannin to set up house or anything."

"So now can ya give me Gloria's address?"

"I'm feelin sorta reluctant, ya get my drift."

"I don't."

"Is Gloria gonna get in any trouble?"

"No more than you."

"Hey. Ya mean I'm gonna be in hot water?" She lit another cigarette. "I need a drink. You want one?"

I didn't have to check my watch to know it wasn't even noon. "No, thanks."

"Suit yerself."

She got up and went to the kitchen again, opened a cabinet above the sink, and took out a bottle of something clear that I guessed was gin. I watched while she poured a couple a fingers into a tall glass. She gulped it down and then poured another, put the bottle on the counter, and came back to her chair.

"So as I was sayin, is this gonna get me in a jam?"

"If I found ya, the cops will. So ya better gimme Gloria's address so I can put her wise to the situation."

"Me and Gloria didn't have nothin to do with nobody croakin or disappearin."

"I think ya should know the stiff was found in Ladd's hotel room."

Her face lost the little bit of luster she'd hung on to.

"When?"

"Yesterday."

"Yesterday I was tied up."

"I didn't say he was killed yesterday."

"Well, it don't matter when the corpse croaked cause like I said, me and Gloria had nothin to do with it."

"Have ya talked to her since ya spent yer evenin with the boys? Compared notes?"

"Who do ya think we are, June Allyson and Deanna Durbin? We don't gab on the horn and I ain't seen her since that night." She took a swig of her gin.

"So how d'ya know she didn't have anything to do with the murder?"

"You kiddin me? Glo's a decent girl, no matter what ya think."

"Whaddaya mean, what I think?"

"I'm not just off the farm, ya know. I can tell when a person's lookin down on me."

"That's what ya think I'm doin?"

"Ain'tcha?"

"No." I wondered if I was. "You think I'm some sorta saint?"

"Betcha yer a virgin."

"Now yer getting outta line, Ida."

She smirked and took a deep drag on her cig.

"I have no opinion about what ya did or didn't do with Charlie Ladd. And I don't care. All I wanna do is find him."

"And what about the stiff?"

"That's why I wanna talk to Gloria."

"See, that's what I mean. Yer gonna get her up a creek without a paddle fer nothin."

"If she didn't do anything, she'll have a paddle."

"Why don'tcha let me give her the scoop?"

"Cause I need to talk to her, that's why?"

"Okay. I'll give ya her address. But when you leave, I'm callin her."

"I can't stop ya from doin what ya think ya have to do. But yer makin me awful suspicious."

"About what?"

"What you girls might know. Lemme ask ya this. We need ya, are ya willin to ID a body?"

"Hell, no."

I didn't think we'd need her cause Cummings was gonna do that. "Then gimme Gloria's address and ya won't have to."

"Ya think I'd sell out a friend for somethin like that?"

I stared at her.

"What the hell. Like ya said, the cops'll be comin

106

here anyways. She lives on East Twenty-eighth Street."

"Building number?"

She gave it to me. Also the phone in case Gloria wasn't in. "You girls don't work, right?"

"You bet yer bottom dollar we work. Just not the hours you work."

"Night shift."

"You got it."

I thanked her for the coffee and the info. For a second it did feel cooler outside than in Ida's place. Then the humidity hit me like a wet towel.

I was hungry and Gloria could wait. After Ida called her she probably wouldn't be home anyway. I decided to grab a snack at Blondell's. It was on West Fourth Street, not far from where I was.

Ida Collier was something else. I didn't think she had anything to do with Ladd disappearing or the body in the hotel room. But I couldn't rule out Gloria till I met her.

I got to Blondell's pretty quick. The gold star in the plate-glass window always gave me a turn when I saw it. Most of the tables and booths were taken. I found one in the back of the room, which was fine by me. I could read my book in peace.

Skip, the owner, came over when he saw me. He looked like he had two black eyes and had been in a fight. But I knew different. I knew the bruising around his eyes was from grief. His brother, Fred, had been killed in action not so long ago.

"How are ya, Faye? Long time no see."

It was true. I had a hard time going to the joint cause everything had changed since Fred's death.

"I'm okay, Skip. How about you?"

"Gettin along." He parked his big body in the chair across from me.

Since Fred's death, Skip'd let his black hair, which he'd always worn in a military cut, grow out. I didn't know what it meant, if anything.

"Ya got any interestin cases, Faye?"

And that was another thing. He'd never called me Faye before Fred died. It was always monikers like Snappy Susan, Delicious Donna, Gorgeous Gladys. Different all the time. But no more. Although Skip was running the eatery, he was just making the moves. It was like he was a blown-out Easter egg, undecorated. Skip died when Fred did.

"Interestin cases? Ah, nothin to speak of. Skip, yer not lookin so good."

"Just don't tell me to pull myself together, okay?"

"I'd never say that." And I never would.

"Alla time customers come in and say things like *You should be over it by now, Skip*. Why? Why should I be over it by now? Who says? Or *Life goes on, Skip*. They think I don't know that?" He fingered the scar that ran down his left cheek.

"People mean well," I said like some dumb Pollyanna.

He gave me a look with those deep dark eyes.

I said, "Yeah, I know. I'm full of it."

He laughed, something I hadn't seen him do for months.

"You're the best, Faye. Guess I better get my behind into the kitchen." He got up and said, "Keep your powder dry, kid. And try the meat loaf."

So that's what I ordered. Meat loaf, mashed, and beans.

NINE

S kip always let me use the phone so I dialed the office from Blondell's.

"Marty called ya," Birdie said.

"He say what he wanted?"

"All he said was to meet him at Smitty's ya got back in time."

"And what time is that?"

"Three."

I checked my ticker. Plenty of time. "Anybody else call?"

"No. We got no clients now ya had me tell em all to go away."

"You didn't put it like that, did ya, Bird?"

"Whaddaya take me for, a dumb bunny? I said what ya told me. Yer outta town."

"Good. I probably won't be back today, Birdie."

"What if somebody needs ya?"

"I'll call ya later, there or at home."

"Sure thing. I'll be home. Pete's comin over for

dinner. I'm makin his favorite. Pork chops and sauerkraut with potatoes."

"Sounds good." It also sounded hot.

"I'll make it for ya sometime."

"Swell." I wasn't sure why but I'd never been to Birdie's apartment. I guess she'd never invited me.

"For a person who warned another person about the weather it seems that first person is stayin outside a lot today."

"No choice. So long, Bird. Hope ya have a good dinner with Pete."

"Thanks."

Gloria Lane was next.

Gloria turned out to be a dud. I was surprised she hadn't ducked out on me, but she said she wanted to get "this stupid thing" over with. She didn't give me much more than Ida had. So I made it short and sweet.

I was gonna meet Marty at Smitty's. Normally I woulda walked it, but the sidewalk was scorching and the air had that shimmer that made everyone longer and gave em blurry edges like looking through a screwy lens. At Twenty-eighth and Lex I went into the subway to get the train to Forty-second. Not much of an improvement. It was airless and roasting. The train came in and I got a seat. Right across from a soldier with one arm.

It felt like a kick in the stomach. This kinda reminder of the war broke my heart. Maybe we'd learn a lesson this time and, when this war was over, there'd never be another.

The soldier looked like a kid. Ruddy cheeks and blond hair, right outta high school. I didn't wanna stare so I opened my book, but I couldn't concentrate. I kept stewing about the soldier and what was gonna happen to him now. Did he have a girl waiting for him back home? Did she know yet? Had she seen him? How would she handle it when she did see him?

I took the last letter I got from Woody out of my pocketbook. There was a paragraph that got me where I live.

It's scary as hell here, Faye. Everybody starts out tough and gung ho, ready for action, and then the truth hits you in the kisser. It's hell on earth. Bullets whizzing past your ears. Kids being blown up right in front of you. And then the ones who lose a body part and are shipped to a hospital. You know their lives are over, in a way. I got to admit I don't think I'd do too well without a leg or hands. Will you love me anyway if I make it back?

I folded it up and put it away. I couldn't help myself from looking up at the soldier. He was staring at me. And then he smiled, like he was the happiest guy in the world. I smiled back, but I was still chewing over Woody's words.

At Forty-second I got off and hauled myself down the sweltering streets. Smitty's was on Forty-sixth and usually it felt like a hop, skip, and a jump to get there. Today it was like slogging through melted marshmallows.

Marty was waiting for me up front cause a dame alone in a saloon like this was a sitting duck for trouble. He steered me to a booth in the back. No ladies allowed at the bar even with an escort. I almost laughed thinking of Marty as an escort.

Not that he looked like a bum; it was *escort* was too highfalutin a word for him. Marty who was your salt-of-the-earth type.

He wore his hat inside or out. His brown hair was straight and a swatch of it hung over his forehead. An ever-present unlit cigar was clenched between his pearly whites and he always looked hung over even when he wasn't.

"You wanna drink, Faye?"

"Kinda early for me." I never drank before five. "I wouldn't say no to an RC, though."

"Lemme get ya one."

He put his own beer on the table and went to the bar. There wasn't any waiter service at Smitty's.

He was back with my soda. "No RC. Coke."

"That's solid. So what's up, Marty?"

"Everybody tryin to ID the John Doe, I thought I'd take another angle."

Sometimes Marty did this for me without me asking. I was glad for any help he could give me. I had no problem telling Marty my clients' names cause he was a cop.

"What angle is that?"

"The Turner angle."

"And?" I lit one up.

"Seems Lucille Turner is on the outs with the old folks at home," he said.

"Yeah, I know that."

"But do ya know why?"

"No. Claire clammed up on that one."

He looked like a little boy at Christmas. "Lucille had a baby."

"A baby? And?"

"And she ain't married."

"Who's the papa?"

"Nobody knows."

"You said Lucille *had* a baby."

"Yeah. She gave it up for adoption."

"How'd ya find this out, Marty?"

"I got my ways."

Marty never tipped me to his sources any more than Birdie did. He almost always got me good stuff, though, so who cared where it came from.

"So yer sayin that the parents don't talk to her cause she had a baby without bein married?"

"Right."

"Claire, too?"

"If she doesn't sling the lingo with her I guess that's why."

Somebody must know who the father was. "When she have this baby?"

"A few months ago. You think it means anything, Faye?"

"I don't know. Might." I took a swig of my Coke. "Hard to see the connection."

"Yeah."

"Hey, Mitchum," the bartender yelled. "Phone for you."

"Be right back."

As he scooted outta the booth I was already batting around what he'd told me and everything else in the vicinity.

Why had Lucille Turner visited Widmark and then stopped? The elevator jockey was mum about Lucille being pregnant so maybe she didn't show and when she started to, she quit her visits. *Maybe* Widmark was the father. *It wasn't good for her.* That's what Widmark said about the end of their get-togethers. Maybe that was exactly what he meant. It was cause she was on the nest.

What if I was right? Did any of this have to do with the missing Ladd and the corpse in his hotel room? I couldn't make any hookup, but I felt there was one. If only cause Claire and Lucille were sisters. I needed to have a chinfest with Lucille soon as I could.

Marty was back. "Guess what? Yer Cummings guy came in early to ID the corpse."

"And?"

"Private David Cooper."

"Can't say I'm shocked. I had a feelin that's who it was."

"Yeah. Me, too. Ya think Ladd knocked him off then did a Houdini?"

"Coulda. But why?"

"Some beef that got outta hand?"

"There were no marks on Cooper except the thumbprints on his neck. He was choked to death. Doesn't seem like a fight."

"Nah. Should be more telltale signs."

"I guess the cops'll find out more about Cooper's life," I said.

"Poor sucker. Ya wanna refill?"

"No, thanks. I need to see the Ladds. St. Moritz, ya said?"

"Right."

"Think Lupino will let me use the phone?"

"Sure. C'mon."

When I'd called, Mr. Ladd assumed I was a detective with the police, which is what I wanted him to think without saying so. He'd given me the room number and I was off to meet them.

It seemed a bit cooler so I set off on foot. I liked walking. It kept me strong and I got to eyeball John Q. Public, which kept me on my toes cause I'd practice my observing skills. I'd take in hair color, outfit, height, eyes if they weren't wearing dark cheaters, and anything else that might be an identifying mark on a person. Then I'd run it past myself and see how many I could remember. Not the best system scoring yourself, but who else was gonna test me?

When I reached the St. Moritz, I was drenched. This wouldn't help me impress the Ladds and I had time so

I went into Rumplemeyer's and snatched a table for two. There were as many fans going as there were customers. I coulda been dreaming but I thought I felt a sprig of cool air pass over my legs.

Rumplemeyer's was known for its ice cream, but they had other desserts. I knew what I wanted the sec I saw it on the menu a waitress had handed me. I could feel myself drying off while I waited for my waitress to come back.

"What can I get you, dear?"

"A cup of joe and a Nesselrode puddin."

"A cup of joe?"

What a phony baloney. "Coffee."

"Oh, I see." She looked like a lizard, a piece of pink tongue poking out for a moment. I guess it was a smile. And then she was off with my order.

I'd never been in this joint but, taking in the room, I noticed a lotta swells at the tables, some with kids, some not. The kids were eating ice cream, which is what I woulda had if I hadn't spotted the pudding.

I'd never had this, but the delicious description sold me. And it was burned into my brain forever. It consists of cream-enriched custard mixed with chestnut purée, candied fruits, currants, raisins, and maraschino liqueur.

I wouldn't forget that in a hurry.

"Here you are, dear." She put a huge bowl in front of me. "And your joe." She looked pleased that she'd learned a new word.

"Thank you."

When she was gone I dipped my spoon into the pudding and slowly brought it toward my mouth, almost scared to try it. Almost. I guess I'd have to say it was one of the most delectable things I'd ever eaten and I was glad I was alone cause I wouldn't have wanted to give anyone a taste.

I took my time, but not as long as I would've liked cause upstairs the Ladds were waiting for me.

They had a suite and we met in what looked like a living room, but a pretty small one. I shared a couch with Mrs. Ladd, and her husband sat in a club chair.

"I was just about to call room service for drinks, Miss Quick. Would you like one?"

I felt I should even though it was still early for me. "A manhattan would be swell." I wondered how that would mix with my Nesselrode.

After he'd made the call I knew I'd better straighten out my identification. "Mr. and Mrs. Ladd, I think you mighta gotten the wrong idea about who I am."

"You told us who you were over the phone," he said.

"I said I was a detective, and I am, but I'm not with the police department. I'm a private investigator."

"Meaning what?"

"Meaning somebody hired me to find your son."

"Who?" she said.

Always the trickiest part. "I can't tell ya that. It'd be unethical."

They looked at me like I was accusing them of something.

He was tall and skinny with receding black hair that gave him a widow's peak. His eyes were blue, like a cloudless sky, and his mouth looked like a scar. The clothes he wore were good ones. You can always tell by the tailoring. His shoes were black wingtips.

She was beautiful, like a movie star, a blonde—and it looked real, not something concocted in a beauty salon. Her lipstick was the color of ripe strawberries. She wore a daytime suit, a short gray jacket and skirt with black pumps.

"Claire hired you, didn't she?" he asked.

"Mr. Ladd, I told ya . . ."

"Call me William."

"I told ya it would be unethical to say who hired me."

She said, "What's the difference, William. Anyway, it has to be Claire."

"Yes, you're right, Jennifer." He turned back to me. "Tell me, what kind of a name is Quick?"

"Kind of name?"

"Yes. Where's your family from?"

"Newark, New Jersey."

They both laughed but it didn't sound real, more like they were doing the scales.

"No, no," he said. "Originally. Were they born in this country?"

"Sure."

"How about their parents?"

"Oh, I get yer meanin now. Both sets of grandparents came from England."

"How nice," she said.

William nodded in agreement.

I had no idea what that was all about. Did they expect me to ask them the same question? I didn't.

"When's the last time ya spoke to yer son?"

"He called when he got to the hotel. I suppose that was Friday."

"And how'd he sound?"

"Perfectly fine. He was looking forward to his time in New York and seeing this girl, Claire," he said.

"Did he tell ya he was goin out with the boys that night instead of seein Claire?"

"No." They looked at each other, then back at me.

She lit a cigarette.

"That's odd," William said. "Charles said he was in love with this Claire, and was all excited about seeing her. Who were these boys he was going out with?"

I named them.

"We know George, but not the other chap."

"David Cooper was the murdered soldier found in Charlie's room."

"Why didn't the police mention that?"

"When did ya talk to em?"

"Around one."

"He hadn't been identified then. George Cummings ID'ed him about an hour ago."

"You're not suggesting that Charles had anything to do with the boy's murder, are you?" William said.

"Nobody knows."

Mrs. Ladd sat up straighter at the end of the couch.

"Well, I'm here to tell you that my son couldn't have killed anyone. He's the most gentle and sweet boy you'd ever want to meet." She started to cry.

"Now, Jennifer, don't get yourself all worked up."

Whenever a girl had a tear in her eye, men thought she was gonna get hysterical. Or *worked up,* as he put it. Why shouldn't she cry? Her son was missing, and maybe he killed someone. Sounded to me like something to cry about.

There was a knock on the door. "Room service."

"Enter."

The waiter carried a round tray. There were three drinks and hors d'oeuvres that looked good. Ladd stood, directed the waiter where to place each drink, then tipped him.

The waiter left on little cat feet, like the poet wrote.

"You've got to find our son," William said.

"I will. Or the police will."

"I'm not sure the police are too worried about Charles," he said.

I took a sip of my drink. "If it was just a missin person case, I might share that outlook. But Cooper makes it murder. The cops'll take that seriously."

"I hope you're right."

"What about Claire? Do you like her?"

Again they looked at each other.

I waited.

"We haven't met her but at least she's not Jewish," Mrs. L. said.

"Yes. I suppose we should be grateful for that." He

took out a gold holder, stuffed a cigarette into it, and flicked a fancy gold lighter.

"What would be the problem if she *was* Jewish?"

"Well, you know how they are." Jennifer Ladd wrinkled her nose, and it wasn't cute.

"No. I don't know how they are."

William said, "Let's not get sidetracked. What else do you want to know?"

"Do ya have any idea why Charlie would disappear?" I eyeballed the hors d'oeuvres.

"I think he was kidnapped," she said.

"I don't," he said. "There's been no ransom request."

"So whaddaya think happened to him, Mr. Ladd?"

"I can't imagine. Whatever it was, it had nothing to do with Cooper's murder. You say he was a soldier, too?"

"A private like yer son."

"It's so awful, so very confusing and awful," Mrs. L. said. She took a swig of her martini.

"Why would Cooper be murdered in Charlie's room?" he asked.

"That's what everybody wants to know."

"Well, we're going to stay here until Charles is found," he said.

"Can ya think of anything that might help me find him?"

"Such as what?" She blew a perfect smoke ring.

"Habits, interests, hobbies."

Mrs. L. said, "He collects stamps."

"Please, Jennifer. That's not what Miss Quick means."

"Well, it is sorta," I said. "Did he have any other hobbies?"

"He collected stamps when he was a boy," Mr. L. said. "He hasn't done that for years. And no. I can't think of any other hobbies Charles was interested in. But you might want to talk to George Cummings, the other gentleman you said was with him last Friday night. He might know things we don't."

"What kinds of things, William?" She seemed alarmed.

Nobody was eating the hors d'oeuvres. What a waste.

"Jennifer, a boy doesn't tell his mother everything."

She downed her drink then reached for a little cracker with a spread on it. Finally she offered the platter to me.

"Thanks, I believe I will." I bagged a shrimp thing. "I've already met with Mr. Cummings."

"What did he say?" she asked.

"He couldn't help me cause he didn't see Charlie often."

"Poor George," she said. "His eyes."

"Yeah, too bad." I wanted another shrimp, but didn't dare reach for one. I drank instead.

I didn't think the Ladds were gonna cough up anything else useful, so I told them I'd be in touch.

Waiting for the elevator, I thought about that business of asking what kind of name Quick was. And their not-so-subtle feelings about Jews.

I didn't think either of them was keeping any serious jelly from me. They didn't want to face the possibility of where Charlie might be and if they'd ever see him again. Who would?

TEN

J could hear Ma Bell calling to me as I tried to get the key in my door. The harder I tried the worse it got. I thought it might be Johnny. I told myself it was only a phone call and that he'd call back.

Finally I turned the lock, opened up, almost tripped over Zachary, who gave me a greeting howl, and shut the door so he wouldn't get out. I ran to the phone and grabbed the receiver.

"Yeah? Hello?"

"What's with ya, Faye? Ya sound like ya been runnin up Mount Everest."

Birdie. "I had trouble gettin in, that's all."

"Yeah. You've been out."

"No kiddin."

"I've been tryin ya for hours, fresh mouth."

"Sorry." I sat down and Zachary jumped into my lap. I knew it wasn't cause he'd missed me. It was about food. He'd have to wait, but I scratched him around the ears. "So what is it, Bird?"

"Claire Turner called about five o'clock soundin crazy."

"Crazy?"

"More hysterical than crazy, I guess."

"And?"

"She wanted ya to call her soon as ya could."

"Didn't say what it was about?"

"They don't tell me secret stuff like that, Faye."

"That's a secret, tellin ya what she wanted?"

"Lemme put it to ya this way. I asked and she said she couldn't yak about it with *me*. She needed you chop chop."

"Don't be hurt, Bird."

"Who's hurt? Ya think I wanna know about their dirty laundry?"

Yeah, I did. I let it go. "I have her number in my pocketbook, but gimme it anyway."

She did.

"Any other calls?"

"If there was, I woulda told ya."

"Right. Sorry. Why don't ya go home now."

"I *am* home. I'm making pork chops."

"Oh, yeah. For Pete."

"For Pete, yeah."

"Hope ya have fun, Bird. And I'll see ya Monday."

"Goodbye," she said.

Was she mad at me? She was never formal like that. I hoped she wasn't gonna quit. I couldn't run the agency without Birdie Ritter. Sure, I could always get another secretary, but not like her. The sugar shortage made it hard to find a box of candy. I'd have to think of something else to take her on Monday.

124

I was planning to go to Claire's anyway, to get the picture of Charlie Ladd. She knew that. What could be so important? I dialed. She picked up on half a ring.

"Oh, thank God it's you."

"What's goin on?"

"I don't want to talk about it over the phone."

Why did they always say that? "Could ya please come here."

"Sure. I was plannin to, remember?"

"I forgot. The picture."

"Yeah."

"This is nothin to be sneezed at, Faye."

"Okay, I'll be there soon as I can."

Zachary looked at me with pitiful eyes. Claire would have to wait. I stood up and he jumped down. I got his food, dished it up, and put it on the floor. I heard him purring. He was one happy guy.

"I hate to do this to ya, Zach," I said, "but I gotta go out again."

He kept eating; I coulda been invisible. I grabbed my stuff and headed out. A neighbor, Jim Duryea, was in the hall. We'd had a strange encounter a few months ago, but since then we'd been friendly enough though he'd never be my favorite guy.

"Going out in this heat?"

"I have to, Jim."

"I'll bet you're on the missing soldier case."

That knocked me back on my heels. How'd he find out?

"Ya know I can't talk about my cases."

"It's in all the papers. Do you think they'll find him? The soldier?"

"I have no idea. I gotta go, Jim."

Outside I walked to Sixth and Tenth and hailed a hack. Something I hardly ever did. But I'd put it down as expenses. I gave the driver the address and sat back to smoke a cig.

Jim's guess made me think of Anne Fontaine, who was a real psychic. I missed her like mad. We'd been friends since high school, but a couple of months ago she'd moved to California. She said she saw the name of the state written on somebody's forehead and knew she had to go. We kept in touch by letter, but it wasn't the same.

At Sixty-first Street and Eighth Avenue the cabby let me out. I paid him the $1.25 and tipped him a nickel. Cabs were getting pricey.

At Claire's building I walked up three flights. She was standing in the doorway.

"Hurry," she said.

She looked around the hallway before she shut the door. The first thing she did was light a cigarette.

The apartment was pretty dark cause her view was another building about two feet away. Mismatched pieces that looked like she'd gotten them at a fire sale made up her furnishings. I gave the room the once-over, but saw nothing that looked like ya could sleep on. Then I noticed a floor-to-ceiling cabinet. A Murphy bed. I figured the one inside door was the bathroom.

"Sit down, Faye."

I sat and took a cig from my pack of Camels, which was running low.

She paced. "He called."

"Who?"

"The person who took Charlie."

"Ya mean he *was* kidnapped?"

"Yeah."

"What'd he say?"

"He said he had him and he wanted a hundred thousand dollars to give Charlie back."

I let out with a whistle. "A hundred thou. That could buy a lotta tamales."

"Where am I gonna get that kinda money?"

"What else did he say?"

"He said he'd be callin back with instructions. I tried to tell him I couldn't get that much money but he wouldn't pay attention to me."

"You didn't get to speak to Charlie, did ya?"

She flashed a smile of pride. "Yeah, I did. I knew enough to ask for that. He put Charlie on for a couple a secs, but I knew it was him."

"Did ya call the police?"

"He said no cops."

"Yeah. They always say that."

Her eyes widened. "You know who they are?"

"I meant kidnappers in general."

"Oh. So what should I do, Faye?"

"I think we have to tell the Ladds. They're in town at the St. Moritz."

"Have ya seen em?"

"I went to their hotel. Naturally I didn't tell em you hired me. But they assumed that anyway."

"They hate me."

"They never met ya."

"They hate me anyway." She pooched out her lower lip. "Why d'ya think Charlie hasn't introduced us?"

"Ya said . . . never mind. When they meet ya, they'll like ya."

She sat on the chair across from me, put out her cigarette, and pulled her feet up under her.

"Look, Claire, ya don't have the money and the Ladds probably do. I mean if they're stayin at the St. Moritz, they're not broke."

She nodded. "Charlie tried to play it down, but things he said made me know they're rich."

"It seems like callin them is yer only angle."

"What if the kidnappers find out?"

"How d'ya know there's more than one?"

"I heard a guy in the background talkin to somebody else."

"Anyway, he told ya not to get the police into it, not the Ladds."

"Yeah, that's true."

"He didn't say when they'd call back, did he?"

"No." She lit up again.

"By the way, ya got that picture of Charlie?"

"I gave the good one to the cops yesterday when they came to see me. But I got another."

She opened the drawer of a table, took something

out, which musta been the picture, and turned back to me.

"He's much better lookin than this, Faye." Her eyes filled up.

"I gotta see it, Claire."

"Yeah." She laid her glims on the pic like she was gonna forget his face if she didn't, then handed it to me.

Private Ladd was a handsome fella. He had big, sad eyes and a straight nose. I couldn't see his hair cause it was under his hat, but she'd told me it was brown. The brim shaded part of his face.

I lit my last Camel and looked for a place to toss the empty pack. I didn't see anything so I dropped it into my pocketbook. "Ya want me to call the Ladds?"

"Would you?"

"Sure." The minute I said it I felt queasy. How d'ya tell parents their son's been kidnapped? Better than telling them he's dead, that was for sure. And he could end up dead if these snatchers didn't get their long green. I walked over to the phone.

The Ladds were horrified but the moola was no problem for William. I told em to wait in their suite until Claire phoned after she heard again from the men holding Charlie.

This setup made Claire one unhappy twist.

"I don't like the idea of *me* having to call *them*."

I wanted to tell her that this wasn't about her relationship with the Ladds and to can it. But I didn't think honesty would be the smart move to make with this client.

"Claire, this is the way it's gotta be done. Unless ya want the Ladds to come here and wait with ya."

"No."

I figured she was probably ashamed of her apartment. "Well, ya can't wait at the St. Moritz with them cause the kidnappers are callin ya here."

"What if they don't call for days?" Now she was getting whiny.

"Ya gotta sit tight."

"Will you stay with me?"

Oh, brother.

"I suppose you have some hot date?"

"I don't."

"Please stay."

She looked so pitiful I said I'd stay for a while or until they called, whichever came first.

They never called. At least not while I was there and I'd been home for half an hour and hadn't had a jingle from Claire. I tried to stay off the phone, but even though it was late it was one of those times when it seemed like everybody hadda ring me.

I talked to Johnny, but after I told him what was going on I kept it short. Him I woulda liked jawing with. Still, it was nice that I had a boyfriend who understood.

Jeanne Darnell called, too. We made a date for the next week to meet for dinner at Fuglio's on Greenwich

Avenue. She was another one who understood if I had to cancel, which I'd done on many a night. She said she had something special to tell me. I wondered if she was tying the knot with her longtime boyfriend.

I shrugged off a few more calls while I was getting out my bobby pins and the strips of cotton I used to do my hair. I was getting sick of this routine. I kept threatening to cut my mop but I never seemed to get around to it.

I turned on the radio to my favorite music station and caught the Mills Brothers right in the middle of "Paper Doll." I liked them a lot and sang along till the end of the tune.

I'd decided if there was no news on Charlie by morning I was gonna head to New Jersey and meet Lucille Turner.

Swell. How was I gonna get there?

ELEVEN

*T*he phone was my alarm clock. I pushed Zach off my head, rolled out of bed, and got to the horn in time. "Yeah?"

"What if it wasn't me?" Marty said.

"Huh?"

"Answerin with a *yeah*."

"Who are you, Emily Post?"

"How much ya wanna know about David Cooper?"

"A lot."

"Then close that satchel mouth and listen."

"Shoot." This was no time to put on the gloves with Marty.

"The hotel geniuses found Cooper's room soon as they were told the ID. Then Powell and company went over Cooper's room and came up with his dog tags, wallet, the usual."

"Nothin else?"

"That's all I could find out. I was hopin there might be a connection to Ladd, beside them bein on leave together. Somethin to tell us if he knocked Cooper off and then took a powder."

I didn't know what to do about telling Marty the kidnapping stuff. But he'd never forgive me if he found out I'd known and didn't tell him.

"Marty. About Ladd. I got some news but ya gotta swear ya won't tell anybody."

"I swear on my mother's grave."

"Yer mother's still alive."

"I was talkin about the grave she's gonna have someday."

"Don't be a saucebox or I won't tell ya."

"Okay. I won't tell nobody. Ya know that, Faye."

"Not yer tootsie or anybody else."

There was a deadly quiet on the line. I'd never in so many words let slip that I knew about his girlfriend.

"That's a low blow, Faye."

"I'm not judgin ya. I don't care what ya do." It was a lie. I did care that he cheated on his wife. I thought he was a heel to do it. But in all other ways he was

132

solid gold and most of the time I could put his double-crossing Bridgett to the side.

"So why'd ya mention it?"

"I guess I'm afraid a pillow talk."

"I don't tell Bette nothin."

First time I heard her name. "Good."

"So what were ya gonna tell me?"

I filled him in on the call to Claire, the kidnapping, and the Ladds, who were ready to pony up with the dough.

"Ya didn't tell Powell?"

"No. And don't you, either. Ya know it could get Charlie killed just as much as I do."

"Yeah. Okay. But don't ever let on I knew."

"Promise."

I pulled out the drawer in the phone table and scrabbled around until I found an old half pack of Camels. I shook one out. Some matches were in the drawer, too. I jammed the receiver between my shoulder and ear and lit up. That was better.

"So who killed Cooper?" I said.

"How do *I* know who killed him?"

"I was talkin to myself."

"As long as ya don't answer yerself that's okay."

I listened to him laughing like some hyena. "That's a good one, Marty. When yer through pattin yerself on yer back at how witty ya are, I got another favor to ask."

He snorted once, then said, "Spill."

"You know anybody with a car?"

"Yeah."

"You know them well enough to ask to borrow it?"

"For you?"

"Yeah."

"Where'd ya learn to drive, Faye?"

"In New Jersey. My uncle taught me. Said it might come in handy one day."

"Thing is, the person I'm thinkin of wouldn't want a dame drivin his jalopy."

That burned me up. All this malarkey about women drivers. I couldn't ask Marty to pretend he'd be at the wheel, so I wrapped up the conversation.

As I was pouring water in my coffeepot I remembered that *I* knew someone with a car. Jim Duryea. I dialed his number.

We said our hellos, but I didn't beat around the bush. I asked him right out if he was willing to let me have his buggy for the day. He asked me where I'd learned to drive and if I had a license. I felt like hanging up on him but I needed the car. So I made nice. He told me to come up for the keys when I was ready.

I called Birdie.

"Why?" she said.

"Why what?"

"Why're ya goin to New Jersey?"

"That's where Lucille Turner lives and works."

"Why would she live in New Jersey?"

"Careful, you're speakin of my home state."

"Yeah, and a place ya love like I love Iowa."

"I never knew you'd been to Iowa."

134

"I haven't. That's my point."

We said goodbye and then I fed the cat, took a shower, and slipped into a casual polka-dot dress and a pair of open-toed shoes. I didn't have a single pair of stockings left and didn't feel like putting on leg makeup and drawing the damn line down the back of my gams. I went bare-legged instead.

I grabbed my pocketbook, left *The Human Comedy* cause I wouldn't be reading while driving—no matter what all those mugs thought. In the hall Dolores was doing her usual sweeping. She was wearing a striped blouse with a checked skirt and her wig was hanging low over her right ear. Par for the course.

I said hello while starting toward the stairs.

"Ho ho," she said.

I stopped. "What ho ho?"

"Yer goin up instead of out."

"And?"

"Who has the pleasure of yer company?"

She was the nosiest woman I'd ever met. But I couldn't get mad at her. "Jim Duryea. Make somethin outta that."

"Me? Me make something outta a visit to Mr. Duryea? Why would I do that?"

"Ya got me there, Dolores."

"It's early for a visit. Ya having breakfast together? A nosh maybe?"

Telling her the reason would only lead to more questions so I just said no and continued walking up.

When Jim opened his door, there was a smile on his

puss, as usual. He was dressed in a blue summer suit and a lightweight striped tie.

Being inside his apartment was like being in a museum's storage space. Every inch was crammed with artifacts. Jim owned an antiques store but couldn't help bringing home pieces he liked.

He offered me a seat and a cup a coffee. I accepted cause I couldn't just snatch the keys to the car and run. Besides, I'd only had time for one cup and I needed another jolt.

The java he brought me was tops. Jim always had the best of everything.

"May I ask where you're going, Faye?"

"I gotta go to New Jersey."

"Business or pleasure?"

"Business." I couldn't imagine anyone going to New Jersey for pleasure. But my attitude was colored by the fact that my ma and pop were there.

"And, of course, I can't ask why."

"You're finally catchin on, Jim."

"I've always understood, but I thought it worth a try."

I took a cig from my bag and Jim lit it with an odd table lighter.

"I see that you're looking at this."

"Yeah."

He handed me the lighter. It was a metal Scottie dog, black with white eyes and a little red nose. Now that I saw it up close it gave me the jimjams.

"Very nice," I said.

He flashed me a satisfied smile.

"So, New Jersey, hmmm?"

I nodded.

"Isn't that where you're from, Faye?"

"It is. Newark."

"Are you going to visit your folks while you're there?"

Gloom settled over me like a foggy day just thinking about doing that. "I don't think so." I took a swallow of coffee.

"So it has something to do with the missing soldier case."

"You're impossible, Jim." I stood up. "Can I have the keys?"

"You haven't finished your coffee."

"It's very good and I hate to leave it, but I have to go."

He actually sniffed. "All right." He walked over to a serious-looking antique desk, opened a tiny drawer, and took out the keys. "I was able to get a B sticker because I said I drove back and forth from my shop."

"Aren't ya afraid 'ya might get caught?"

"No. I can't imagine who would care about my comings and goings. Take my ration book, just in case you need gas."

"I hadn't even thought about using up yer gas. You sure ya don't mind?"

"For you, Faye, anything."

"Thanks, Jim." I didn't like the sound of that at all.

"I'm parked on Charles near Seventh. You know

what the car looks like, don't you?"

"Who could forget? Burgundy roadster, right?"

"A LaSalle. And it has a rumble seat."

"Well, I won't be needin that."

"I know it's nine years old but I like it. Be very careful when you put the top down, and I'm sure you'll want to on a day like this."

"I promise I'll return it as I found it, Jim. I'm really a good driver."

"If you say so."

I could feel the slow burn making its way up from my toes. "I do say so."

He handed me the keys and the ration book. "When do you think you'll be back?"

"Sometime in the afternoon."

"You can slide the keys under my door if I'm not home."

"I can't thank ya enough."

"Think nothing of it."

When I got downstairs, Dolores was still sweeping. I was sure she was clocking me.

"That was a short visit."

"Yeah? How long was it?"

"How should I know?"

"Just wonderin."

"About twenty minutes."

I went out into the sunshiny, hellish day. First thing I had to do was pick up a fresh pack of cigs from my local store.

Village Cigars was at the intersection of Christopher, West Fourth Street, and Seventh Avenue. The shop was shaped like a triangle and run by Nick Jaffe, a funny little guy who always wore a cap. Some people thought it was because he was Jewish but didn't want to wear a yarmulke. I knew he wanted to cover his bald head. But maybe he had religious reasons, too. Who could say?

The store was empty. Unusual. "Hiya, Nick."

"Faye, my darling. Pack of Camels?"

"And the papers." I hoped I'd have time to read them later.

Nick leaned toward me over the counter. "It's getting worse, Faye."

I knew what he was talking about cause he told me every time I went into the store. I always humored him.

"Worse? How could it be worse?"

"They think they're going to the showers but it's gas comes out of the sprinklers. Poisoned gas."

"No."

"Yes. They say it's hundreds at a time. Women and children, too. Ya gotta get the word out, Faye."

"I'm tryin, Nick." I didn't tell a soul cause I was afraid they'd take him off to the funny farm. I hated lying to Nick, but I felt I was protecting him. "Ya tell anybody else about this?"

"Only the ones I trust. Which ain't many."

I thought the others felt like me but kept mum or Nick woulda been picked up by now.

I paid him for the Camels and the papers.

"Don't let the information get in the wrong ears, Faye. Ya know what they say: 'Loose lips sink ships.'"

"Don't worry. I won't tell the wrong people." I felt like a rat. "I'll see ya, Nick."

Walking up Seventh, I wondered why Nick made up this stuff. He seemed normal in every other way.

I crossed Seventh and on the other side, at the corner of Charles, there it was. It was swell looking, a red dazzler. I wished someday I could sit in the rumble seat. I slipped the key into the driver's door, stepped up on the running board, and got in. The dashboard had dials trimmed in shiny chrome, and the steering wheel had a big chrome horn in the center with the initials LAS across it. The seats were soft tan leather, the color matching the top, which I woulda put down, except for the time I'd lose, so I gave it skips.

I threw my papers on the passenger seat, turned the key, pulled out the choke, and put my left foot on the clutch. I shifted into first, and put my right foot on the gas pedal, and pushed it down while I let the other pedal up. I pulled out a bit and waited at the corner until I could turn down Seventh Avenue toward the Holland Tunnel to New Jersey. Whenever I went through the tunnel, which wasn't often, I thought of my mother's story about the day it opened.

My grandfather had insisted that his son, Humphrey, take the whole family in their car and drive them through the tunnel, each way. My mother said it was quite an experience, but it wasn't fun cause her mother was terrified that the walls would crumble and they'd all drown in the water that would come gushing in from the Hudson River.

I wasn't nuts for going through the tunnel myself. Maybe I inherited my grandma's fears cause it didn't take much to make me think I heard crumbling or rushing water.

At the booth I paid the toll. Soon I passed the sign on the tunnel wall that said NEW YORK/NEW JERSEY. It gave me the same feeling as sitting in the house in a wet bathing suit.

Before long I saw some light and then I was out of the tunnel. I was in New Jersey. Always a thrill. I wasn't far from my family's house. It was closer than the bookstore where Lucille worked. I guess I'd known all along that I couldn't be in NJ without dropping in at 1240 Seymour Avenue. The question was, before or after the bookstore? I figured I'd have a better chance of catching my mother a little sane in the morning than later in the day.

So I headed to Seymour Avenue.

TWELVE

Seymour Avenue wasn't the ritzy part of Newark but it was nearby. Two blocks over was Van Ness Place, which once had gates at either end. The gates were gone but the houses were still the biggest around.

Our house, *their* house, was small. I'd only lived in it my last two years of high school. Soon as I graduated from Newark High I amscrayed out of there PDQ. I'd spent my whole life wanting to get away from my family. When I was little, I daydreamed of having a magic pogo stick that would take me far and wide, almost like flying. Up, up, and away.

I sat in the car and stared at the house. It needed paint. But it had always needed paint. The small front yard wasn't mowed. Had it ever been?

I'd left the motor running and I reached for the shift to put it into first and skedaddle. But the front door opened and my pop stood there eyeing the car. He was wearing a white shirt with the sleeves rolled up, a pair of gray trousers, and brown oxfords.

I coulda left. I knew he didn't know who was in the car. But like somebody else was running the show, I turned off the motor and got out.

When I came around the car to the sidewalk, his face lit up and he came down the three front steps.

"Faye. I can't believe it."

"It's me, Pop."

"A sight for sore eyes."

He put his arms around me and gave me a big hug. It felt nice.

"What're ya doin here, toots?"

"I'm seein you."

"C'mon in."

My heart was pounding cause I knew my mother was inside. And even though it was still early in the

142

day, I didn't honestly know what condition she'd be in.

Pop and I walked up the steps together, his arm around my shoulder, mine around his waist, and we crossed the narrow porch to the front door.

"That's some snazzy car ya got there, Faye."

"Not mine. I borrowed it."

"Well then, ya got snazzy friends."

He gently pushed me in front of him and we went through the doorway. Once inside the blue funk settled over me. There seemed to be too much furniture in the living room, and all of it was dark. I hadn't remembered that.

"Let me get your ma," he said.

I grabbed his sleeve. "How is she?"

He shrugged. "She'll be okay this time a day. I know she'll want to see ya."

I wasn't so sure. He left the room and I froze, unable to sit down, like maybe I'd catch something if I did. There was a *Reader's Digest* on the coffee table and a racing form stuffed down between the seat cushion and arm of a chair. Not much had changed.

Then I heard them coming down the stairs. They were moving slowly. She was setting the pace. They reached the bottom and walked slowly to the living room. When I felt them in the doorway I turned around to face them.

Pop had an arm around her waist as he guided her in. I knew she wouldn't look good; she hadn't as long as I could remember. But this was a whole new dimen-

143

sion and it knocked me for a loop.

Mostly the Bowery was peppered with men, but sometimes you'd catch sight of a lady on the street, too. That's where my ma looked like she belonged. Her salt-and-pepper hair was now totally white. It hung down the sides of her face, lifeless and dull. Her skin had a yellow cast to it, and under her vacant eyes were dark patches like smears of tar.

"Here's Faye, Helen."

"Hello, Ma."

She stared at me like I was a stranger, or a ghost.

"Let's sit down. Over here, Helen."

He steered her away from the chair with the racing sheet.

"Take the load off yer feet, Faye."

I sat on the edge of the sagging couch so I could bolt if I had to.

"How are ya, Ma?" Stupid question.

"Just grand."

What could I say to that? "I had to be over this way so I thought I'd pop in."

"Pop in," she said.

I felt myself shrinking. I was about fourteen now.

"Ya want some coffee or somethin, Faye?" he said.

"No, thanks."

"Pop in," she said again. "Sort of the way ya popped out."

I didn't like how this was going or what I felt. Twelve now. I didn't have an angle on what to say, what to ask her. It was like a minefield.

"Faye's a private investigator, Helen."

I was stunned Pop knew what I did. "How'd ya know that?"

He smiled, making his dimple show, but he didn't answer me. Not that my line of work was top secret. Easy to find out, if you wanted to know. And that's what got me. I wouldna thought he'd care enough to know.

"What do you investigate?" she asked.

"Different things. Depends on the case I get."

"Like missing persons?"

"Yeah, exactly like that."

"Missing people."

I nodded.

"Missing children?"

"Sometimes."

"Missing babies?"

Oh, no.

"I haven't had a case like that."

"Sure you have."

"Helen, don't."

"Why don't you look for your brother."

I stood. "I gotta go. I'm meetin somebody." I started toward the door and she grabbed my wrist.

"Your brother's missing, you know."

Her grip was tight, like she'd clamped my wrist in a vise. "Ma, he's not missing. He's dead. Ya know that."

"Dead."

"He died in the influenza epidemic twenty-five years ago. Let go of my wrist, okay? I gotta leave."

"Find him," she said.

I was very young now, but I was strong and pulled out of her grip, ran from the room and the house. By the time I got to the street Pop was on the porch and coming down the steps.

"Faye. Faye, please don't go this way."

"I gotta," I said, dashing to the other side of the car to get in.

He tried to open the passenger door but it was locked. I started the car.

"Faye, please."

I looked at him and he had tears in his eyes. But I hadda keep going. I hadda leave to save myself. I shifted, worked both pedals, and moved away slowly so I wouldn't hurt him. When he stepped back, I floored the damn thing.

I drove down Clinton Avenue. I wasn't going to let this kayo me. I'd always known Ma wished I'd died instead of Jimmy. She went around the house moaning that she wished *she'd* died instead of her son. But that was a lie. *I* was the one she'd trade for him. She never said so, but I knew. I pushed it to the back of my mind and homed in on where I was going and who I was gonna see.

I passed the Roosevelt movie theater. I wished I was going there instead of seeing Lucille Turner. The theater was showing *Shadow of a Doubt* and *King of the Cowboys*, a Roy Rogers movie. I liked Roy better than Gene, but I liked Trigger better than either of em.

The traffic wasn't bad so I got to Market and Broad

pretty quickly. I found a parking spot on Edison. Still shaken by the dustup with my mother, I lit up in the car. I knew I couldn't get out and walk while I was smoking cause Aunt Dolly told me nice girls didn't do that.

Thank God for Aunt Dolly and Uncle Dan. They'd raised me from the time Jimmy died until I was about four. Then everyone thought my mother was okay and I moved back home. But she was a stranger to me. And she wasn't okay. My pop wasn't home much, so I spent a lot of time alone with books.

On weekends I stayed with my aunt and uncle and they took me to the movies, gave me books, and, when I was about twelve, started taking me into New York City to see plays. My first show was *The Shannons of Broadway* and from then, right up until I left Newark, we went every other Saturday. My Uncle Dan also taught me to play chess.

I didn't let most people know I played or how good I was. Chess wasn't a girls' game and though I mostly didn't give a rat's behind about stuff like that, I figured I'd leave that one out. No guy would play with me anyway. I watched the big-shot roosters play in Washington Square Park and knew I coulda beaten a few of them.

I stubbed out my cig in the chrome ashtray and got out of the car. Mostel's Bookstore was on Market, which wasn't far. I hoped Lucille would have lunch with me.

The store had two show windows on either side of

the door, and when I opened it a little bell chimed. The place was stuffed with both old and new books. There was a U-shaped counter in front, but no one was behind it. A couple of customers browsed the shelves.

A tall girl, her dark hair cut short, came outta the back. I knew right away this was Lucille. She wasn't as beautiful as Claire but still a knockout.

She wore a knee-length, peach-colored dress belted at the waist. It had large lapels and was puffy at the shoulders. The sleeves were short. She smiled as she came up to me.

"May I help you?"

I had to ask to be sure. "Are you Lucille Turner?"

She looked frightened, like a startled cat. "Is something wrong? Who are you?"

I showed her my license.

"What do you want with me?"

"Have ya read in the papers about the missin soldier?"

She nodded.

"Yer sister's boyfriend. I believe ya met him once."

"I don't know anything about his disappearance."

"I'm not sayin ya do. But I'd like to ask ya some questions all the same."

She looked over her shoulder toward the back of the shop. "Not here. I don't want Mr. Mostel to know."

"Okay. Will ya meet me for lunch?"

She mulled it over. "All right. Do you know where Child's is?"

I did.

Lucille checked her watch. "About twenty minutes."

"Ya sure you'll show?"

"Yes. Of course."

"Mind if I . . ."

"Miss Turner?" A man's voice came from behind us.

"I'm with a customer, Mr. Mostel."

"When you finish, come back here."

"Yes, sir."

"Not a *please*," I said.

She rolled her eyes. "Or *thank you*."

We smiled at each other.

"I was gonna ask if ya minded if I looked around."

More mulling. "I guess that's fine. But I don't want to leave together."

"You think I look like a PI? Why couldn't I be a friend?"

"You could, but it makes me nervous. Please meet me at Child's, okay?"

"Sure. I'll give the browsing a pass."

"Thanks." She scurried off to the back.

I left and made my way to the restaurant.

Aunt Dolly used to take me to Child's for lunch on Saturdays when we didn't go see a show. I always had the buckwheat cakes with sausages and a Chero-Cola root beer. Every time she'd ask me if I wanted to try something else, but I never did.

I was smoking a cigarette and drinking an RC when Lucille came in. She found me right away and took the seat across from me. I couldn't get a booth.

"Thanks for comin, Miss Turner."

"Sure. Call me Lucille."

We agreed to use first names. I let her look at the menu before the smiling waitress came over, dressed in a white starched uniform with a little white cap.

"What can I get you ladies?"

At last, a nice waitress. I ordered my buckwheat cakes and Lucille asked for tuna salad on white and a Coke.

She lit her cigarette with a Zippo and blew out a long stream of smoke. "Fire away," she said.

"I've been hired to find Private Ladd."

"By Claire?"

"I can't tell ya that."

"Well, who else would it be? It doesn't matter, anyway. Did she tell you to come talk to me?"

"Lucille, like ya said, it doesn't matter. I wanted to meet ya."

"Howdayado," she said, and gave a big throaty laugh. "So we've met. What's next?"

"I have a few questions."

"About Charlie?"

"Yes."

"I don't know what you think I can tell you." She turned her lighter around and around in her hand.

"Maybe nothin. But maybe somethin you don't know is important."

"Like what?"

"That's what I'm here to find out. Did ya like Private Ladd?"

"I liked him fine."

"And ya met him how many times?"

"Only once."

She answered very quickly, as if she wanted me to be sure how little she knew him.

"And where was that?"

The waitress brought Lucille her Coke and left.

"I had dinner once with Claire and Charlie. She'd broken off with another guy and Charlie was the new one."

"Van Widmark."

She looked at me suspiciously. "Claire told you about Van?"

I didn't answer.

"She tell you what happened to him?"

"He told me ya used to visit him."

"You've met Van?" This seemed to upset her.

"Wanna tell me why ya visited him and then suddenly stopped?"

"It wasn't sudden. And what does Van have to do with anything? With Charlie?"

"You tell me."

"I don't know."

"So why'd ya visit Van?"

"I felt sorry for him."

"If ya felt sorry for him, why'd ya stop droppin by?"

"I don't think that's any of your business."

"Was it because you were pregnant?"

She glared at me and pressed her lips together so tightly they disappeared.

I waited.

"I think I should leave." She put out her cig.

I reached across the table and put my hand gently but firmly on her wrist. "Please don't do that. I'm not yer enemy."

"How do you know about the baby?"

I didn't say anything.

"I suppose you can't tell me that, either?"

"That's right."

"Well, I know it wasn't Van because he'd never tell anyone."

"Who was the father?"

"None of your beeswax, Miss Quick."

"Did the father know you were pregnant?"

Ever so slightly, she shook her head.

"But your parents knew and cut you off, didn't they?"

She nodded and her eyes teared up.

"Why didn't ya tell the father?"

"I don't see what this has to do with Charlie missing."

She was right. "I'm sorry."

Our lunch came. My buckwheats looked the same as when I was a kid. I couldn't wait to dig in.

Lucille stared at her sandwich as though *it* might bite *her*.

"Did ya ever meet a soldier named David Cooper?" If she'd read the morning paper, she'd know his name from that source and say so.

"Sounds familiar."

"Where'd ya hear it?"

"I'm not sure."

"Try to think where ya heard it, Lucille."

"Oh, yes. I remember. From Charlie."

"Was that at the dinner with Claire?"

"Yes."

"Not when ya met Charlie alone?"

"How do you know about that?"

Good guess, Quick.

THIRTEEN

*W*hy don'tcha tell me about that meetin with Charlie, Lucille."

"It was nothing."

"Some reason you were seein your sister's boyfriend alone?"

She stalled, lighting up again. I knew she was trying to think of a story that'd throw me a curve.

"Charlie wanted to give Claire a surprise birthday party."

"When did ya say this was?"

"I didn't. But it was for her twenty-first and that was a little over a year ago."

"You and Claire were friends then?"

"Yes."

"When's Claire's birthday?"

"June first."

"So when were you and Charlie makin these plans?"

"He was home on leave in April. He knew he wouldn't be able to do much about a party, except pay for it, and he asked me to do the planning."

I'd ripped through my lunch, but Lucille hadn't touched her sandwich.

"Ya haven't eaten anything," I said.

"I'm not hungry."

I wondered what that was like. Lotsa these dames claimed they were never hungry. I didn't know much about that. Practically nothing.

"Charlie was sure he was gonna be home for her birthday?"

"He must've been."

"Lucille, soldiers fightin a war got no idea when their next leave is gonna be. There was no way he could count on bein anywhere, much less home for Claire's birthday."

"Are you calling me a liar?"

"Yes."

She looked like I'd slapped her and then she began to cry. I waited.

"This is so awful," she said.

I was beginning to think it might be. "What ya tell me is confidential. And it's probably not as bad as ya think."

"Oh, but it is."

"Let's start with how you and Charlie happened to get together alone."

"He called me. He said he had a friend he'd like me to meet."

154

"David Cooper?"

"Yes."

"Then what?"

"Well, I wasn't seeing anyone at the time so I agreed to meet David. I thought it was going to be a double date with Charlie and Claire."

"But it wasn't?"

She shook her head and her eyes started filling again. "He asked me not to tell Claire about it, cause she might not like him fixing me up."

"Did that seem right or odd to you?"

"Claire has funny ideas about things. It was a little strange but I knew she didn't approve of blind dates."

"Why not?"

"I think she had a bad experience once."

"But this would be a blind date that her boyfriend arranged."

She shrugged.

"Okay. Go on."

"When I got to Charlie's room—he was staying at the Commodore then, too—there was no Private Cooper. At first I didn't think anything of it. He could've been late."

"But he wasn't. He never showed up, right?"

"Right. Charlie said David would be there any minute and fixed us both a drink."

"What'd ya talk about?"

"Claire mostly. He indicated that she was frigid. It made me very uncomfortable to hear him talking that way."

"Did ya tell him that?"

She nodded. "But he kept on going. He said she wouldn't even French-kiss and he couldn't get to first base with her. I tried changing the subject but he'd always come back to Claire and how she wouldn't give him what any soldier, who might be going off to be killed, needed. Deserved, he said."

I felt sorry for Lucille cause I thought I knew what was coming. "Go on," I said.

"We'd finished our drinks and I asked about Private Cooper. Charlie laughed and came over to me, pulled me out of my chair, and dragged me to the bed." She began to cry again.

"Did he rape ya, Lucille?" I asked.

She nodded.

"What a louse Charlie is. A real skunk. I'm so sorry," I said. "What happened afterward?"

"He threatened me. Said if I told Claire he'd say I tried to seduce him but failed and now I was trying to get revenge. Then he called me a whore and told me to get out. I did. I wanted to get away from him as fast as I could."

"And ya never told Claire?"

"I dropped a few hints to go slow with this guy, but she was already sold on Charlie and anything I said put her back up all the more."

"Was the baby Charlie's?"

"Yes."

"Did ya ever tell him about it?"

"No. I thought about having an abortion but I was

too afraid. I'd heard so many awful stories. And some part of me didn't think it was right. But I didn't want a baby, and certainly not his. So that's why I gave him up."

"Ya didn't tell Claire or yer parents who the father was?"

"I couldn't."

"You've been keepin this story to yerself all this time?"

"No. Van knew about the rape. He was furious. And even more furious that he was unable to do anything about it."

"And he knew about the baby?"

"Yes."

"Did he know that Charlie was the father?"

"He figured it out. He wanted me to tell Claire, but I just couldn't."

"It was his idea for ya to stop visitin him, right?"

"Yes. When I started to show. That was when I moved here from New York and it wasn't so convenient to stop by Van's. He thought it was too much for me. We talked on the telephone."

"What'd ya do for money?"

"My grandfather, on my mother's side, left both Claire and me a bit of cash. We're not swanky people or anything, but he made money in scrap metal. He would've made more with the war, but he died a few years ago."

"Why are ya workin in the bookstore?"

"I wasn't left that much money. And I want to work.

What am I going to do all day, stay in my apartment and stare at the walls?"

"Couldn't ya have told yer parents and Claire that ya were raped by someone else?"

She gave me a smirk. "You know better than that. I couldn't say it was Charlie, but no matter who I named I'd still be blamed."

It was true. That was how people looked at girls who were raped. They always said she was asking for it. I'd never bought that.

"Yer right. But why didn't ya go back to New York after ya gave birth?"

"I don't know. My parents wouldn't speak to me and neither would Claire."

"You didn't have friends there?"

"Oh, sure. Maybe I didn't want to be in the town where it happened. I'll go back someday. Working in the bookstore isn't my destiny."

"You're different from Claire. For one thing ya speak different. Why's that?"

"My grandfather sent me to college in Colorado. I wanted to go but Claire didn't. I guess my accent got mixed up with a western one."

I switched gears. "Did ya know that David Cooper was the person found dead in Charlie's room?"

Her hand flew to her mouth.

"They identified him yesterday."

"I don't understand."

"Yer not alone. And now we know Charlie's been kidnapped."

"What?"

"Claire got a ransom call. Charlie's father is at the ready to pay when they call back."

"Poor Claire. Don't kidnappers usually kill their victims?"

"Often." I wondered if she wished somebody *would* kill Charlie Ladd. Couldn't blame her.

"So what's everybody doing? Waiting?"

"That's about it."

"Who knows about the kidnapping?"

"Only the people who need to know. I'd appreciate it if ya kept this info to yerself."

"Of course."

"I should call Claire right now and see if she's heard anything more. Excuse me, okay?"

"Sure."

The restaurant phone booth was occupied by a very large woman squeezed inside. She couldn't quite close the door, so I could hear her part of the conversation. Any other time I wouldna been able to keep myself from listening, but I couldn't stop thinking about what Lucille had told me.

My picture of Private Charlie Ladd had changed once again. First I'd thought he was a murderer or murdered himself; then a victim of kidnappers, which he was. Now a rapist.

After the Ladds anted up and Charlie was free, was it my responsibility to tell Claire that he'd raped her sister? She was my client but I wasn't hired to protect her *from* her boyfriend. I was hired to *find* her boyfriend.

Anyway, there was always the possibility that Lucille was lying. But she had nothing to gain from me by making up a story like that.

The huge woman finally signed off and maneuvered her way out of the booth. She looked at me with disgust when she passed me, as though I was responsible for her girth.

I went in the booth, got the operator, gave her Claire's number, dropped some nickels in, and waited. She answered right away.

"Have ya heard anything?" I asked.

"Nothin."

"Okay. I won't stay on. I'll check with ya later."

"Faye, do ya think ya could come over for a while?"

"Not right now, Claire. I'm interviewin somebody."

"Another case?"

"No. Your case."

"So who is it?"

Damn. "I'll tell ya when I see ya. We should keep the line free now."

"Yeah. So I'll see ya later?"

"I'll call ya first. Gotta go now." I put the earpiece in its cradle.

When I got back to the table, Lucille was smoking a cigarette and she'd ordered herself another Coke.

"Did you get her?"

"Yeah. No word yet."

"Oh, poor Claire. She must be a wreck. She's very fragile, you know."

"She is?" That was something I hadn't noticed.

Course she'd started stretching my job to include babysitting duties.

"Is someone with her? Waiting for the call?"

"I'm gonna go over when I leave ya."

"I guess that should be about now. I have to get back to work."

She began gathering her things: pocketbook, lighter, cigarettes.

"May I come back to see you again if I need to?"

She hesitated. "Sure. I don't see why not. You want my number in case you need to ask me a quick question? That's funny. A quick question."

I smiled. "Yeah, I gotta lot of quick questions. But I have both yer numbers."

"Oh, of course you do."

I motioned to the waitress to bring the check.

"You wanna take yer sandwich home?"

"No, thanks."

I wanted to, but I knew that wouldn't look good.

The waitress brought the check. "Oh, dear, something wrong with the sandwich?"

I said there wasn't and that Lucille wasn't hungry. I paid the check and told her to keep the change. She smiled and thanked me.

"I didn't expect you to take me to lunch."

"Expense account. Don't worry about it." This would be an item in my expenses or not, if I didn't want Claire to know about it. But who knew where we'd be by the time this case was over?

Outside, I thanked Lucille for being honest with me.

She asked me if I'd keep her updated now and then, and I said I would. We said goodbye. Then she headed toward the bookshop and I went over to Edison Street to pick up the car.

When I got back to the Village I found a parking spot on Morton Street, locked up the LaSalle, and went home. When there was no answer at Duryea's apartment, I slid the keys under his door like he told me to.

As usual, Zach was hungry. But I told him it was too early. I called Claire. Still no word. I'd said I'd be over soon. I relented about feeding Zach cause who knew when I'd get home? Besides, too early for what? It wasn't exactly like having a drink before five.

What I'd learned about Charlie nagged at me. I didn't know much about rapists but what was to know? If they forced themselves on girls, they were the lowest of the low. Snakes in the grass. And if Charlie raped Claire's sister, who was to say that he wouldn't do it to some other dame. Maybe a friend of Claire's. Maybe he already had.

Maybe the kidnappers knew he was a rapist. Maybe he'd done it to one of *their* sisters. And David Cooper? Where did he fit in? Had he learned about Charlie and confronted him? Then Charlie killed him and along came some kidnappers? Something was smelling like Gorgonzola.

Then again, Charlie's character might have nothing to do with Cooper or with the kidnappers. Maybe they killed Cooper cause he was in the way.

I knew I was going around and around cause I didn't want to go uptown to Claire's. Not telling her about Charlie's true nature was gonna be tough. Almost impossible.

FOURTEEN

*J*t was almost eleven P.M. Claire and I had drunk cup after cup of java waiting for the phone to ring. She let me sit in the one comfortable chair, a big flowered club whose springs had hit the skids. I felt like I was sitting on the floor. Mostly Claire paced and looked over at the phone every fifth or sixth step.

"Why don't ya give it a rest," I said.

She stopped. "I'm so nervous."

"Yeah, I know. Ya think pacin and lookin at the horn is gonna make those bums call ya?"

"I guess I do. Stupid." She sat on what passed for a sofa. "I don't get it. How do they think they're gonna get their dough if they don't call?"

"Nobody ever said crooks were smart."

"Yeah."

"I don't think they're gonna call tonight, Claire."

"Based on what?"

Ouch. "A hunch."

"That's not helpful."

"You're right. Sorry. But if they don't call by midnight, I think ya should go to bed."

"You think I could sleep?"

"Maybe not but ya hafta rest, Claire."

"And where will you be if I go to bed?"

I knew she wanted me to say I'd stay right there but I couldn't. "I'll hafta go home."

"Why? It's not like ya have anyone waitin for ya."

"I know yer nervous and scared, Claire, but I'm not yer punchin bag. Yer startin to be real nasty to me."

"Oh, you're right." She put her hands over her face and started bawling.

I didn't go to her cause I thought she needed to cry and I've noticed if ya go to a person who's crying, it stops them. After a while her crying petered out.

"And by the way, I do have somebody waitin for me."

"Who?"

"His name is Zachary."

"How come ya never mentioned him?"

"I'm not much fer blabbin." I didn't bother pointing out that we weren't girlfriends no matter how much Claire wanted to do let's pretend. Our relationship was strictly a professional one.

"Is he handsome?"

"I think so. He has black hair with a small patch of white in the front."

"That sounds cute. He's waitin for ya at your place?"

"Yeah."

"Does he stay . . . I mean . . . do ya . . ."

It wasn't too hard to get her drift. "No."

"Can't ya call him, tell him you're stayin here?"

"He'd never answer my phone." Everything I was saying was true about Zach. "Look, Claire, I can't stay all night and that's that. If they call, ya listen carefully, write everything down, and then ring me."

"Will ya come back then?"

"I'll do what the circumstances call for. Okay?"

"I'm payin ya to find Charlie, ya know?"

"Sittin here watchin ya pace back and forth isn't findin Charlie."

"Oh, Faye. I'm so sorry. I don't know what's wrong with me."

That one left me cold. People who used this in tight situations were hoping to wheedle comfort out of anyone who'd bite. But they knew exactly what was wrong with em. I said nothing.

Claire gave up waiting for a reply. "Faye, just tell me one thing. Do ya think he's alive?"

"Honestly, I don't know. When they call ya should ask to speak to him again."

"And what if they won't let me?"

"Say ya need proof that he's still alive. And if they won't give it, we'll talk it over, then ask the Ladds what they wanna do." I put down my coffee cup and pushed myself outta the chair.

"Yer goin?" She sounded surprised, like we hadn't been talking about this for the last ten minutes.

"Yeah."

"I know the minute ya hit the street they'll call."

"Might. But whatever they ask ya to do I'm pretty

sure it won't be for tonight. Ya should try to get some sleep. At least lie down. Want me to help pull the bed down?"

"No. I do it every night. Thanks."

I picked up my pocketbook, put my cigs and matches inside, and closed it.

"You'll take a cab this time of night, won't ya?"

"This all goes on my expense account, ya know."

She waved a hand as if to say it didn't matter.

I reminded myself about her small inheritance. "Okay. If I don't hear from ya, I'll call ya in the A.M."

She nodded and I headed for the door.

At home I debated whether it was too late to call Johnny. He was a night owl but it was almost midnight. If he was asleep I'd tell him I'd call back in the morning.

But he wasn't asleep.

"I was wondering where you were. I called a few times."

I brought him up to speed on the case. Then I asked his advice about telling Claire what kinda man Charlie was.

"You only have Lucille's word for it. And it's not your place to tell Claire. That's not what she hired you for."

I knew all that but I needed him to reinforce my thoughts. "But what if I could find out that Lucille was tellin me the truth? Could I tell Claire then?"

"How would you do that? There were just two people involved and one's Lucille and the other's missing."

"You have a point."

"You believe Lucille, don't you?"

"Yeah. I mean, why would she say Charlie'd done that to her if he hadn't?"

"Ah, Faye. You know better than that. Why would anyone say anything? Or do anything?"

"Yeah, yer right, Johnny. I still can't get it that people do things for no reason, or a reason I can't figure."

"I could tell you some stories that'd make your jaw drop."

"Bet ya could."

"You're still new to the deceits and tricks of some people."

"Guess so."

"I think that's sort of nice."

"Are you patronizing me, Johnny?"

"No, not at all. I mean it. Thing is, there's gonna come a time when your trust in people won't be so natural."

"You mean I'm gonna get callous and crusty like Detective Powell?"

He laughed. "You'd better not get like Powell. Here's my suggestion. Get Claire talking about Charlie, see if she's as naïve as you think."

"I tried that tonight but she was too squirrelly to concentrate."

"Try it again. Maybe she'll lead you down a path that opens the way for you."

"I'm not sure what path that'd be but I'll try. Meanwhile Charlie Ladd's bein held somewhere and these kidnappers aren't callin. Plus, I don't think Powell has any suspects for Cooper's murder."

"I heard through the grapevine he's convinced it's Ladd. Thinks Ladd's flown the coop. Course he doesn't know this latest wrinkle. The kidnapping."

"And yer not gonna tell him, are ya?"

"Would I do that?"

I realized then that I honestly didn't know, cause I didn't know Johnny Lake that well. It'd been months, not years.

"Why the silence?" he asked.

"I don't *think* you'd do somethin like tellin Powell about the kidnappin, but I don't *know* ya wouldn't."

Now *he* was silent.

"Johnny?"

"I was just thinking about how well I know you, and if the tables were turned what would I believe? Okay. I give you my word and that's the best I can do."

"I do believe yer a man of his word."

"Thanks."

"I think I better get to bed."

"You might have a lot on your hands tomorrow."

"I got a question. Has anybody been in touch with David Cooper's family?"

"Don't know. You'll have to talk to Powell about that."

I didn't say anything.

He caught on. "You want me to ask him, right?"

"I know we agreed not to get into each other's cases, but he'd be more likely to tell you."

"True. I'll have to think up a good one for why I wanna know."

"I have complete faith in yer ability to do that, Johnny."

We both laughed.

"I'll try to find out about the Coopers tomorrow."

"Thanks."

We said our good nights, but not the words I knew we both wanted to say. I wondered how long it would take us to get to that point, or if we ever would.

Zach was twirling around my ankles. I laughed when I thought of what I'd told Claire about him. And how easy it all fit. Good thing she didn't actually say the words *do you sleep with Zachary?* cause I woulda had to either lie or say yes. Zach never let me sleep alone.

Saturday was my day to do chores and clean my place. Before I started, I drank a cup a joe and smoked a cig. I'd called Claire first thing but she still hadn't heard. She was bawling her head off but I calmed her down a little.

Saturday was also a day I'd think on a case if I had one. And boy did I have one. I hadda wonder what Claire's parents were thinking. They musta known about it from the papers if not from Claire. But she never mentioned them. Did they know Claire's army private? Did they care that their daughter's boyfriend was missing?

Someone knocked on my door. I hoped it wasn't Dolores cause I wasn't in the mood. And please, not Jim Duryea. I put down my cup and went to answer the door. Standing there were two soldiers with bands on their arms that identified them as military police. The shorter one looked me up and down. I had on a short-sleeve blouse, slacks, and sandals—my Saturday duds.

"See anything ya like?" I said.

"Are you Miss Quick?"

"Yeah. What's up?"

"I'm Sergeant Cagney and this is Sergeant Grahame."

"How can I help ya, soldier?"

Cagney's eye twitched. "May we come in?"

"What's this about?" I was pretty sure I knew.

"We'd like to talk to you about privates Charles Ladd and David Cooper."

I opened the door wider and they filed in like schoolkids, each removing his hat and tucking it under his arm.

"Can I getya anything?"

"No, thank you," Cagney said.

"Wanna sit down?"

"Thank you," Grahame said.

They spotted my cup in front of the sofa so they took the opposite one, each of them sitting like they had rods up their backs, feet flat on the floor, hands on their knees. Real relaxed.

I offered them coffee but they thankfully refused. I picked up my java and had a swallow, put it back on the table. Then I went for my cig. "So what can I do for ya?"

Grahame said, "It's come to our attention that you're a . . . a . . . private investigator. Is that true?"

You woulda thought he was asking me if I was a member of the Mafia. "That's right."

"And you're working on a case that includes both Ladd and Cooper?"

"My case has to do with Ladd, but since Cooper was found in Ladd's room it's hard to separate the two."

"Miss Quick, we're here to ask you to drop that case."

People telling me what to do didn't go down easy with me.

"The Ladd case?"

"And anything to do with Private David Cooper."

"Why?"

"This is a government case," Cagney said.

"Cause the boys are in the army?"

"Exactly."

"I don't see what that has to do with me. My client is a civilian."

"Miss Turner. We know."

I kept my trap shut.

"Miss Turner hired you four days ago to find Private Ladd, didn't she?"

"I can't answer that. Privileged information."

"Yes, but we're government employees."

"So?"

"That gives us the right to know anything we want."

"I don't think so. Anyway, I'm not tellin you who my client is."

They looked at each other and Grahame took over.

"Will you tell us if you've found Private Ladd?"

If I answered one question, would I have to answer them all? Whether I found Charlie or not wasn't privileged. "No. I haven't found him. Have you? Cause if ya have, I sure would like to know."

They looked at me like I'd given em a right hook.

"Miss Quick, I don't think you understand."

"Oh, sure I do. You wanna get info from me, some of which I can't give ya. Some I can. I said I haven't found Charlie, so what else?"

"You found the body of Private Cooper, is that correct?"

"Correct. You call his parents yet?"

"We're asking the questions."

"Isn't this a give-and-take?"

"Did you identify him?"

"I'd never seen him before."

"Then did Claire Turner identify him?"

"She didn't identify Private Cooper cause she didn't know him, either."

"She'd never *met* Private Cooper."

"Correct."

They looked at each other again.

172

Cagney said, "Who *did* identify him?"

"How come ya don't know?"

"We're not at liberty to tell you that, Miss Quick. We have privileges, too."

"That must be nice for ya."

"Again. Who *did* identify him?"

"I believe it was a George Cummings. A friend of the deceased."

"Are you trying to find out who killed Private Cooper?"

I was and I wasn't. My job was to find Charlie and if along the way I found out who knocked off Cooper, that'd be a bonus to the cops. But these turkeys? "No, I'm not tryin to find Cooper's killer."

"Why not? Never mind," Cagney said. "We want you to stop looking for Private Ladd."

"Why?"

"I thought you understood. Ladd is the government's problem."

"So what? Wouldn't it be a good thing if I found him for ya?"

"Miss Quick. You must cease and desist."

"And if I don't? The stockade for me?"

They stood up like they were Siamese twins. "We've warned you, Miss Quick. You may no longer search for Private Ladd."

"Or?"

"We'll have you arrested."

"So it is the stockade then." I stubbed out my butt.

"You're a private citizen. You'll go to a regular jail."

173

I thought they were full of it, but I went along so they'd get outta my crib. "Okay. Now ya got me worried."

Grahame said, "Somehow, Miss Quick, I very much doubt it. But don't underestimate us. Good morning."

When they were gone, I called Marty at his precinct, and miracle of miracles the mug was there. I told him about my visit.

"They can't stop ya, Faye."

"I didn't think so. But I wonder why they'd want to."

"Probably routine. I'll try to find out. But I got some news. Mrs. Ladd's gone home. Couldn't take it. Mr. Ladd's still here. Also, Raymond and Thelma Cooper are in town."

"Where?"

"The Hotel Astor. They got in last night."

"Ya know the room number?"

"Fourteen twenty."

"Thanks, Marty. You're the top."

"Ya goin to see the Coopers?"

"Guess."

FIFTEEN

The Hotel Astor was in Times Square between Forty-fourth and Forty-fifth on Broadway. The streets were crowded with Saturday tourists, there to see the shows and eat in the restaurants. Maybe take in a double bill. I took a look-see at the zipper going around the Times building. It said: RAF BOMBS GERMANY ROCKET BASE PEENEMUNDE. I didn't wait to see what was coming next.

The hotel was red brick and had a mansard roof. Its lobby was jam-packed with lots of Chinese curios, Louis the something furnishings, geegaws, and stuff I couldn't name. It reminded me of pictures of Victorian parlors, only much bigger.

Since I had the room number I didn't have to bump heads with the clerks behind the desk and went directly to the elevators. Although I'd changed from slacks to a dress the bunch waiting with me looked like they were coming from either a wedding or a funeral except they weren't wearing black.

When the elevator came, we all rushed in like it was the last elevator on earth and yelled out our floors.

A tall, stylishly dressed woman said to another, "Well, the summer's over."

"It is?"

They talked as loud as if they were in their own house. Everyone else was silent.

"Once you've passed the Fourth, that's it. You'll see. We'll be celebrating Christmas before you can say Jiminy Cricket. You have plans, Hazel?"

"For what?"

"Christmas, of course."

"You know, Frances, sometimes I think your head's not screwed on right."

The operator called five and the women got off.

175

When the doors closed behind them, I heard snickering. A lotta glances and smiles were exchanged and I felt like I was in cahoots with these strangers. I sorta liked the feeling.

After that, each person getting off said goodbye to the rest of us, so when we got to fourteen I did the same.

Right next to the elevator there was a plaque pointing one way to 1401 to 1410 and the other way to 1411 to 1420. I went to the right, all the way to the end.

When I knocked and a man asked who it was, I said, "Room service." I wouldna tried that except for the war. This was a man's job ordinarily. Now any job could be had by a girl.

"I didn't order . . . ," he said as he opened up. "You're not room service."

"No, I'm not." I gave him my spiel about who I was and why I was there and he let me in.

Mr. Cooper had a small mustache, like Charlie Chaplin, and his brown eyes were set close together with bushy brows above them. He wore a dark blue suit, white shirt, and blue tie. Around his arm was a black band. He had a prissy look about him, as if he'd been dressed by his mother.

"Would you like to sit down?"

"Thanks." There were two armchairs in the room. I took the one facing the windows and he took the other. I wondered where Mrs. Cooper was gonna sit when she came outta the bathroom, which is where I assumed she was.

"First, let me tell ya how sorry I am about your son."

"Thank you." He reached into his pocket and took out a nice-looking cigarette case. "Would you care for one?"

"I have my own, thanks." I took my Camels from my pocketbook, shook one out. Mr. Cooper was ready with a match. After he lit his own he dropped the dead match in the ashtray between us on a little table.

"Do ya know Private Ladd, Mr. Cooper?"

"No. Our son wrote to us about him but we never met him. David never brought home any of his army friends."

"Where are ya from again?"

"Pittsburgh."

"Were ya expectin to see David on this leave?"

"Yes. We were very worried when he didn't appear on Sunday. We knew he was in New York, but he only planned to stay two nights. He was coming home on Sunday because that's when he could travel."

I wasn't sure what he meant by that, but I wanted to get to other questions. "You didn't know what hotel he was stayin at?"

"Yes, I did. David called us on Friday when he got in. I asked where he was staying and he told me."

"Did he say anything that might be important?"

"I don't understand." Irritably, he blew out a puff of smoke.

"Somethin that might be a clue as to what happened to him."

"What could that possibly be?"

"I don't know. That's why I'm askin you."

"He reversed the charges as we'd told him to do. It was a short conversation. He confirmed that he'd be home Sunday. He was taking an early-morning train."

"Did ya go to pick him up at the station?"

"Yes. Thelma was with me. She was so excited to see him."

I knew he was, too, even if he couldn't say it. "What happened when David didn't get off the train?"

"Well, Thelma was naturally in a panic. We drove straight home and phoned the Commodore. I had them ring his room. No answer so I signaled for the desk. They said he hadn't checked out and his key was not in his box."

"Did ya ask for Ladd's room?" I took a drag.

"Not then. It didn't occur to me. But about an hour later I called back, and after trying David's room to no avail I asked for Private Ladd's room. No answer there, either, and he hadn't checked out."

"What'd ya think had happened?"

"To tell you the truth I was baffled. I kept trying to contact my son and Private Ladd, and finally Ladd picked up."

"Did he know where David was?"

"He said as far as he knew he'd taken the train for Pittsburgh. I told him David hadn't checked out. Ladd seemed evasive."

"Whaddaya mean?"

"I asked more questions and he danced around them.

Finally I confronted him. I told him I thought he knew where David was."

"And what'd he say?"

"He hesitated, said he did but he'd be betraying David if he told us. That made me very angry and I threatened Ladd with the police." He crushed out his cig in the ashtray.

"He didn't like that, did he?"

"Who would? So he told me. He said David had met a girl and he was probably with her. He didn't know where the girl lived or who she was."

Gloria Lane. Maybe she knew more than she'd let on.

"Was that it? I mean did ya talk anymore?"

"No. Thelma wanted me to go to New York right then. But I said he was sowing his wild oats and didn't need me to butt in."

"And when ya couldn't reach him for days?"

"I got very angry. Thelma was hysterical."

"Did ya call the police?"

"Of course not. I didn't want to embarrass the boy. I made plans to come in myself. And then we got the call." He slumped like a sunken soufflé.

"It musta been terrible for ya."

"Thelma needed to be sedated right away."

"What did David write to ya about Charlie Ladd?"

He pinched the bridge of his nose and closed his eyes. When he opened them, he said, "Not much. Just that they were good buddies, as he put it."

"Did he write about anyone else?"

"I suppose so but I can't think of their names right now."

I nodded in understanding. What I didn't understand was why Mrs. Cooper didn't come out of the bathroom.

"Do ya have any idea who coulda done this to David?" Did he know his son was found naked?

"I can't imagine, Miss Quick. I simply can't imagine."

I hadda ask. "Is Mrs. Cooper gonna join us?"

"Thelma didn't come with me. She's still under sedation. David was our only son."

"So ya have a daughter?"

"Two. I don't understand why he was found in Private Ladd's room. Why wouldn't he be left in his own room?"

"Have ya talked to the police about this?"

"Yes. I spent yesterday afternoon with them before I saw David's body."

What could it be like to have to view your dead son? "I thought he was already identified."

"Yes. Or they never would've called us. Cummings I think. I don't know him."

"George Cummings. He only met David once. But he was able to identify him. Why did the police need ya for that?"

"They didn't. I wanted to see him. I had to see him. To be sure. To never wonder."

"I understand." And I did. "I know that life will never be the same for you and Mrs. Cooper."

He looked at me strangely.

"What did the cops say about David bein in Charlie's room?"

"They didn't know why he was there. But it was clear they thought Ladd did it, because he's missing. Did you know that, Miss Quick? Did you know Private Ladd was missing?"

"Yeah. I did."

"So what does that suggest to you?"

"I'm not sure."

"I'll tell you what it suggests to me. It suggests that Ladd had something to do with my son's murder."

I wanted to tell him that Charlie'd been kidnapped, but I was afraid he'd tell the police.

"And I'll tell you what's completely baffling. David wrote me that he was going to share a room with Charles. They'd save money that way."

"When did he write ya that?"

"In his last letter."

Come to think of it, why *hadn't* they shared a room? Maybe Charlie being Charlie wanted to get Claire into his lair and ravage her.

"In his letter did David say sharin a room was all planned or was it an idea he had?"

"I can't remember the exact words. I'd have to look at the letter."

"It's at home in Pittsburgh?"

"Yes. With all his other letters. Thelma keeps them in a beautiful box with jade inlay that she inherited from her mother."

"Do ya think she could find the letter and read ya that part?"

"I don't think Thelma can do much of anything now. No. That's out of the question. You know, Miss Quick, I'm not certain I understand what your connection is to David's murder."

"It's to do with Private Ladd. Since David was found in his room their cases have gotten mixed up together. To get back to the letter. What about one of your daughters findin it?"

"Why is this so important?"

"If yer son wrote that it was a definite that they were gonna share a room and then they didn't, that could mean the boys had a fight."

"A fight is different from murder, Miss Quick."

"Yes. But maybe it could tell us if they fought or not?"

"Even if David did write that it was a fait accompli, anything could have happened. They're young boys and perhaps they decided they needed privacy." He blushed.

"Ya mean girls?"

He nodded. "Didn't Private Ladd have a girlfriend?"

"Yeah, he did."

"David didn't, but that doesn't mean he didn't want to find one. And apparently he did, according to Ladd. His mother would be horrified to hear that, but I'm realistic."

"When ya talk to yer daughter, do ya think ya could ask her to read that part from his last letter?"

"Yes. I will. Perhaps there's something in it I don't remember."

I was glad to hear him say that. Maybe there was. "How long will ya be in town, Mr. Cooper?"

"Until the police release his . . . his body. He should have been buried the day after he was found."

"It's just been a few days."

"But our custom is different."

"Excuse me. I don't understand."

"We bury our dead the next day."

I finally caught on. "Are you of the Jewish faith, Mr. Cooper?"

"Yes. If you're wondering about our name, it was changed from Kupfermann when my parents came to the United States through Ellis Island."

"Were ya born here?"

"Yes. A year after they settled on the Lower East Side."

"Are ya religious, Mr. Cooper?"

"Yes."

"Was David?"

"As a child. He had his bar mitzvah, but in high school I knew he was drifting away from it even though he went to temple with us every week. But what does our religion have to do with anything?" He stood up, his face turning a reddish color. "Everything always comes back to that, doesn't it?"

"I don't know what ya mean. I was curious, that's all. I didn't mean to insult ya, Mr. Cooper."

"My cousins are still in Germany. Do you have any

183

idea . . . never mind. Is there anything else?"

My cue to beat it. I grabbed my Camels and pocket-book and stood up. "I'm very sorry to have upset ya, Mr. Cooper."

"You didn't upset me. You wouldn't understand, that's all."

"Will ya still ask your daughter about that letter?"

"Yes, of course."

"Lemme give ya my number." I wrote down both office and home numbers in my notepad, tore the sheet out, and handed it to Mr. Cooper.

He looked at it like I'd written in hieroglyphics.

"You can call me anytime. Day or night."

He nodded. "Look, Miss Quick, I'm sorry I acted the way I did a few minutes ago."

"Think nothin of it."

"But I do. I know you weren't being . . . anti-Semitic."

"No. Never."

"Anyway, I'm sorry for my behavior."

"Okay. Thanks for talkin with me."

He nodded, his eyes looking somewhere past me. I left.

Back on the street my head said, *What's goin on here?* I thought of Nick Jaffe at Village Cigars. It seemed like Jewish people were getting real sensitive. I never thought about whether somebody was Jewish or not. It didn't occur to me. But what occurred to me now was that I had no idea whether I knew a lotta Jews or not. I started thinking.

Dolores was Jewish. One. That's all I could come up with. Why didn't I know more Jews? Why didn't I have any Jewish friends? I didn't put Dolores in the friend category. Had I been naïve about this Jewish thing? I knew there was anti-Semitism in the world, but I never thought of it as being in my little world. Was I an anti-Semite? Is that why I didn't have Jewish friends? I didn't believe that. But what was clear was that people like me didn't mix with Jews. Or maybe Jews didn't mix with people like me.

Suddenly some of the things the Ladds said came flying back to me like bricks through a window. I knew their remarks made me uncomfortable when they were saying them, but I didn't connect it.

If the acorn didn't fall far from the tree, then was Charlie Ladd an anti-Semite?

And if he was, did it have anything to do with David Cooper's death and Charlie being kidnapped?

SIXTEEN

J decided to go to my office since I was so close, even though it was Saturday. On my way I saw a small crowd at Duffy Square. When I got closer, I saw that it was a war bond rally. I'd bought three so I felt I'd done my part on that front.

Sometimes they had movie stars selling the bonds, but I could tell by the size of the group there weren't any stars.

Behind the makeshift platform was the huge statue of Father Duffy, a war hero—in World War I. I'd seen the movie with Pat O'Brien and James Cagney.

The guy trying to sell the bonds didn't look like he was doing such a great job cause people were walking away. I felt sorry for the poor schlemiel and I almost bought one. Then a pretty twist stepped up and flashed some long greens, which I felt freed me to go on my way.

First thing I did when I got into my office, after I lit up, was to call Claire.

"Thank God it's you," she said.

"What's happened?"

"They called. I gotta go to Pier Eighty-eight with the hundred thousand."

The luxury liner the *Normandie* sank there when it was being turned into a troopship. Eighty-eight had been a ghost pier since then.

"When?"

"Tomorrow."

"What time?"

"Three."

"And yer supposed to bring the cash?"

"Yeah. Me and no one else. If I tell the cops or anybody else comes along, the guy said he'd kill Charlie."

"You supposed to meet somebody or leave the loot somewhere?"

"There's a green metal barrel there, musta been for trash or oil once. Anyway, it's about three feet past a warning sign that tells ya the pier is dangerous. I'm supposed to drop the dough there and leave. Soon as they've got it, they'll let Charlie go."

If only it would be as simple as that. But with kid-nappings, something almost always went wrong.

"Faye, I'm so scared."

I wanted to tell her she should be scared for Charlie, but I knew that would make things worse. "Ya afraid they might do somethin to *you*."

"I don't know. The whole thing, it's a mess and a half."

"You'll be okay. Don't worry about that now. Did ya call the Ladds?"

"No. I was waitin for you to tell me what to do."

"When ya got the call, did ya ask to speak to Charlie?"

"Sure. They let him say hello, that's all."

"Could ya tell if it was him?"

"It was him."

"Ya could really tell this from a hello?"

"He said, 'Hello, Bambi.' That's what he calls me." I held my tongue. "So yer sure it was Charlie?"

"Yeah. I knew, too, by the tone of his voice."

"Okay. I'll call the Ladds."

"Thanks."

"Call ya back."

I dialed the hotel and got connected to the Ladds' room right away. He answered. I laid out the setup for him. He said he'd get the scratch that afternoon.

"My lawyer's bringing it. He's a Jew, but I trust him."

I didn't know what to say to that, so I didn't say anything.

"I think I should deliver the money," he said.

"They want Claire to hand it over, Mr. Ladd."

"But I'm his father."

"I guess that's not a high priority with the kidnappers."

"Who is this Claire, anyway? We don't even know her."

"Mr. Ladd. In these cases ya gotta follow instructions or serious things can happen."

"You think they might kill Charles?"

"If ya get em mad or don't deliver to order, there's a strong possibility of that. Kidnappers are funny that way. Sticklers for rules."

"Can you and I hide somewhere nearby?" Ladd asked.

"You mean while Claire hands off the ransom?"

"Exactly. I could hire a car."

"They're gonna be watchin everything."

"How many are there? Do we know that?"

"No. And that's the point. We can't risk doin anything that might set their teeth on edge."

"Are you sure you know what you're doing?"

I was waiting for that one. "It's not too hard to follow, Mr. Ladd."

"What I mean is, maybe we should tell the police."

"Not a good idea."

"They could have an *expert* hidden at the scene."

I got the scorch. "Look, I can't tell ya what to do, but

my best advice is *not* to bring the cops into this."

"Is it some sort of professional jealousy?"

"Is what professional jealousy?" I asked, starting to steam up.

"You and the police. You want to solve this on your own, don't you?"

"Mr. Ladd, I'm not solvin anything here. I'm just tryin to get yer son back alive."

Silence.

"How do I know you're telling the truth about all this?" he said.

"Ya don't. Ya hafta trust me."

"That's not much comfort."

This guy was getting in my hair. If it hadn't been for Claire, I woulda walked away from the whole thing. But she'd hired me, not this meathead.

"I'm not on this case to comfort ya, Mr. Ladd, although I feel for ya havin yer son kidnapped. I'm workin for somebody else. The kidnapper wants Claire to deliver the money alone and that's how it's gotta be."

"I'll call you when the money arrives here." He hung up.

I put the phone back in its cradle. What a goulash. I couldn't be sure that Ladd wouldn't bring in the cops, but I had to go along with the kidnappers' demands. There wasn't any other choice.

I called Claire. I told her that the money was on its way to Mr. Ladd, but I kept the rest to myself. It'd only give her the jumps.

"Faye, d'ya think I could go out now? I'm gettin bats in the belfry stayin cooped up here."

If it was me, I wouldn't wanna be away from the phone one minute even though the arrangements were all tied up. You never knew; they might change the plans. I suggested that to Claire.

"Ya think?"

"It's possible."

"I'm gonna go bonkers if I don't get out for some air. I'll just walk around the block. If they call while I'm out, they'll call back. Won't they?"

"Probably."

"Then I'm gonna take that walk. I need some ciggies, too."

"Okay. But keep it short, Claire."

"I will." She sounded almost happy.

"One more thing. How does Charlie feel about Jews?"

"Jews? I dunno. I mean he says stuff, but who doesn't?"

"What kind of stuff does he say?"

"Lemme think. Oh, yeah. Once we were in a club and some guy banged into us when we were dancin. Charlie called him a *clumsy kike.*"

"What'd the guy do?"

"Nothin. He looked mad, but he moved away from us. Everybody says stuff like that."

"They do?"

"Sure."

"I didn't know that."

"Charlie didn't mean anything by it."

"All in fun, right?"

"Well, I wouldn't put it that way. It's just how people talk. It's like *wop* or *mick*. Why're ya askin, Faye?"

"Just curious. Nothin important. Go take yer walk."

We hung up.

As I'd suspected, Charlie Ladd was probably as anti-Semitic as his parents. He probably hadn't known David Cooper was Jewish or he wouldna been friends with him.

I lit another butt. Speaking of David, which I was to myself, I thought I better go back and take another crack at Gloria Lane. I'd let her off too easy. I had a feeling she knew more than she'd owned up to when I interviewed her the first time.

Gloria lived on the top floor of a five-story walk-up. And the only way up was stairs. Her crib was down the hall at the end. I rapped on her door. Nothing happened. I put my ear to the wood. I heard rustling. I knocked again.

"Hold yer water," she said.

I waited.

"Who is it?"

"Faye Quick."

"Who?"

"We spoke before. I'm the PI on the Ladd case, remember?"

"Oh, yeah. The girl dick. What now?"

"Gotta fill in a few blanks, Gloria."

"I told ya what I know."

"I got some new questions."

She unlocked and let me in.

Gloria Lane was a bleached blonde and one of those broads who had a bosom like a shelf and made me wonder if I could park an ashtray on it. Her eyes were hazel with well-plucked brows. She was wearing a green silk lounging outfit that she musta gotten before the war.

Her place struck me the same as when I'd first seen it, decorated like what I imagined a brothel would look like. A lot of reds. Couches, chairs, pillows, even the wallpaper. We sat across from each other. She didn't offer me anything to drink.

From the table next to her chair, Gloria picked up a long black cigarette holder, stuck one in, and lit it with a table lighter. I got out my butts and lit mine with a match.

"So what's cookin?" she said.

"I'd like to ask ya a little more about the night ya spent with David, Charlie, and Ida."

"I told ya what happened."

"I know ya did. But other stuff's come out now."

"Yeah? What kinda stuff?"

"Did you know David was Jewish?"

"Yeah. And what's that got to do with the price a beans?"

"I just wondered if ya knew. How about Charlie?"

"How about him?"

"Did he know David was Jewish?"

"Why would I know that?"

"How'd Charlie act toward David?"

"Ya asked me that last time and my answer's the same. I wasn't payin attention to how the boys were treatin each other. My spotlight was on David, poor mutt."

"Did David *tell* ya he was Jewish?"

She blew a plume of smoke like a drunken dragon. "Not in so many words."

"What's that mean?"

"Just what I said."

"I don't get it," I said.

"So ya don't get it. Who cares?"

"Why're you actin like this, Gloria?"

"Like what?"

"Obstreperous."

"Come again?"

"It's like yer a different person from last time. Ya were real cooperative then. Now yer fightin me on every question."

She looked away, at the wall to her right, at the door, even the ceiling. Anywhere but at me.

"C'mon, Gloria. What's wrong?"

"I'm not a Hershey bar, ya know."

"A what?"

"That's what the soldier boys call it."

"Ya lost me."

"A floozy, chippy . . . oh, hell. I'm not a prosty."

Boy, did I feel stupid. "I never thought ya were, Gloria."

"If I tell ya what ya wanna know, you'll think I'm one."

"I won't, I promise."

"Yeah. Ya say that now."

"Just tell me how ya knew David was Jewish."

There was a long silence while she took another gander around the room. Then she gave a look-see right in my peepers like she could read em.

"Okay. Me and David? We had a roll in the hay."

"Yeah. So?"

"Jeez, Faye. I hafta draw ya a picture?"

I was trying my damnedest to figure this out, but I was still coming up blank. Gloria was getting her dander up and I didn't wanna make her any madder. So I kept quiet and just waited.

Finally, she said, "We kept the lights on. I saw him in the altogether. That's how I knew he was Jewish. Get it now?"

I did, and felt like a dunce.

I went home and, sure enough, Dolores was on the stoop. I almost didn't recognize her cause she had on a new wig. This one was brunette and was slipping over her left ear. I'd last seen her with her right ear nearly invisible.

"Dolores. You look different."

"I lost some weight."

And that was the end of that line of talk.

"Ya going out with yer fella tonight?"

"I sure hope so."

"Tell me, Faye, this is the real thing, ain't it?"

"Depends what ya mean?"

"I mean yer k'velen when yer around him."

"I make it so obvious?"

"Maybe only to me."

I heard my phone ringing through the open window. "I gotta get this, Dolores."

"Go, be happy. It's probably him, such a mensch." I ran up the steps and through the outside door. I got my key in the lock, ran in, and grabbed the phone.

It was Marty.

"Why didn't ya tell me, Faye?"

"Tell ya what?"

"That the cops got the skinny about Charlie."

I sorta fell into the chair at the phone table.

"Where'd ya hear that? And don't say ya got yer sources."

"I heard it from the sarge at my precinct."

"How'd he know?"

"Got me. But I checked around and found out old man Ladd called Powell and asked for help."

Charlie was as good as dead.

SEVENTEEN

*M*ore than anything I wanted to call William Ladd and rake him over the coals. But what good would that do? The whole thing was fouled up. I had to tell Claire. Claire! The cops had probably gotten to her already.

I dialed her number and a man answered. It had to be one of the boys in blue so I cut the connection. I wondered if the FBI had been brought in yet.

Claire was my client and I had to help her. Help Charlie. Zach's big green eyes stared at me as I paced my small kitchen, trying to figure what my next step should be.

I called Marty but he wasn't at the precinct or any of his usual haunts.

Then I dialed Claire's number again and got another man.

"Is Claire home?"

"Who is this?"

"Faye Quick."

"Just a minute."

I could tell he was covering the mouthpiece, checking with another cop.

"Hello, Quick." Detective Powell. I'd recognize that growl anywhere.

"Who's this?" I said to irritate him.

"Powell."

"Thank God," I said, hoping that'd throw him off his game.

"Huh?"

It worked. "I'm lookin for Claire Turner. Is she with you?"

"So happens she is. What about it?"

"I was worried about her."

"Don't be."

"I need to stop by."

"Do what ya want. We won't be here." He hung up.

Yeah, I really had Powell in my pocket. If they weren't gonna be at her apartment, they must be taking her to Powell's precinct. I didn't think they'd be booking her for anything. Just a lotta talk trying to figure what to do to get Charlie back and catch the kidnappers at the same time. A stupid and dangerous idea.

I woulda given anything to get outta my duds, but I couldn't show at the police station in slacks. I needed to look serious.

I left my crib and thanked my lucky stars Dolores wasn't on the steps to slow me down. But it was so unusual that I had a mad moment of thinking I should see if she was okay. Then I decided that was borrowing trouble and I had enough as it was.

I hurried toward Sixth Avenue and hailed a hack. This riding in cabs was getting to be a habit. I told him which precinct to go to.

The cabbie was silent for a while and then he said, "Why're ya goin to a police station, ya don't mind me askin? I mean, a nice-lookin gal like you."

I didn't get why my looks had anything to do with me going to the station.

"No, I don't mind ya askin. It's my mother. She tried to rob a bank."

"No kiddin? Yer mudder, huh? A regular Ma Barker."

"Somethin like that."

"So yer puttin up bail?"

"Nah. I'm gonna make sure they keep her in there."

"Huh?"

"She's a menace to society."

"But she's your mudder."

I didn't like the curve this was taking. Joke or not, it made me think of my real mother and I didn't wanna do that.

"I hope ya don't mind, but I don't wanna talk about it," I said.

"Yeah. Sure."

I could see the side of his cheek, and the muscle jumping under the skin told me he was crazed with questions.

We pulled up to the curb.

"Here we are," he said. "Buck thirty."

I gave him the do re mi and a nickel tip.

"Ya know somethin, girlie? A mudder is a mudder and if mine was Lizzie Borden, I'd still be behind her. Yer a disgrace."

"Thank you," I said, and got out, sorry I'd tipped him.

The station looked like any other with its globes of green light on either side of the door. And inside coulda been any station, too: the usual high desk with the cop behind it and a lotta gray chairs against one wall with a lotta gray people sitting in them.

I went to the desk and waited for the cop to finish whatever he was writing. And I waited. And waited. I cleared my throat. Nothing. It was beginning to get my dander up.

"Officer," I said. Nothing. Making a scene was outta the question. It was the old honey-or-vinegar routine.

"Officer?" Sweet as pie.

He looked up. I batted my long lashes.

"What can I do for ya, miss?"

"I'd like to see Detective Powell."

He squinted his tiny eyes, which pushed his eyebrows together, making them look like one. "What's yer name?"

Uh-oh. "Miss Quick."

He looked down at his desk again and fumbled some papers. "Faye?"

"Yeah."

"He don't wanna see ya."

"What?"

"He don't . . ."

"I heard what ya said. I wanna know why."

"How should I know? He give me my instructions. That's all I gotta know."

"Could ya tell him I'm here?"

"Why would I do that?"

"Maybe he changed his mind."

"Detective Powell don't change his mind."

That sounded right. "Can ya tell me somethin else?"

"No."

"You haven't even heard what I wanna ask ya?"

He pursed his mouth into the size of an eraser, then said, "What? Whaddaya wanna ask?"

"Is Claire Turner here?"

"This I ain't got the skinny on."

"When Detective Powell came in, did he have a girl with him?"

"Ya think all I gotta do all day is watch who the detectives bring in with em?"

I could see I was getting nowhere and that things weren't gonna change. I walked away and sat on one of the gray chairs to figure out what my next move was gonna be.

Maybe Claire needed a lawyer. She never woulda thought to get one. Looking around, I spotted a pay phone on the wall. I strolled over, put my nickel in, and dialed 0. I gave the operator the number I wanted.

"Joel Sheridan's office," a girl said.

I told her who I was and that it was a matter of life and death that I speak to Sheridan now. She told me to hold on.

I waited. And waited. The operator cut in and told me to fork over another buffalo head. Finally Sheridan picked up.

"Whatcha got goin on, Faye?"

The voice of an angel.

Half an hour later Joel appeared. He came over to me, kissed me on the cheek, and took off his straw fedora. His head was shiny, like a peeled egg. He wore a light-weight blue pin-striped suit with a colorful tie. And he had bright brown eyes that shone with smarts.

"Fill me in," he said.

I did.

"So you want me to represent Miss Turner?"

"For now," I said. "Who knows what paces they're puttin her through."

"Okay."

He started to get up from his chair, and I put a hand on the arm of his suit.

"What?"

"She doesn't have any loot, Joel."

"She payin you?"

"A little."

"That's good enough for me."

"My point bein is that I don't know if she can afford another expense."

He smiled. "You called me, you knew I wouldn't care."

"It's just for now."

"Gotcha."

I watched him go up to Officer Charming at the desk. There was a back-and-forth, but I couldn't hear what they said. Then the sergeant picked up his phone. In a minute he was waving Joel up the stairs where I knew the detectives had their offices.

I hoped Joel'd get Claire outta there right away, but knew it could take a while. Meantime, I had plenty to keep me entertained. Drunks were hauled in, and penny-ante types, and . . . William Ladd. He was walking toward the desk when he saw me and did an about-face.

"What are *you* doing here?" he said.

"Claire is bein quizzed by the cops."

"Good. We have to pull together on this."

"Who does?"

"Everyone but you."

I felt like I'd been slapped across the face. "I don't think that's up to you to decide."

"We'll see about that."

"Claire's got a lawyer now."

"What does she need a lawyer for?"

"To protect her."

"From who?"

"You for one." I could get my licks in like any other bully.

"Do I have to remind you, Miss Quick, it's not your son's life on the line."

"Mr. Ladd. I'm tryin to save Charlie's life."

He ignored that. "Where did Miss Turner get a lawyer?"

"I got her one."

"What's his name?"

I wondered why he cared cause I was pretty sure he wouldn't know any New York lawyers.

"Joel Sheridan."

"What kind of name is that?"

"What is it with you and names?"

"Never mind. A girl like you would never understand."

"What's a girl like me?"

"You live in Greenwich Village, don't you?"

"So?"

"I know you people associate with any type."

"You people? Any type?"

"Communists, Jews, radicals, and God knows who else."

I was ready to mix it up with this nasty little man, but then I saw them. "Here they come," I said.

Joel's hand was under Claire's elbow as he guided her toward us.

"Oh, Faye. Thank you so much for Mr. Sheridan."

I smiled. "They ask ya a lotta stuff ya felt ya hadda answer?"

"I'm afraid so. Until Mr. Sheridan came in. Then I didn't answer anything."

Ladd said, "Why shouldn't she answer questions?"

"Who's this?" Joel asked.

"Mr. Ladd. The father of the soldier who was kidnapped."

"Oh." Joel stuck out his hand.

Ladd looked at it with suspicion; then he took it for a second but let go fast.

"I don't think ya know Claire, either, do ya?" I said.

"I haven't had the pleasure. How do you do, my dear?" He gave a little bow from the shoulders. What a phony.

"Hello," she said. "We spoke on the phone."

I could smell his disapproval of her. I hoped she couldn't.

"And I want to thank you for informing me of the latest development in my son's kidnapping."

So that's how it happened. Claire. Why hadn't she listened to me? How could I ask?

"You're certainly a girl I can trust."

"I'm not sure everybody thinks I did the right thing."

"You mean this shyster and this poor excuse for a detective?"

"Excuse me, Mr. Ladd," Joel said. "I don't think you understand the jeopardy your son is in now. Bringing in the police wasn't too smart in a situation like this."

Ladd looked at him like he was a pesky persistent bug. "I have no interest in anything you have to say. I'm going to see Detective Powell now and we're going to work out the details of how to get my son back."

"I can guarantee you, you won't get him back if you bring the police into this," Joel said.

"Mr. Sheridan, I don't know what it'll take to get you to mind your own business. In case you don't know, I'm a lawyer myself. I know how to handle these issues."

"I knew ya were a lawyer," Claire said. "Charlie told me."

Why hadn't she forked over this little tidbit to me? "He was very proud of ya," she said.

He smiled, as if to say: *Of course he was.* "I hope Charles will join my firm someday."

"Oh, no," Claire said.

We all looked at her.

"He wants to be a writer."

"A what?" Ladd said.

"A writer. Ya know, like Hemingway or that dead one, the Fitzgerald guy."

"F. Scott," Ladd said.

"Yeah, that's the one." Claire wasn't helping herself with William Ladd.

"A writer. I've never heard such nonsense. Charles never expressed to me any desire to be a writer. Had he, I would've put paid to that."

"What Charlie is gonna be isn't too important now cause if we don't work somethin out he's not gonna be anything," I said.

"That's a brutal thing to say, Miss Quick."

"Sorry. I'm only tryin to point out the truth."

"I'm going to see Detective Powell now and get this whole mess straightened out and expedited."

"You mean to get the hundred thousand to the kid-nappers?" Claire asked.

"Exactly."

"Don't ya think I should take the cash to the place they chose?"

"I'll be doing that," Ladd said.

"The kidnappers want *me* to do it."

"How do I know you won't run off with the money?"

We were all quiet for a moment. Stunned, I think.

"Look, Miss Turner, you're being kind to offer, but I think this whole matter is better left to the men." He gave me a knifelike glance.

"She isn't bein kind," I said. "She loves your son."

"That's very charming."

"What's charmin about it?" Claire asked.

"For you to have loving feelings toward Charles when he's engaged to another woman."

EIGHTEEN

J don't know whose jaw dropped lower, mine or Claire's.

"How come ya didn't mention this when I came to your hotel, Mr. Ladd?" I asked.

"Frankly, I didn't think it was any of your business."

"But Charlie and me were gonna be engaged."

Ladd showed some teeth when he snickered. "I'm sure you misunderstood, Miss Turner. Now, if you'll excuse me . . ."

"Who's he engaged to?" I asked.

"You mean her name?"

"Yeah."

"I don't want you bothering her."

"I'd just like to know who Charlie's engaged to."

"Why do you want her name?"

"Call me nosy."

"I'd be glad to."

"Mr. Ladd," Joel said. "Do you have something to hide?"

"No. Of course not."

"Then tell us the fiancée's name."

"Barbara Swanson of the Rhode Island Swansons. May I go now?"

No one objected, and he walked toward the desk. Charlie Ladd was some kind of Dr. Jekyll and Mr. Hyde. I started wondering if it might be better for me, and especially Claire, to get outta this.

"I can't believe it," Claire said.

I could. I knew what Charlie was capable of. "He never said word one to ya, right?"

"Nothin."

It was hard not to tell her about Lucille. But she didn't need any more bad news right then.

"I have to go," Joel said.

"I'm sorry, Joel. I didn't mean to keep ya."

"It was worth it to see Mr. High and Mighty in action."

"Mr. Sheridan, I don't know how to thank ya."

"Don't give it a thought, Miss Turner."

"Thanks for comin down here, Joel."

"Glad to help out." He kissed me on the cheek, put his forefinger and thumb to the brim of his hat to Claire, and left.

Claire said, "I don't wanna cry here, Faye."

"Let's get some coffee."

We left the precinct and walked to Lexington Avenue, where we found a coffee shop. We took a booth in the back.

Claire pulled a white lace hankie from her pocket-book and dabbed at her eyes. "I just can't imagine Charlie bein engaged to some Barbara Swanson or anyone else. I can't."

I didn't know what to say cause I *could* imagine it.

"The main thing now, Claire, is ya gotta be the one to make the drop. I hafta convince Ladd of that. And I don't know how to keep the cops and the FBI outta this."

"I meant to tell ya about those G-men who came to my house. There were three of those monkeys and they scared me silly."

"They can do that. You gotta make that drop, Claire. Cops or FBI on the scene or not. The kidnappers hafta think you're on the level."

"I can't make the drop if Mr. Ladd won't gimme the money."

"Good point."

"I don't know what we can do."

"Yeah. Ladd's determined to do it his way."

"So what'll happen?" She blew out smoke that was like a soft puffy cloud.

"I don't know for sure. What they'll try to do is have Ladd make the drop while they're watchin so when someone picks it up they can nab him."

"But that might not work, huh?"

The waitress came for our order. Claire wasn't hungry, but I was. I hadn't eaten since breakfast. I ordered an English muffin with my java. Then I said make it two.

When the waitress left, Claire said, "I told ya I wasn't hungry."

"I know. They're both for me. Where were we?"

"I asked ya whether the police plan might work or not."

"If the kidnappers have any suspicion or see anybody, they won't pick up the spinach in the barrel."

"And what'll happen to Charlie?"

"I can't be sure." This was tough.

"Whaddaya think will happen?"

"The worst is they'll kill him."

She didn't blink an eye. "And the best?"

"They'll try again."

The waitress brought our order. She put one of the English muffins in front of me and one in front of Claire.

"It's for me," I said.

"I gave ya yours."

"They're both for me."

She looked at me like I was a pig in garbage.

"I'm hungry," I said. I coulda kicked myself for thinking I needed to explain.

She picked up the plate in front of Claire and put it in front of me. "Happy eatin," she said.

There wasn't any butter but there were a couple a jams that looked okay. What I wouldn't give to see real butter again.

Claire picked up her cup in two hands like she was warming herself. She brought it to her lips, then set it back in the saucer without having any.

I wasn't gonna push her. She was a grown-up girl and if she didn't want to eat or drink, that was her choice.

Me? I slathered on some strawberry jam. I knew it wouldn't be very sweet cause nobody made jam with sugar these days. I took a bite and it tasted like ambrosia to me, I was that hungry.

"I'll find out about this Barbara Swanson if ya want me to."

"Find out what?"

"If Charlie's really engaged to her?"

She shrugged.

"Yeah. I guess it doesn't make any difference right now. And when he comes back, you can ask him yourself."

"Don't ya mean *if* he comes back?"

"Claire. I don't want ya thinkin like that."

"I'm tryin to be realistic, Faye."

It was so hard not to spill the beans about that bum. I didn't want him to be killed but I didn't want Claire to marry him, either. "You're right. I guess it's good to be realistic."

"From what I've read in the newspapers and heard on the radio, kidnappin victims usually don't come home alive. Isn't that true?"

"Yeah. It is."

"Even if they get the money?"

"Even then."

I kept going back and forth on this damn thing. Maybe it would be easier on Claire if I told her the truth about Charlie. On the other hand it might devastate her to hear about her sister and Charlie. And to hear how it happened? No, I couldn't tell her yet. If Charlie didn't come back, she would never need to know. If he did, I'd have to warn her about who this guy was.

When we . . . I . . . finished my English muffins and java, Claire said she wanted to go home. Outside, I put her in a cab.

I had a friend whose mother always said, *There's nothing as hot as hot cheese.* She was wrong. Soaking wet and panting like a dog, I made it back to my office. I put my key in the lock and right away I knew the door was not zipped up. Had I forgotten to lock it when I was there earlier? I was pretty sure that wasn't the case. It was times like this I wished I carried a gat. But I didn't. I heard Woody's voice. *Yer on a case, Quick, and it's got violence in it, ya carry a piece at all times.* So much for listening to my boss.

I couldn't decide whether to go in or leave. I wasn't calling for the cops. I had my pride. Then I heard the toilet flush. I tried to tell myself this was just a person who needed the WC. Myself wouldn't buy. Okay. I hadda take a chance. Slowly, I turned the knob and carefully opened the door inch by inch. When I got it open enough to let myself in, the bathroom door opened and we both screamed.

It was Birdie.

We spoke at the same time and said the same thing. "What are you doin here?" Then we laughed.

"You go first," I said. Being boss sometimes had advantages.

"I had a fight with Pete and I didn't feel like talkin about it with any of my girlfriends, so I thought I'd come here and sit and think for a while."

It was hard to picture Birdie sitting and thinking cause some part of her was always moving. "What was this fight about? Or don'tcha wanna talk to me, either?"

"Ah, Faye. It's the same old stuff. Ya don't wanna hear it."

"Another woman?"

"Nah. He's pushin me to get married. I guess maybe there's somethin wrong with me, huh? I mean what girl doesn't wanna get married?"

We sat down in the waiting room that doubled for Birdie's office. Then we reached for our smokes.

"I bet there's lotsa girls don't wanna get hitched," I said.

"Yeah, well, I don't know any. *You* wanna get married, don'tcha, Faye?"

Did I? "Eventually."

"What about Johnny? Don'tcha wanna marry him now?"

"No. I don't know him well enough."

"So if he asked ya, you'd say no?"

"He's not gonna ask me."

"Yer duckin the question."

I thought of telling her about our new arrangement, but I decided to keep it to myself for now.

"Faye?"

"I know twenty-six isn't too young to get married. But I feel like I'm a kid."

"There ya go."

"You feel that, too?" Birdie was thirty. She wouldn't tell her age, but I had my ways of finding out.

"Nah."

"So why *don't* ya wanna, Bird?"

"I don't see the point. What's in it for me? I don't

wanna have kids, I know that's another strange thing about me, and I don't feature bein a housewife. I mean, me home all day waxin the floors, or whatever those married dames do? So what I'd end up doin is takin care of Pete. This way I get to have him in my life and I don't hafta wash his dirty socks and cook every meal for him. See what I mean?"

I nodded.

"Course there's one catch like always. He might fly the coop and marry someone else."

"You really believe that?"

She blew smoke through both nostrils like somebody on the silver screen. "Yeah. Pete wants someone to take care of him even though he doesn't say so."

"And ya think he'd be willin to give ya up?"

"Lemme put it this way: if I was a man, *I* would, ya get my drift?"

I did. "I'm sorry, Bird. But it's not happenin today, so maybe ya should make it up with Pete." It went against the grain to push Pete, cause he wasn't a favorite, but I wanted Birdie to be happy.

"Yer probably right, Faye." She stubbed out her cig. "But I think I'll let him stew in his own juices for a while. So whaddaya doin here?"

I brought her up to date on the case.

"No kiddin? This is a doozy. Sounds like Charlie maybe wants *two* gals to take care of him."

"I'd laugh but then I think about him rapin Lucille."

"Yeah. I forgot about that for a sec."

"As long as yer here, Bird, would ya mind tryin to

get a phone number for Barbara Swanson in Rhode Island?"

"My pleasure, I'm sure."

"I'm gonna go. Ya can reach me at home later, okay?"

"Okay. One thing, Faye. How d'ya know Lucille is tellin the truth? I mean she probably had a baby, but who says it was Charlie's?"

"There was somethin about her that rang true."

"Wasn't it you who told me when ya hired me, *What they tell ya isn't always the truth*?"

"You're right. I better investigate Lucille a little closer. But the first thing is to get Charlie Ladd back safely. I hafta convince his father that even though the police are involved and it's too late to change that, Claire should be makin the drop."

"How're ya gonna get him over to yer side?"

"If I was a guy I'd take him out to dinner and get him plastered then get him to agree."

"Why can't ya get him to take you out to dinner and get him plastered anyways?"

"What would I do without ya, Birdie?"

"You'd close up shop," she said.

When I got home, I called Claire and told her to be ready the next day to make the drop, but I couldn't promise. She said she was ready for anything.

Then I called Ladd at his hotel. After a few snipes from him, I got him calmed down.

"Mr. Ladd, you and I want the same thing for

Charlie. We're not enemies here."

"I want my boy back. I want him safe, unharmed."
He sounded like maybe he'd been bending his elbow
already.

"That's what I want," I said. "That's why I think we
should work together."

"How?"

"Could we meet? It's so . . ."

"Impersonal this way."

"That's it."

"Why don't we have some dinner?" he said.

"Oh, that's a terrific idea."

We made plans to meet at seven at the 21 Club. I'd
never been there, but I knew enough to know I'd need
to borrow something dressy from Jeanne Darnell. The
21 Club was no Blondell's.

Then I called Johnny and broke our date. He understood. He was an A number one kinda guy. But if I
married him, everything might change. I was getting
Birdie's philosophy more and more.

What was I thinking? The guy hadn't even hinted at
marriage. Well, why the heck hadn't he?

NINETEEN

J spent an hour with Jeanne going through her
closet. We were basically the same size. Half an
inch here or there didn't matter. Good thing she was a
clotheshorse. My wardrobe consisted of one nice

black cocktail dress I'd bought before the war, and clothes for work, simple and comfy.

There were a hill of dresses on Jeanne's bed. We'd discarded one after the other. Too dressy, not dressy enough, too sporty, too revealing, and so on.

Finally we found the perfect one. It had a sweetheart V neckline and short, set-in sleeves. There was a decorative design all over the dress that was hand-stitched. It was blue but not blue. The rayon fabric kept changing.

"This is you," Jeanne said.

"I don't know about those little things around the neckline."

She looked at me, surprised. "They're rhinestones, Faye, and they're in good taste. Trust me."

I trusted Jeanne in everything and especially when it came to clothes.

"Try it on," she said.

"Okay." I was already in my slip, having tried on about five other things. Jeanne zipped me up in back.

"Yes. Perfect," she said. "All eyes will be on you tonight. And Johnny's going to adore it."

I smiled. I hadda lie. It was too complicated to explain.

"I bet he's going to propose, Faye. I mean, how often do girls like us get taken to 21?"

"I don't think this is about marriage." Not a lie.

"You think it's just a regular date?"

"No." Not a lie.

"Then what?"

I felt like a louse when I looked into her eyes. "I'm not sure."

"Whatever it is, I get the first phone call tomorrow."

"You bet," I said.

"Oh, dear." She clapped a hand over her mouth.

"What?"

"Shoes. And an evening bag."

"I don't have any shoes that'd go with this dress. And I don't own an evenin bag."

She smiled, showing her dimples. "I have both. What size shoe do you take?"

"Five."

"Mine might be slightly big on you, but you can adjust, can't you?"

"I think so. How much bigger?"

"Only half a size."

"Let's see." Jeanne went back to her closet to pick out a pair from her shoe rack. She'd admitted to me once that she'd never met a pair of shoes she didn't like.

"These will be just the ticket," Jeanne said.

The shoes she held out had a wide high heel and were a dark blue with ankle straps. The top was cut into a pattern and had an open toe.

"Before the war," she said. "You wouldn't find anything like this now."

I thanked my lucky stars that Jeanne kept everything she bought. I tried on the shoes and though they were a little big it wasn't anything I couldn't handle.

"They look swell on you, Faye."

"Thanks."

She was back in her closet and from a rustling of tissue paper she pulled a dark blue sequined bag with a gold-colored frame, a brass clasp, and a brass chain.

It couldn't have been more on the button.

Jeanne said, "Suits you to a *T*."

I didn't know how to thank her.

"Now let me do your face."

I knew this was coming and I dreaded it. I wore lipstick, powder, and rouge like any girl, but the big makeup job didn't knock me out. Jeanne, on the other hand, made it an art.

While she was working on me, I asked her what it was she wanted to tell me.

"You'll never guess so I'll give it to you straight. I've joined the Wacs."

I grabbed the hand that was about to do something to my eyebrows. "Are ya serious?"

"I leave in two weeks."

"Yer on the level?"

"You bet."

"Have ya thought about what yer gonna hafta wear?"

She laughed. "That's one of the reasons I joined. I won't have to think about what to wear anymore. You don't know how much energy it takes out of me, Faye."

I'd always thought it was a snap for Jeanne. Always envied her ease with looking smart.

"I didn't know that, Jeanne. Ya make it look so easy."

"Well, it drives me crazy to make it look that way. I'm hoping wearing khaki will break me of my obsession. But that's not the only reason I joined up. I know it's corny, but I want to give something to the war effort."

"Couldn't ya have bought a war bond?" I hated the thought of Jeanne leaving, maybe getting hurt. "And what does Ronald say?"

"I can't say he's pleased as Punch, but he understands I have to do what I have to do."

I felt guilty as could be. What was *I* doing for the war effort? I wasn't even rolling the tinfoil from my cigarette packs and chewing gum wrappers into balls. Maybe if I understood what they wanted it for, I'd do it. Nah. I was a selfish person. Too busy to have a Victory Garden or collect scrap metal. And here was my good friend going off to war.

"I'm nothin but a yellow belly," I said.

"Oh, knock it off."

"I don't even have a Victory Garden."

She looked at me like I was crazy. "You're right. I think you should start one right away. In your bedroom. Now stop this. Catching bad guys is important. Besides, everyone isn't the same. I could never do what you do, Faye."

"You mean that?"

"You bet I do. Now hold still or we'll never get this done."

By the time she was finished I had to admit she'd made me into one swanky-looking dish. I barely recognized myself and I hoped William Ladd would like this look.

It had gotten late and I couldn't see any way to meet him on time if I didn't go right to 21 from Jeanne's.

"Can I leave my stuff here and pick it up tomorrow?"

"Sure."

I went through my pocketbook to get my keys and smokes and transferred them to the evening bag.

"Jeanne, I think yer the bravest dame I know, and even though I'll miss ya, I admire yer courage."

We hugged and said our goodbyes. Walking along Barrow toward Seventh I kept making my case to myself. Sure I wanted to help the war effort, but I figured the best way I could do it was to stand in for Woody. So I didn't get a job in a war plant like Stella Dallas, or join the Wacs like Jeanne. I was doing my part another way. At Seventh, before hailing a cab, I overheard two passing sailors.

"A real glamour-puss."

"I saw her first, buddy."

I looked around to see who they were talking about and was struck dumb. It was me. I could get used to this.

There were jockey statues lining the walkway into the restaurant. And once inside, there were two more. A maître d' showed instantly and gave me an obvious look-see.

"May I help you?"

I raised my chin so my nose was in the air and tried for the lockjaw sound blue bloods used in the movies. "I'm meetin Mr. Ladd."

"Oh, yes. He said to expect you. He's in the main dining room. Follow me, please."

Everywhere I looked I saw something beautiful. The wood itself, a painting, a silver tray. I felt dizzy. Who'd a thought I'd ever be in a joint like this. And even though it'd been a speakeasy during Prohibition, it sure wasn't that now.

As we threaded our way through the tables, I couldn't help but notice the glamorous customers. I was sure I was dressed all wrong, but then I spotted a woman wearing something like my getup. And I didn't spot anyone giving me the fisheye.

William Ladd was sitting at a small round table and rose when I came near. He was wearing a dinner jacket and a black tie. We smiled at each other. The maître d' pulled out the plush red satin chair for me, bowed slightly, and left. Mr. Ladd listed on the way down but landed back in his chair.

"What would you like to drink, Miss Quick?" He pronounced the words carefully as if they were all new to him.

"A manhattan, please."

A waiter materialized out of nowhere. Mr. Ladd gave him my order and asked for another martini. Then he opened the gold cigarette case lying on the table and offered me a cigarette. My best instincts told me to forget my Camels and take his offering. With a matching lighter he fired up my cig.

We both took big drags and I let the smoke out very slowly. Then I said, "I'm a little late because . . ."

He put up his hand to stop me. "Never apologize, never explain."

I stared at him. "Never apologize?"

"That's correct."

"But what if I bump someone, step on somebody's foot."

"That's different. By the way, you look lovely tonight, Miss Quick. I wouldn't have thought . . . yes, very lovely."

"Please call me Faye." What he wouldn't have thought didn't get past me.

"Certainly. And you must call me William."

I smiled and nodded.

"So, Faye, let's get to the point of our little rendezvous? You said you wanted to work with me on getting Charles back."

"Oh, yes. I do . . . William."

In the nick of time a waiter came with our drinks. Playing my part wasn't like rolling off a log. I hadn't thought about how I'd work my wiles; I'd only been worried about what to wear.

"Shall we toast?" he said.

"Why not?" I gave a toss of my head, trying for a devil-may-care air, but I wasn't sure it worked.

"To having Charles returned safely."

Our glasses clicked and I took a dainty sip while he took a gulp. Good.

"So what do you propose, Faye?"

It was too early in the game to suggest he let Claire make the drop. "Plenty of time for that, William. Tell me what it's like to live in Rhode Island."

"Why, it's like living anywhere, I suppose."

"Oh, I don't think so. Isn't it the smallest state in the Union?"

"Well, yes. But I don't see what that has to do with what it's like to live there."

"What town do ya live in, William?" I sipped my drink, then puffed on my cig.

"Newport."

"Isn't that where all the rich people built their summer houses?"

"Cottages. But we don't live in anything like that. Newport is a lovely comfortable town on the sea. Our home is modest."

What this guy considered modest would probably be like a palace to me. But I wouldn't wanna live in Rhode Island, no matter how nice it was. Let's face it, I wouldn't wanna live anywhere but New York City.

"Is that where Charles grew up?"

"Yes. Now what's your plan for getting him back to us?"

He'd finished his drink and was looking a little glassy-eyed. I couldn't decide whether to take the plunge or wait. Just in time the waiter arrived.

"Do you wish to order, sir?"

"I'd like another drink, William."

"Yes, of course. Bring us two more," he said.

I smiled at William, happy that he'd have a third martini. For all I knew it mighta been his fifth or sixth. I'd sip at my manhattan.

"Now what were we saying?" he asked.

"You were gonna tell me about Barbara Swanson."

"I was?"

"Yeah. Ya said she was takin this whole thing real hard."

"I did?"

"Why didn't she come with ya, William? I mean she's his fiancée and all."

"Her parents wouldn't let her. They considered the whole matter sordid. It's all so embarrassing."

"Embarrassin that Charlie was kidnapped?"

"You don't understand the Newport attitude about privacy. They don't look kindly on being splashed all over the newspapers. Bad form."

"Ya got a picture of Barbara?"

"Why would I have a picture of Barbara?"

"I thought maybe ya had one with Charlie in it."

"No."

"What about Mrs. Ladd? Tell me about her."

"Fragile. She's a very fragile girl."

By the time he finished talking about Jennifer and how she didn't understand him, and he'd tossed down his fourth martini, William was mine.

"I think we gotta talk about Charlie."

"Who?"

"Charles. Your son."

"Oh, Charles. Yes."

"The kidnappers demanded that Claire make the drop and I think that's how we should do things."

"No."

"Why not?"

"He's my son. I'm doing it."

"Could I let ya in on some of my experience, William? Only cause it may be helpful to you and to Charles."

"Of course, Faye. Yes. Please do that."

I felt Mr. Ladd could slip away, or under the table, at any time.

"Kidnappers are a strange breed. Once they've decided on something, it's set in stone, and when a kidnapper is disobeyed he sees red, if ya know what I mean."

"You look very lovely tonight, Faye."

Oh, brother.

He put a hand over mine. I gave him a swift smile. I'd wanted this to happen, but now it didn't seem like such a great idea. Still, I left my hand where it was.

"William," I said. "You gotta let things go the way they're supposed to. The police and FBI shouldn't be in on this, but the boat's sailed on that one."

"What boat?"

This was harder than I'd imagined.

"Ya want Charlie back in one piece, don'tcha?"

He nodded, his eyelids drooping like they had tiny barbells on em.

"Then ya gotta let Claire do this, William."

"My son."

His head hit the table with a terrible crack.

So much for my disguise as a femme fatale.

The people at 21 had been very nice and helped me put William in a cab. I rode with him to the St. Moritz, and from there the doorman and bellboys took over. I kept the cab and went home.

It was still hot and sticky and Dolores was on the steps with her fan. The window to her apartment was open, and from the radio on the sill Dick Haymes was singing "You'll Never Know." In my window Zach sat on his pillow observing.

"Oh, a taxicab now. And look at you, bubele, dressed fit to kill."

"Never say that to a detective, Dolores."

I could tell by how she looked at me that she didn't get it. I wanted to get inside and have some food. The manhattans were swell at 21, but I hadn't had a bite to eat.

"Dolores, I'd love to gab, but I've had a terrible night. I gotta go in."

"Johnny didn't do something bad, did he?"

"I wasn't with him."

"You was with another one?" Her eyebrows vanished under her wig, which was hanging low on her forehead.

"Business."

"And yer all dolled up like that for business?"

"I am. I gotta eat."

She started to get up. "Lemme feed ya, tootsie. I

have leftover kasha and some nice blintzes, and . . ."

It sounded great, but if I let her feed me, I'd have to talk to her, and I wasn't in the mood.

"I just wanna grab somethin. And I gotta be alone. Ya understand?"

She sat back down. "Yup."

I knew she didn't. She was hurt and I felt like hell, but there was nothing I could do about it now. Like Scarlett, I'd worry about it tomorrow. I gave her a halfhearted wave and went inside.

Zach turned his head, but he didn't jump down when I came through the door. He thought the street was much more interesting than I was. I agreed.

I headed for the icebox. I was starving, tired, and feeling down and out. Not to mention my worry over Jeanne. I found some old lettuce and Velveeta. A perfect meal for a bungler like me. Dick Tracy woulda been ashamed of me cause William Ladd was gonna sober up, the brass were gonna take him to the drop, and they were all gonna put Charlie's life at risk.

There wasn't a thing I could do about it.

TWENTY

I slept in dribs and drabs, then got up and smoked a butt or two, which was not my routine. It was seven A.M. I lay in bed staring at the ceiling and wishing there was someone in the kitchen to bring me a cup of java. Well, not just anyone. Johnny. Who else? I wondered if he was the kind of guy who'd make a gal a cup, or if he'd expect me to do all the deliveries. I put that on my mental list of things I wanted from a mate. It was getting pretty long. But not unreasonable to my way of thinking. Number one was a sense of humor. Johnny had that in spades. In fact, he'd been batting a thousand on my list. The addition of coffee in bed mighta upped even that stat.

Zach was on top of my head, but he was getting too heavy for this habit. I reached up to take hold of him, then transferred him to my stomach. Even though he looked at me like I was crazy he began to purr in no time.

I wanted to go back to sleep. I wanted to find a way out of this day. But there wasn't any. I'd have to call Claire and tell her the bad news. And now she understood the damage Mr. Ladd could do by making the drop. But there was an outside chance we'd get away with it. Maybe the kidnappers would just be glad to get the dough whoever dropped it. Nah. Even if they didn't spot John Law they'd know the cops were there. A substitute for Claire would tip em to that and they'd scratch the pickup. Unless they were stupid, and we couldn't count on that.

The phone rang. When I moved, Zach leapt from the bed like a volcano had erupted. I padded out to my phone and got it on the third ring.

"Did I wake ya, Faye?"

"No. I wish ya had." I sat down.

Birdie said, "What's that mean?"

228

"I didn't get a lotta shut-eye last night."

"Ya don't mean . . . Mr. Ladd?"

"Course not."

"Did ya get him plastered?"

"Yeah. He passed out on the table at 21."

"Before he was face-first in the soup, did he say he'd let Claire make the drop?"

I liked her picture and didn't see any reason to tell her it wasn't exactly what happened. "That's the thing. He refused."

"Ya think he'll be sober enough to do it himself today?"

"Oh, sure."

"So whaddaya gonna do?"

"I don't know yet. Why ya callin me so early?"

"Ya said I didn't wake ya up."

"Ya didn't. That's not the point."

"What is the point?"

"Bird, just tell me why yer callin."

"It's about Barbara Swanson. I found her. She lives here."

"Whaddaya mean?"

"Here. New York. Barbara Swanson. Lives."

"How d'ya know?"

"I talked to her mother in Rhode Island. She gave me Babs's address and phone number."

"Babs?"

"That's what she called her."

"How come she gave ya the info so fast?"

"Who said it was fast? I was on for a half hour

before I got Mrs. S. to trust me."

"And how'd ya do that?"

"I think I'll keep that one to myself."

"Yer kiddin me."

"Nope."

"Ya get this from Marty?"

"Get what?"

"Playin close to the vest."

"Faye, yer workin on a mystery so I'm gonna be mysterious."

It made no sense but trying to get something out of Birdie Ritter, once she'd made up her mind, was like getting gold from a monkey. So I dropped it.

"So tell." I grabbed a piece of paper and a pencil.

She gave me the info on Babs. "Did ya make up with Pete?"

"Yeah. He won't bring up gettin hitched for a while."

"Glad to hear it. Thanks for gettin all that info."

"You bet. See ya tomorrow."

Barbara Swanson lived on the Upper East Side. She would. If there was one place in the city I didn't care for, that was it. I always felt I hadn't bathed enough when I walked around those streets.

I put water in the pot, spooned coffee into the top half of the pot, lit the burner along with a cig, and sat down to wait.

It was a little too early to call Claire, and I dreaded giving her the lowdown. All of a sudden I realized how hungry I was. Lettuce and Velveeta weren't

230

gonna fill the bill. I washed my face, brushed my teeth, put on lipstick, blotted it on a tissue, and threw on a pair of slacks and a short-sleeve white blouse. I slipped my feet into a pair of sandals, took the coffee off the burner, grabbed my pocketbook, and was out the door.

It was a little early even for Dolores to be sweeping or sitting on the stoop. But I knew the bakery on the corner of Bleecker and Seventh would be open.

Inside, the smell of fresh bread hung in the air. There was an old man ahead of me so I had time to clap my eyes on the rolls and loaves of bread. Before the war the case had been loaded with sweet stuff. Napoleons, éclairs, cookies, you name it. But now Clifton, like everybody else, had a devil of a time getting sugar. Still, once in a while . . . well, I hoped this was one of those days.

The old man left with a loaf of bread in a brown bag.

"Faye. I've missed you. Where have you been, dear girl?"

"Here and there."

"I hope that doesn't mean another bakery."

"Course not. I'm on a case and it's takin almost all my time."

"But you must eat."

"Couldn't agree with ya more."

"See anything you like?"

I stared into his eyes until he smiled, held up a finger, and disappeared behind a curtain that separated the shop from the bakery. He came out holding a white box tied with string. "Eighty cents, please," he said.

I forked over the coins, thanked him, and almost ran back to my apartment where I cut the string and opened the box to see what he'd given me.

I thought I'd died and gone to heaven. There was a slice of apple coffee cake with pecans, and a chocolate éclair for later. Maybe for later. It hadda be for later. I wouldn't have time for all this now. What a sweetheart Clifton was. I hadda think of something nice to do for him.

I put the coffee back on the stove, went to my folded dining table, and lifted up one side. I got out a plate covered with rosebuds—one Aunt Dolly'd given me—for the coffee cake, and a knife, fork, and spoon. I brought everything to the table.

When the java was ready, I poured it into a good cup and took it to the table. My record of Stravinsky's Rite of Spring went on the phonograph. I wasn't a big classical music lover, but there were a few things that I liked and this was one of them.

Then I pulled a chair over and sat. I had delayed as long as possible. But I couldn't anymore. The first bite of the coffee cake was scrumptious. It seemed like forever since I'd had anything like it.

Sitting there listening to the music, drinking coffee, and eating my cake, I felt I could spend the rest of my life this way.

But wouldn't you know. The phone rang.

It was Claire. "Lemme turn the music off," I said. On the way back from the phonograph I picked up my cup and sat down at the telephone table.

"I was gonna call ya in a few minutes. I wanted to let ya sleep a little longer."

"Sleep? I haven't slept a wink all night."

People always made this claim—like the old finger-smith who boosted my wallet—but it was hardly ever true.

"I don't have good news for ya, Claire. Mr. Ladd's insistin they do it his way."

"Oh, no."

"I'm sorry."

"Charlie's gonna die, isn't he?"

I took a swallow of my coffee. "Anything could happen."

"Don't lie to me."

"I'm not. I'm not makin any promises, but I honestly don't know what's gonna happen."

"I know ya don't *know*. But we talked about this before and ya admitted the chances were slim to nothin."

"I don't know about every person who's been kid-napped, Claire."

"Don't bother soft-pedalin, Faye. I know what I know. So what's gonna happen next?"

"The FBI will be stakin out the pier, and at three o'clock Ladd will put the money in the barrel. Then he'll leave and the FBI will wait till somebody picks it up."

"But what if the kidnappers spot the FBI? They won't pick it up, will they?"

"No. The fact that Ladd is droppin the money is gonna tip the kidnappers anyway."

"Then what?"

"Then when the bad guys call ya again, we can hope Mr. Ladd wises up and lets ya do it without gettin the FBI or cops involved."

"Won't they be mad, the kidnappers?"

"Yeah. I would be, wouldn't you?"

She didn't answer.

"Claire? Ya there? Claire?"

"Yeah. I'm here. I was just thinkin. Maybe they won't bother to call me again. Maybe they won't trust me anymore."

"I think they'll give ya another chance." I wasn't sure of that, but I hoped it was true. Charlie Ladd was worth more to them alive than dead. Unless he was dead already, which wasn't outta the question.

"I don't guess we can go and hide out somewhere and watch, can we?"

"I don't think that's a good idea. We'll find out what happened later. How're ya gonna spend the day?"

"Why?"

"I don't want ya sittin in your apartment twiddlin yer thumbs."

"Whaddaya want me to do?"

"Ya like movies? Go to a movie."

"I couldn't do that. It wouldn't seem respectful."

"Call a friend who ya can be with." I hoped she wasn't gonna ask me to stay with her.

"Okay. I'll call Rita Welles. She's been a pal for years."

"Great. I don't think we'll know anything before about five. I promise, soon as I know I'll give ya a jingle."

"Okay."

"Try not to worry too much, Claire." What a dumbo thing to say.

"Sure."

"I know. Sorry. I'll call ya later."

After I hung up I poured another cup a joe and went back to the table. My slice of cake was still there. Where would it go? I dug right in.

I managed to save the éclair for later. Then I called Jeanne and gave her the phony baloney about my date with Johnny. I said he didn't propose and I was glad. He just felt like taking me to a special place. She thought that was hunky-dory.

Then I phoned Johnny and we had a nice tête-à-tête. Depending on what happened, at seven we were gonna meet and have a bite at John's Pizzeria on Bleecker.

Next was Marty. I asked him to keep his big ears open about the Ladd case and what happened when William Ladd coughed up the ransom. Then I rang Barbara Swanson and asked if we could meet. She was iffy at first, but when I told her it was about Charlie Ladd she changed her tune.

The subway was stifling. I don't know why I bothered to bathe. I felt like I was in a bath all the time. I tried to read but it was too hot so I did my perusal of the other riders. Part of me kept hoping I'd run into the old lady who'd lifted my wallet. And what would I do if I did? Could I prove anything? No. Would I even be able to confront the old grifter? No. That was that.

Sunday the crowd was different on the subway. Lotsa kids with their parents all dressed up to go to Grandma's for dinner. A few singles, but a lot more couples, the girls with their soldiers and sailors. It wasn't as interesting as during the week.

I tried my book again but no go. Eventually we got to Forty-second where I took the shuttle to the East Side. And then I hopped another train to Eighty-sixth. From there I hadda walk almost all the way to the East River. The powers that be were always saying they were gonna build a subway far east, but they never did. By the time I got to where I was going, I could have wrung out my dress. I may as well have swum the river, the way I looked.

Swanson's building looked snazzy. Nothing I'd like but it was new and expensive. And, of course, it had a doorman.

"Barbara Swanson," I said. And when I said her name it hit me like a ton of bricks.

Claire hadn't said word one about Swanson. Zip. And that didn't make sense.

TWENTY-ONE

*B*arbara Swanson's apartment was as interesting as the inside of a Kleenex box. I guessed it was a two-room joint, but I only saw the living room. White walls and tan furniture. No pictures on the walls, not a book in sight, as if she'd just moved in.

Barbara herself, at least the way she looked, was more interesting. She was shorter than I and wore her brown hair like Veronica Lake. The style was better blonde, but it still worked on Babs. Whenever she turned to her left I couldn't see her face cause the sheet of hair cascaded over her right side completely. I knew she couldn't be working in a factory with hair like that. Machines loved it, but the bosses didn't.

She wore a patterned light blue poplin dress with no collar but open at the neck and belted at the waist. On her feet, white open-toed shoes with a low heel.

There was no engagement ring on her left hand.

She handed me my cup of tea and sat on a very expensive and uncomfortable-looking chair.

"You wanted to know something about Charles?"

No *Charlie* for her.

"Yeah. How're ya feelin about the whole thing?"

She blew a stream of cigarette smoke straight at me, but I was far enough away so it didn't make the trip.

"What whole thing?"

"That he's missin."

"Miss Quick, I don't have any idea what you're talking about."

I believed her. "Miss Swanson, are you engaged to Charles Ladd?"

"Of course not. And call me Babs."

"Why d'ya say *of course not*?"

"Charles and I are like brother and sister."

"You are?" I stubbed out my cig.

"We've known each other since we were children. There's never been anything romantic between us."

"Can ya explain why William Ladd said ya were engaged?"

Her laugh was like the trill of a canary.

"That's funny, huh?"

"Amusing, yes. I can't imagine why Mr. Ladd would say such a thing. And frankly, Miss Quick, I'm not so sure he did."

"Meanin?"

"How do I know who you are, really?"

"I showed ya my license."

"Yes, you did. But you could be telling any tall tale. I don't know what it is you want from me. What's this about Charles missing?"

"Charlie disappeared almost a week ago."

"And you thought he was with me?" Her eyes were glittery, as though they'd been polished.

"No. I didn't think that. But I thought you might know where he is. *Do* you?"

"How dare you." She shot up but her height made this stunt seem silly.

"Look, Babs, I came here to find out your connection to Charlie."

"And now you know. We're friends. Anything else?"

"When's the last time ya saw him?"

"Before he was drafted."

"Not since then?"

"No."

"Why don't ya take the load off." I gave her the high sign to sit down.

She wasn't an eager beaver about it, but after a few seconds she took my advice.

"If you and Charlie were such good friends, how come ya didn't see him when he came into town?"

"I've only lived in New York for a month. Before that I was at home."

"In Rhode Island?"

"Yes."

"So why'd ya come here?"

She fired up another smoke and rested her head against the back of the chair. "Why does anyone come to New York?"

"To get away from their parents?"

She gave out with the warble again. "That, too."

"What else?"

"Do you have any idea how boring it is to live in Rhode Island?"

"Sorta like livin in New Jersey, I guess."

"At least New Jersey's close to New York. I wanted to feel alive. I was dying at home."

I nodded cause I understood. "So Charlie didn't phone ya over the weekend?"

"He doesn't know I'm here. Unless his parents wrote him. But no, I haven't heard from him. And I had no idea what was going on. Are his parents here?"

"Yes. Mr. Ladd is. Mrs. couldn't handle it and went back home."

"Poor Jennifer. Are the police involved?"

"Yes. And, of course, Claire."

"Claire?"

"Didn't you and Charlie write each other?"

"Yes. For a while. Then he stopped answering my letters." Her face was draining of color.

"Why d'ya think that happened?"

"I don't . . . I don't know."

"I think ya do."

She turned away, her Veronica Lake masking her face from me. But I could see her shoulders shaking and I knew Barbara Swanson was crying.

I waited.

She turned back to me after she'd taken a hankie from the pocket of her dress and swiped at her face with it.

"I was in love with Charles but he didn't feel the same way. Our parents always assumed we'd marry. We were a couple in high school. I knew he didn't really care for me."

"You wrote to each other when he was first in the army?"

"Yes. I shouldn't have told him how I felt. It was

after that that he stopped writing."

I hated having to tell her. "So ya didn't know that Charlie had a girlfriend named Claire Turner?"

"No."

"Do ya know if Charlie had any enemies?"

"How could he?"

"Meanin?"

"Charles is the nicest, kindest man I've ever met."

Charlie Ladd had everybody fooled. Except maybe the kidnappers. I toyed with the idea of telling her the truth about what'd happened to Charlie. Then I rejected it cause the less people who knew what was going on, the better.

I stood up.

"Where are you going?"

This took me aback. "You've been real helpful, but I hafta go now."

"Are you going to see this Claire person?"

"Why?"

"I'd like to go with you."

"I don't think I can do that. I mean, that'd be sorta a mess."

"I want to be somewhere where I can know what's happening."

"Frankly, Babs, I was goin home."

"Won't you be searching for Charles?"

I couldn't tell her I'd be waiting to hear how the ransom drop went.

"I'll be followin some leads from home," I said.

"Then let me come home with you."

This was some wacky broad.

"Please. I don't want to be alone." What was it with these girls? I liked my time alone.

"Can't ya get a friend over?"

"I don't have any friends."

This was malarkey. "That's not true."

"How do you know?"

"You seem like a nice dame, why wouldn't ya have any friends?"

"I told you, I just moved to New York. I haven't had a chance to make friends."

"Not even at work?"

"I don't work. I have a trust fund."

What did she do all day? I couldn't picture not working. I'd go loco with nothing to do.

"Look, Babs. Comin home with me is not a good idea. I promise I'll call ya as soon as I know anything."

"You hate me."

"Huh?"

"You think I'm vile."

"Wait a minute. I don't know where yer gettin this hogwash, but I don't hate ya or . . . or think yer . . ."

"Never mind. Just go."

"I'll call ya, Babs."

"I might not be here."

"I'll try ya again."

"If I'm still alive."

I wasn't falling for this. I walked to the door, opened it, said goodbye, then closed it behind me.

To say this meet gave me the blue devils wasn't the half of it. I'd never come across anyone so manipulative and loony. I wasn't sure what her game was, but I wasn't playing.

My wristwatch said two-thirty. Half an hour till the drop. I hadda argue myself outta heading for Pier Eighty-eight and playing the invisible girl. Deep down I knew that might make things worse. So I decided to go home and wait for the call.

Dolores wasn't on the stoop, and she hadn't left her pillow there. The shade was down on her window. Everything looked exactly like it had when I'd left that morning. Something was out of whack and the butterflies were making mincemeat outta my stomach.

I hurried up the steps into the building and right to her door. I knocked hard and loud.

"Dolores? Ya in?"

I put my ear to the door. Nothing. That was pretty scary, too. She always had her radio on when she was there. What was I thinking? Maybe she just wasn't home. I was getting to be a worrywart in my old age.

I knocked again and called her name. I'd just about decided she was out somewhere when I realized that was tommyrot. Dolores never went anywhere. To the store, but that was it. And if she'd gone to the store she wouldn't pull down the shade and her pillow'd be on the top step.

A cold sweat started running along my spine. I banged on the door and yelled her name. Finally I tried the door. It was locked. Dolores never locked her door. I'd nagged her about that, but she always waved the idea away.

"What's wrong?"

It was Jim Duryea.

"Dolores doesn't answer." I quickly told him all the reasons we oughta be worried.

"You think we should call the police?"

"Yes. And I think we should try to get this door open." I gave him the keys to my apartment. "Could ya go to my place and make the call?"

"What about getting the door open?"

"Leave that to me."

He gave me a funny look, then went to my apartment, where he unlocked the door. While he was inside my place I got out my ever-loving picks and went to work. By the time Jim came back I was opening the door. I hated going into people's apartments. I never knew what I'd find.

I called Dolores's name and listened. Nothing.

"The bedroom," Jim said.

I nodded and we tiptoed toward it. I don't know why we thought we should be quiet. If she wasn't there, she wouldn't hear us—and if she *was* there, she probably wouldn't, either. I got a knot in my stomach when I thought of that.

I knocked on the bedroom door and called her name once more, hoping. Nothing. I looked at Jim.

"We have to go in," he said.

"Yeah."

I turned the knob and opened the door. We saw her right away.

She was facedown on the floor. I ran to feel her pulse. It was there. And she was breathing. There was a little blood on the side of her head but I figured that coulda happened when she fell. I didn't think this was a crime scene.

"Where are those police?" Jim asked.

"I think I hear em. Run out and tell em we need an ambulance."

"Okay."

"Dolores? Can ya hear me? Dolores?" I felt guilt weighing me down, like some ape was sitting on my chest. All the times I'd found Dolores annoying, tried to duck her, thought she was batty.

"Please wake up."

She didn't stir.

Two cops came thundering in.

"Move back, lady," one said.

I didn't move. "I don't know what's happened to her. I found her like this."

"I said to move back." He looked like a package of unshelled walnuts.

"Okay." I stood up as he moved in.

"She's alive," he said.

"Yeah, I know."

"Slezak, go call an ambulance."

"My friend's doin that," I said.

"Look, girlie, I'm in charge here. I don't even know who ya are."

"I'm her neighbor."

"Go on, Slezak, don't just stand there like a department store dummy."

Slezak left.

"Now you, girlie, you stay outta the way. In fact, ya said ya were a neighbor, go home."

"Not on yer life."

"What'd ya say?"

"I said, I'm not leavin. She's my friend." And she was.

"Listen, sister, you better . . ."

There was a racket in the other room and then two guys came in with a gurney. Both of us moved outta the way.

I tried to watch while they took her vital signs. But I couldn't see a thing. Then they got her on the gurney and carefully carried her out. I followed.

There was a crowd on the street. I knew most of them, and they'd be asking me a trillion questions after the ambulance left. St. Vincent's Hospital was the closest, so I started walking in that direction.

"Faye? Where are you going?" Jim asked.

"To the hospital."

"I'll come with you."

"Suit yerself."

And we were off.

TWENTY-TWO

There's only one thing worse than sitting in an emergency waiting room and that's sitting in it with Jim Duryea. The man never stopped flapping his jaw. I wasn't much of a gabber anyway and I sure didn't feel like yapping now.

Finally I couldn't take it anymore. "Jim, would ya put a cork in it, please?"

He looked at me like I'd spit in his face.

"Look, I don't mean to hurt yer feelings, but I'm just not in the mood to talk. I'm real worried about Dolores."

"I was trying to take your mind off it."

"That's nice of ya. But it's not workin."

"I'm worried, too."

"I appreciate that. I do. But I wanna sit here, quiet. It's noisy enough. I need to think."

"Do you wish me to leave?"

"I want ya to do whatever ya want."

"Well, I do have an appointment at seven."

"Seven?" I looked up at the big clock on the wall. It was six-thirty. Johnny. I didn't wanna stand him up but I didn't think I should leave even long enough to explain to him. "Jim, could ya do me a big favor?"

"I will if I can."

"Could ya go to John's on Bleecker and leave a note with the owner for my boyfriend, Johnny, and tell him where I am."

"All right. And you'll be fine alone here? I mean there are some pretty strange-looking characters sitting around."

There were. "I'll be okay. Ya seem to forget what I do for a livin."

"I never forget that, Faye." He stood up. "I'll try to find Detective Lake at John's."

It didn't get past me that Duryea knew Johnny was a detective and that his last name was Lake. And I knew that it was Dolores who told him.

"Thanks, Jim. You're a peach."

His face reddened a little as we said goodbye.

I had a bad feeling about Dolores. Even though nobody knew how old she was, she was no spring chicken. She coulda had a heart attack or a stroke. A stroke was most likely since women hardly ever had heart attacks. And what if she died? She never talked about her past so I didn't know if she had any relatives or what her wishes were about burial.

Ah, no. I had to stop thinking like that. Dolores wasn't gonna die. The blood hadda be from hitting her head. Maybe she'd only fainted from something. Not from lack of food, that was one thing I knew.

I saw a nurse I'd talked to earlier so I got up and walked over to her.

"I was looking for you," she said.

"Is she all right?"

"Fortunately, the bullet went in just below her shoulder."

"Bullet?"

"Didn't you know?"

"No. She was lyin facedown and I couldn't see her cause she was surrounded by all the emergency people. I thought maybe she'd had a stroke."

"She was shot."

"But there was so little blood."

"I'm told she fell onto a slipper so that must've stanched the flow."

I pictured Dolores's big fluffy slippers, now red with her blood.

"At any rate, she's going to be fine. They've taken her into surgery to remove the bullet and then she'll be in recovery for several hours. So I suggest you go home because you won't be able to see her until late tonight or tomorrow morning."

"Have the police been notified?"

"Yes, of course. I understand you're a neighbor of Mrs. Sidney's?"

"Yes."

"I think you'd better go home. The police will want to talk to you."

I nodded. "How will I know she's all right?"

"Call in a few hours."

"Okay. Thanks."

I looked at the clock. Quarter to seven. Maybe I could get to John's before Johnny got the note.

On the way over I was racking my brain for a reason anybody would shoot Dolores. A burglary gone bad. But on a Sunday in broad daylight? Didn't seem logical. Also her place didn't look like it'd been tossed. I

249

didn't know anything about her past. Maybe the shooting had something to do with that. Somebody with a long-running beef. Dolores Sidney, the swindler? Grifter? Thief? Murderess? I couldn't see it.

So what *had* happened? I kept dodging the thought poking up its ugly head. Finally I had to give in. Did it have anything to do with me? That didn't make sense, either, but it wouldn't be the first time a suspect in a case had tracked me down. And then what? Shot at Dolores cause I wasn't home? There was no use trying to figure this thing. The main point right then was that Dolores was gonna be okay.

When I got to John's, it was starting to get crowded, customers sitting at the wooden tables and chairs or near the back of the room in wooden booths. In the middle of it all was a big brick oven where their famous pizzas cooked, over a coal fire. I looked around but Johnny wasn't there. I saw Red Conte, the manager, at the back of the main room. I waved to him and he waved back as I waded through the tables in his direction.

"Hey, Faye, how ya doin?"

"Okay."

Red always wore a tie even if he had an apron on, and today it was the usual type. Dancing girls in Hawaiian skirts with leis around their necks. Very colorful and nothing offensive. Except maybe the tie itself.

He was a big guy with a shock of red hair and huge

shoulders holding up suspenders over a dark blue shirt. Red gave me a kiss on the cheek.

"Long time no see."

"Yeah. I've been busy. Have ya seen Johnny?"

"Funny ya should ask. A weird guy left a note for him."

"Yeah, I know. I sent him here." I had a hard time keeping a straight face about Red calling Jim weird.

"I got the note right here." He reached into a pant pocket and pulled it out, handing it to me. "I guess ya can deliver it in person."

We shot the breeze for a few more minutes and then I went outside to wait for Johnny. Forget about frying an egg on the sidewalk. Tonight you could do a whole chicken. Johnny was late by fifteen minutes.

I told him everything. But we decided to eat before going back to my building and a possible grilling. Dealing with most coppers was done better on a full stomach.

Red waved us to a wooden booth in the back, shaking hands with Johnny before we sat down. We didn't have to tell our waiter what we wanted cause we always had the same pizza: mushrooms on one side, sausage on the other. We also ordered two beers, which came almost immediately.

"You look real nice, Faye."

"Thanks. I don't know how I could look anything but a mess cause I've been runnin around and then to come home to Dolores on the floor . . . well, it's been some day."

"You still look nice."

I smiled at him. "You do, too."

We looked in each other's eyes for a few seconds and then I could see the blush creeping up his neck. I looked away so he wouldn't be uncomfortable.

"How was *your* day?" I asked.

"Pretty dull."

"How come?"

"I wasn't with you."

"Ah, Johnny. What a sweet thing to say."

"It's only the truth."

"I missed you, too." My truth was I hadn't had time to miss him, but I knew if I'd had time, I *woulda* missed him.

Our pizza arrived, unlike any other pizza in town. That brick oven made it aces. We dug right in.

There were still little knots of people across the street from my building. I waved to some of them. A uniformed cop stood in front of the outside door to my building.

"Sorry, you can't come in here."

"I live here."

"Can you prove that?"

"She lives here," Johnny said. He took out his shield.

"Oh, okay. Sorry, sir."

"That's all right. You were doing your job."

"Yes, sir."

We went in. The door to Dolores's apartment was

open. I saw two detectives from the Sixth on Tenth Street standing in her living room. I didn't know em well, but we'd met.

"Detective Davis, hello," I said.

"Who're you?"

He knew who I was, the mug who looked like a bread that came out of the oven too soon, but he liked to play this game. He had hooded blue eyes, a nose that'd been broken a few times, and a mouth that was made to hold the smoke that was always in it. His brown suit was shiny and was probably made during the First War.

"Faye Quick. I'm a PI."

He laughed. "Everybody wants to play detective. Must be all those radio shows."

Detective Ryan said, "She's the broad who lives across the hall."

I could hear Johnny breathing hard. It was one thing to step in with the uniform outside on the door, but he knew I wouldn't want him to do it here.

"That right."

"Yeah, she's the neighbor found the vic." Ryan was younger than Davis. He had a red face like he'd already become the drunk he was destined to be.

"Come on in," Davis said.

I stepped into the living room. And Johnny did, too.

"Who're you?"

Johnny flipped open the holder with his shield.

"This ain't your turf."

"He's with me," I said.

"Oh, yeah? Well, it don't matter. Wait in the hall, Lake."

There was nothing Johnny could do. Ryan kicked the door shut.

"So tell me about findin Mrs. Sidney," Davis said.

I did.

"How do I know you didn't shoot her yourself?"

"Don't start that, Detective."

"What'd ya say?"

"I'm not the perp and you know it."

"I don't know nothin yet. Go on with yer story."

"The ambulance came and that was that. Story's over."

"Where'd ya go then?" Ryan asked.

"To the hospital."

"In the meat wagon?"

"No. I walked."

"Why?"

"Why did I walk? To get there before the ambulance." I didn't like calling it a meat wagon.

"And did ya?" Davis said.

I nodded.

"Ya got any idea why somebody would shoot the old lady?"

That threw me for a sec cause I didn't think of Dolores as an old lady. Old lady was another type of person. "I don't." I wasn't bringing myself into this unless I had to, especially with this meathead.

"Ya know her good?"

"Yeah."

"Ya know her friends?"

"Some."

"What about family?"

"I don't know."

"What don't ya know?"

"I don't know if she has any."

"Oh, real chummy, were ya?" The cigarette kept bobbing in his mouth when he talked.

"She never mentioned any family. Dolores asks a lotta questions, but doesn't talk about her past."

Davis looked at his notepad. "Ya know where Mr. Sidney is?"

"No."

"*Is* there a Mr. Sidney?"

"I guess there was."

"And now?"

"Haven't the vaguest."

"Kids. She have any? Any come to visit?"

"I never met any."

"Ya sure ya even know this lady, Quick?"

I buttoned up.

"What about friends. Ya said ya knew some."

"Yeah."

"Names." Ryan held a runty pencil over his note-book.

"Eve Raines, Evelyn Granger, Ella Carnovsky."

"Why do they all have first names startin with *E*?"

"Ask their mothers."

"Don't crack wise, Quick."

"How should I know why they have first names startin with *E*?"

Ryan said, "Sounds like a ring to me, Davis."

"Yeah. They Americans?"

"Far as I know."

"Could be spies," Ryan said.

"Yeah. They spies, Quick?"

This was getting ridic. "They're little old ladies like ya said Dolores is," I said.

"Even so. Ryan, find those dames."

"Ya got addresses for them?"

"No."

"Who else visited her?"

I wasn't getting anyone else involved in this stupidity. I was sorry I'd given him names. None of those girls had anything to do with shooting Dolores.

"I don't know who else. I gave ya what I know."

"You on a case now?"

I had to tell the truth. "Yeah."

"What case?"

"Ya know I can't talk about it."

"A couple a nights in the cooler could change that."

He was bluffing. "So book me."

"You're obstructin the law."

"I'm protectin my client."

"Ah, you private dicks turn my stomach."

I had plenty a answers to that, but I kept em to myself.

"I think ya know more than yer tellin," Davis said.

"I've been cooperative, given ya names, what more do ya want?"

"I want to know about yer case. It might have somethin to do with this shootin.'"

"That's baloney." I wondered how Davis had gotten so smart all of a sudden. I didn't know for sure Dolores had been shot cause of me, but I wasn't ruling it out.

"Don't leave town."

"I can't believe ya said that. Must be all those radio shows yer listenin to."

"Get outta here."

I turned to go and the door opened. A man I didn't know came in.

"Who're you?" Davis said.

"I'm Morris Sidney. Dolores is my mother."

TWENTY-THREE

*M*orris Sidney was what Dolores would call a schlemiel. I'd seen the types she'd called this as they walked by the stoop. I decided Morris took after his father.

He was skinny and wore a paint-stained white shirt, the sleeves rolled up, no tie. His gray pants were wrinkled and baggy and held up with a worn black belt. His black clodhoppers were cracked and dirty.

I figured he was somewhere between thirty-five and forty-five, with a hairline that started on the top of his head and only wisps of what had been showing above his ears.

Droopy brown eyes, a crooked nose, and a mouth

257

you could hardly make out. Above it, a pencil mustache needing a trim completed the picture. All in all Morris Sidney was a look-alike for a starving rodent.

Davis said, "You know what happened to yer mother?"

"Not exactly. I just came from the hospital and they told me she'd been shot."

"How'd ya know to go to the hospital?" I said.

"Shut yer hole," Ryan said. "So, Morris, how'd ya know to go to the hospital."

"A neighbor called me." He pulled a crumpled pack of Raleighs and a small box of matches out of a pocket, then shoved a smoke in his mouth and lit it.

"What's the update on your mother's condition," I asked.

"She was in intensive care when I was there. They wouldn't let me see her."

"Stop jawin, you two. Was the neighbor who called ya yers or yer mother's?"

"My mother's. Mrs. Kilbride."

"I know her," I said.

The detectives ignored me.

"She phoned ya?"

"Told me my mother was in St. Vincent's."

"How'd she happen to have yer phone number?"

"Ya got me." He shrugged.

"I know Ethel Kilbride. I can find out," I said.

"No, thanks," Davis said.

I was really getting cheesed off by this attitude. It was clear Davis and Ryan were bent on locking me out. Maybe I wouldn't get help from them, but they couldn't keep me from running my own investigation.

"Where do ya live, Morris?" Davis asked.

"The Bronx."

"Whaddaya do there?"

He looked at the detectives, then at me.

"I live there."

Davis squeezed his lips so tight the skin around them turned white.

"What do ya do there to make a livin?"

"Who says I make a living?"

"How do ya eat, Morris?"

He smiled and I could hear him saying something like: *With a fork*. But he resisted.

"You mean where do I get money?"

"Right."

"I don't see why that's your business. I came here because I wanted to see what happened to my mother's apartment and what anyone knew, not to be asked a lot of dumb questions about my life."

Hooray for you, Morris.

"Did it ever occur to ya that ya might be a suspect?" Davis said.

"No, it never did."

"Right now yer number one on the list."

"I always wanted to be number one on some list."

"You got a smart mouth, Morris."

"Thanks."

"Ya wanna answer questions here or at the precinct?"

259

"You sound like somebody on a radio show," Morris said. "If we were uptown you'd probably say, *I'm taking you downtown.* But we're already downtown so you can't say that."

"Yer peevin me, Morris."

"Yeah? The feeling is mutual. This is my mother's place and she was shot here. I want some answers."

Maybe I'd misjudged Morris. He might look like a schlemiel, but he wasn't acting like one.

Davis and Ryan looked at each other. I could tell they weren't sure what to do next.

Morris turned to me. "What's your name?"

I told him.

"Oh, you're her neighbor, aren't you?"

"I am."

"She likes you a lot."

"I like her a lot."

"She probably never told you about me."

"Fraid not."

He waved a hand at me. "Nah. Don't worry about it. She never talks about me or my brother."

"You have a brother?"

"Larry. He lives in California."

Davis said, "Are you two finished?"

"Only if you fill me in on what happened here."

"Somebody came in and shot yer mother."

"That much I know."

"It wasn't a break-in. Seems like she musta known her assailant."

"Why were they in the bedroom?" I asked.

"Bedroom? My mother's in her eighties."

"She is?" I'd always thought seventies. Good for Dolores.

"Eighty-four."

"You'd never know it."

"I know. Anyway, we want to know why she was in the bedroom with the person who shot her?"

"*We*. Now it's *we?*" Ryan said.

"Don't eschew the question," Morris said.

"Eschew?"

"Look, I'm running out of patience here. If there wasn't a break-in, then what was my mother doing in the bedroom with the guy who shot her?"

"Yer just gonna have to ask yer eighty-four-year-old mother, ain'tcha?" He wiggled his eyebrows in a suggestive way.

"You're disgusting," Morris said. "Basically what you're telling me is that you don't know anything. You know somebody shot my mother, you don't know why they were in the bedroom or why she was shot at all. That about it?"

"Listen, bub, we just started our investigation. In case ya don't know, it takes time to gather info, build a case. This is now a crime scene, and it's time the both of ya left."

"Just like that," he said.

"Yeah. But before ya do, I want yer address and phone number, Morris."

He rattled them off.

"Ya get that, Ryan?"

He handed Morris the notebook. "Write it down here."

He did.

"All right." Davis grabbed the notebook outta Morris's hands. "I'd like to search yer apartment, Quick."

"Get a warrant."

"Don't think I won't."

"I think ya will. I've got nothin to hide, Detective." I had a gun but it was licensed and obviously not used to shoot Dolores.

"Get out. We have police work to do here."

In the hall I introduced Johnny to Morris, and invited them both into my apartment. Inside I offered them drinks. The boys had beer and I had a rum and Coke. We sat in the living room. I filled Johnny in.

"This is a nice place," Morris said when I was finished.

"Thanks."

"Same layout as my mother's, but you'd never know it. She's a collector." His smile made him less funny looking. He picked up his pilsner glass and took a sip, white foam clinging to his mustache for just a second before the tiny bubbles popped.

"Morris, can ya think of anyone who'd want to kill yer mother."

"You think somebody tried to kill her?"

"I think that was the idea."

"Yeah. Sure. Of course. My father would've, but he's dead."

"Any living person?"

"No. I really can't think of anyone."

Johnny said, "You mean those two blockheads didn't ask you this?"

"Nope."

Johnny shook his head.

"Far as I know, my mother has a lot of friends and no enemies. She runs her mouth a lot, but I think that's harmless."

"It is," I said. "I've heard her gossip but never say anything vicious."

I thought it was time to bring myself into this. "It's occurred to me that Dolores gettin shot might have somethin to do with my case."

"Why do you think that, Faye?" Johnny asked.

"I don't know. A feelin."

"That's not enough," he said.

"What case is that?" Morris said.

"You know about the missin soldier and the dead body in his room?" It'd been in all the papers.

"Sure."

"Someone hired me to find Private Charlie Ladd. This is what I see," I said. "Somebody came here lookin for me, and Dolores was in the hall, sweepin. She got talkin to the somebody. This happened once before. The somebody asked to use the phone and Dolores bein Dolores let that somebody in."

"Even if that's true, Faye, why would he shoot Dolores?"

"That part I haven't figured out yet."

"Maybe she got suspicious of the guy," Morris said.

"That's possible," Johnny said.

"I don't know. She's pretty open to people. Was she always like that, Morris?"

"Yeah. Talking to people she didn't know in stores and on the street. It embarrassed me as a kid."

"That's what she does now. When she's on the stoop, people she doesn't know walk by and she talks to em."

Johnny said, "Do any of them get annoyed?"

"You wanna be annoyed by Dolores sometimes, but it's hard." I got annoyed plenty of times. Strangers didn't, though. They thought she was charming. And she was, in her way.

"Anything could've happened, I guess," Morris said.

"I think we should go across the street and ask Ethel Kilbride why Dolores gave her Morris's number." This didn't have much to do with the shooting, but I wanted to know why Dolores gave the number to Ethel instead of me. I couldn't believe how petty I was.

"What's that got to do with anything?" Johnny asked.

"Ya never know," I said.

"If you say so," Johnny said.

We downed our drinks and left the apartment. A uniform stood in front of Dolores's door. Outside, we marched to one of the brownstones across the street.

Ethel Kilbride lived on the fourth floor. We went up

the three flights and knocked on her door. Ethel was a woman of a certain age and I hoped she wasn't asleep cause it was almost ten.

She asked who was there and I think that mighta been a first. We all opened our doors to a knock, but now, I guessed, the neighborhood people were afraid. I told her and she unlocked and let us in.

It was pretty clear that the décor of Ethel's apartment was inspired by her trips to India. In her younger days there'd been a slew of them, according to Dolores.

Sitting on the paisley sofa, covered with brightly colored Indian shawls draped over the arms, was Jerome Byington, her neighbor from across the hall.

"How's Dolores, Faye?" Ethel asked.

"She's in intensive care. This is her son Morris, and I think you've met Johnny Lake."

Ethel made eyes at both men. It was her MO, like an automatic reflex. She was about four feet eleven with gray hair that she wore in a snood, bangs in front. Dolores didn't like the bangs cause she thought Ethel was trying to look young.

Jerome was younger than Ethel by about twenty years. He wasn't married, and there was constant speculation among the neighbors about why that was. He combed his dark hair straight back and was always impeccably dressed. Even though he was only at Ethel's, he wore a suit and tie. Jerome's outstanding feature was that he had a deep baritone voice, which was a good thing cause he was a radio announcer. He stood by the couch.

"Sit down. Would you like some refreshments?" Ethel said.

"We just had some, thanks. And we're not stayin long."

Jerome said, "Is it true that Dolores was shot?"

I told him it was. "What I want to know, Ethel, is why ya had Morris's phone number."

"Oh, she gave it to me a while back in case."

"Of what?"

"This very kind of thing. But she expected it to be a stroke or something more mundane. I must say, I never heard of a shooting in this neighborhood."

"I don't think there's been one," Johnny said.

"Well, you're a detective, I guess you should know." A tiny giggle.

"Had Dolores been afraid of anything lately?" I asked.

Ethel and Jerome chorused a firm no.

"She didn't mention any strangers hangin around or anything like that."

"Oh, no," Ethel said. "And I think if she'd noticed something like that she would've told me. She might've even have told you, Faye."

"Why do ya say *even*?"

"Well, Dolores didn't like taking advantage of you."

That made me sad. If she was scared about something I'd hope she woulda let me in on it. Maybe I didn't give her the chance.

"I guess we have what we need, Ethel."

When Ethel and I stood, so did the men.

"Is she going to be all right?" Jerome asked.

"The doctor assured me she'd recover," Morris said.

"Should we send flowers?"

"That's up to you."

"We don't have a room number," Ethel said. "We'd better wait until she's out of intensive."

Byington nodded in agreement.

"It's so nice to finally meet you, Morris. I wish the circumstances were different."

I was jealous that Dolores had confided in Ethel and not me. How childish could you get?

We said our goodbyes, then went downstairs and across the street where we stood in front of my building.

"You have a long way to go home, Morris?" Johnny asked.

"It takes about an hour. But it's worth it. I have a big studio in my apartment."

"A studio?"

"I'm an artist. I paint."

Some of the paintings Dolores had on her walls must be his.

"Morris, do ya have any idea why Dolores would keep ya a secret from all of us except Ethel?"

"She doesn't like me."

That shut me up fast. I'd never heard of a parent who didn't like their own kid. Except Ma, of course. But she was one of a kind. At least I'd thought so.

Johnny said, "Do you like her?"

"It's a funny thing. I do. My brother doesn't, but he's her firstborn and she likes him. It's always the way, isn't it?"

"Maybe she likes ya and ya don't know it?"

"It's okay, Faye. I've lived with this for over forty years. I'm used to it. I think I'll call it a night. Nice to meet you both, and I guess I'll probably see you at the hospital," he said to me.

Johnny and I watched him walk to Bleecker and turn. When he was out of sight, Johnny said, "That's sad."

"Yeah, it is. I don't think he did it, do you?"

"Nah. But I think you might be on to something with your theory of how it happened. Somebody after you. And I don't like that."

I felt all warm inside. "With Dolores gettin shot I haven't had a chance to find out how the drop went today. Let's go in and call Claire."

"Good idea." He grinned at me.

Heart, don't melt.

TWENTY-FOUR

*C*laire answered on one ring.

"They haven't called," she said.

"That's not right. It's been eight hours. Somethin musta happened by now. Lemme see what I can dig up."

I looked at Johnny as I hung up.

"She doesn't know anything?"

"Right."

"Want me to make some calls?"

"I thought we agreed not to mix in each other's cases."

"That's true. Why don't you try whatever it is you'd do now if I wasn't here. If that doesn't pan out, I'll see what I can dig up."

"That'd be swell, Johnny."

Zach appeared and did an *S* around Johnny's legs, leaving a trail of hair on the bottom of his trousers. I was glad he didn't seem to mind. In fact, he leaned down, picked Zach up, and cradled him like a baby, scratching his stomach.

I reached William Ladd at the St. Moritz.

"I was callin to see how it went today."

"It didn't. Well, not yet."

"Ya didn't make the drop?"

"Oh, yes. I did that right on time. Then I came back here to wait. But as of this point no one has picked it up."

"They probably eyeballed the cops."

"The police have decided to wait until morning . . . well, there's one FBI agent on site . . . and if no one picks up the ransom, he will."

"And then what's their plan?"

"I don't think they have one. At least they haven't told me. I think you were right, Miss Quick. Claire Turner should have gone."

This was a big admission for someone like Ladd.

And I had no desire to rub it in. "The kidnappers may try to contact Claire again, give her strict orders."

"Do you think they've killed Charles?" His voice shook on the last words.

"Cause of the foul-up?" I didn't wanna make it all his fault. "I've got no way of knowin, but I doubt it."

He didn't ask me why I doubted it cause he wanted to believe I was right.

"So you're saying if the kidnappers don't pick up the money by morning, they'll get in touch with Claire and we can try again?" he said.

"That's what I hope will happen."

"And now we just wait?"

"I'm afraid so. Why don't ya try to get some sleep, Mr. Ladd."

"Ahh. There's no way I can do that."

I understood. "Okay. Could ya call me if anything happens?"

"Yes. Yes, I will, Miss Quick."

We were back to the formalities. "Good. And I'll call you if they contact Claire."

"Yes."

"And Mr. Ladd, you'll keep the cops and the FBI outta this?"

"I will. I promise."

"All right. That's good. Let's not tie up our lines now in case anybody is tryin to get us."

"Yes. Miss Quick?"

"Yeah?"

"Thank you."

"Yer welcome."

After I hung up, Johnny said, "He thanked you?"

I nodded.

"That must make you feel good." He smiled and put Zach down.

"It would if I didn't feel so sorry for him."

Johnny came over to me and gently pulled me to him. "You're a special girl, Faye."

He leaned down and kissed me and that's when the phone rang. It startled us both. I hated to leave his arms but I knew I had to.

It was Claire.

"They called."

"Who?"

"The kidnappers."

"What'd they say?"

"They said I hadn't followed orders but they were gonna give me one more chance. No cops. No one else deliverin the dough."

"When and where?"

"They said they'd be callin back with those instructions."

"Okay. This is good news, Claire."

"What should I do now?"

"Go to sleep."

"I'll never be able to sleep."

"Get in bed and try. They won't call back tonight."

"Ya sure?"

"Yes." I wasn't sure at all. But if I was wrong, I'd admit it.

After we hung up Johnny said, "They didn't tell her where or when, did they?"

"No."

"I'm glad. If they had that all set up, I'd be nervous about Charlie's chances."

"I know what ya mean."

"I'm gonna go, Faye."

"Okay." I was disappointed that he was leaving so soon. But it was late and tomorrow might be a big day. I walked him to the door.

"Don't forget to call back Ladd."

"I won't."

We kissed good night. It was long and loving and made me feel good all over.

When he was gone, I went right to the phone and called William Ladd with the skinny.

First thing Monday morning I called St. Vincent's Hospital. Dolores was no longer in intensive care. She wasn't out of the woods, though she'd been moved to a room. She couldn't have visitors, but that might change later in the day.

Claire hadn't heard anything more and neither had William Ladd. He said the cops seemed suspicious, but he thought he'd convinced them he was telling the truth.

When I left my apartment, it seemed strange not to see Dolores sweeping. I didn't like the way it made me feel. I walked to the subway and went uptown to my office.

. . .

I stopped at Stork's for smokes and all the boys were there, lounging around, shooting the breeze, flipping through magazines: *Collier's* and *Life*, sheets on the nags. Fat Freddy was marking up the racing form, per usual.

"Hey, hey, Faye, Faye," Larry the Loser said.

"You're in fine fettle," I said. Even a smile from him was scarce as hen's teeth.

Fat Freddy said, "The dirty dog inherited a nice bundle of long green."

"It ain't that much," Larry said.

"It's enough to lend a friend a Benjamin."

"I ain't lendin ya a Donald Duck, Freddy."

"Can ya believe that, Faye? Some friend."

"He's just smart," Blackshirt Bob said.

"Who'd ya inherit from, Larry?"

"My aunt Elsa. Haven't seen the broad in years and she up and leaves me a nice piece a change."

"Good for you," I said.

"I'm gonna move outta my SRO, get a real apartment."

Stork said, "I wouldn't be too quick. You'll probably lose it all before the day's over."

He wasn't called Larry the Loser for nothing.

"Whaddaya say, Larry? Ya gonna gamble it away?"

"Nah. I've changed my ways, Faye."

"No kiddin. How'd ya do that?" *Once a gambler always a gambler* was my thinking. I'd lived it. My pop might be working at the theater for now, but it was only a matter of time before he got in a game, bet on the ponies, tossed the dice.

Larry wasn't interested in the track; his downfall was poker.

Blackshirt Bob said, "He got religion."

They all laughed except Larry.

"That true?" I asked.

Larry looked sheepish, like he'd boosted an old lady. "I took a meal at the Salvation Army. Ya gotta listen to the preacher afterwards. So these mugs think that makes me a knee bender."

"It's nothin to be ashamed of if it's true, Larry."

"It ain't true."

"What's true is the guy's got a lot of do re mi now," Stork said.

It wasn't like I saw a blinding light or a major revelation smacked me in the puss. More like seeing something from a different angle.

"What's the matter, Faye?" Bob asked.

"Hmmm?"

"Yer starin at nothin."

"I am? Yeah, I guess I am. Stork, gimme a pack a Camels. I gotta make tracks."

"You okay?"

"Sure."

"On the level?"

"You bet. I gotta get to work, is all."

"Okay. Cigs and the papers?"

"Just one today." I paid him and grabbed the *Post*

274

from the rack. "So long, boys. Don't lose that money, Larry."

"Ya can count on it, Faye."

Outside, you could feel the temp rising, like a pot of boiling water getting the flame turned up. I ankled around the corner to my office. Birdie was typing away.

"As I live and breathe, a boss returns."

"What's that supposed to mean?" I hung my straw hat on the coatrack.

"Seems like I ain't seen ya in a dog's age."

"Ya saw me Saturday. This is Monday. Same as always we had a Sunday in between."

"Yeah. I know. And what a Sunday it was."

I didn't ask her what she meant cause I knew it was about Pete and I wasn't in the mood.

"Any calls?"

She shook her head, sulking.

"Pete do somethin heinous?" What a softie I was.

"Heinous?"

"Yeah. Heinous."

"Is that got to do with sex?"

"Nah. It means somethin really foul."

"I guess it depends how ya look at it."

"How do *you* look at it?"

"Heinous."

"What happened?"

"We were supposed to spend a nice Sunday together, the park, a movie, dinner. All like that."

"And instead?"

"Sunday mornin he wouldn't get outta bed. Pulled the covers up to his chin. He said he had the flu."

"I suppose ya hadda wait on him all day, too."

"Yeah. That was the heinous part."

"Sorry, Bird."

"Thanks. What's up with the case?" She lit a cig.

I filled her in best as I could.

"So what yer sayin is that it's not much different from Saturday."

"Guess I am. Except for the meetin with Barbara Swanson."

"From what ya said that didn't tell ya too much, did it?"

"It told me that lies and deceit are more a part of the picture than I already thought. And I gotta look at the whole case from a new angle."

"What kinda angle is that?"

"I was in Stork's and Larry the Loser was talkin . . . ah, it doesn't matter what he was sayin . . . but he inherited some lettuce and he thinks he's a changed palooka."

"So?"

"People think they get money, their life is gonna change . . . they're gonna have natural curly hair instead a straight."

"Larry's got a new hairdo?"

"Never mind, Bird."

"Yer losin me here."

"That's cause I don't know what I'm talkin about."

"You feel all right?"

"I'm fine. Somethin hit me at Stork's but I don't know what exactly. It's gone now."

"Lemme know when it comes back."

"I will. Somethin else happened Sunday, too. Ya know Dolores, my neighbor across the hall?"

"Yeah, sure. The sweeper lady."

"Somebody shot her. She's in the hospital." I got my Camels from my pocketbook.

"Was she burgled?"

"No. That's why I think there's a connection."

"To what?"

"Me. The case."

"I don't get it."

"I don't, either. I mean, I can't figure out the thing or who coulda done it, but I'm as sure as death and taxes there's a link. Maybe it was meant as a warnin for me." I opened the pack and shook one out.

"That's some warnin."

"I'll never forgive myself if that turns out to be true."

"Ah, Faye, even if it is, it's not yer fault."

"Maybe I oughta get outta this line of work."

"You kiddin?"

I thought for a few seconds. "Yeah."

"That's a relief."

"I didn't know ya cared about me so much, Bird."

"Who said I did? I'd be out of a job."

"Yer all heart."

The phone rang and Birdie answered.

"Who's callin, please? Just a minute." She covered

the mouthpiece with her hand. "It's the Turner dame."

I stubbed out my cig in Birdie's ashtray and went into my office.

"Hello."

"Faye?"

"Yeah."

"They called again."

"And?"

"They wanna do it today."

"Where and when?"

"Grand Central at two P.M."

So now they were trying a crowded place instead of a secluded one. It didn't make much sense, though. The cops could so easily be watching.

"Where in Grand Central?"

"Nowhere."

"Whaddaya mean?"

"I gotta catch a train there?"

"To where?"

"I go get my shoes shined, say the magic words, and the shoe shine boy gives me a piece a paper that tells me what train."

"What're the magic words?"

"Has Charlie gone home?"

I didn't like the sound of this at all, but I didn't let on to Claire. "So that's it. Ya take the train on the paper? How d'ya know where to get off?"

"I go to the bar car and say the same thing to the bartender. He gives me another piece of paper, which tells me where I should get off."

"Then what happens?"

"I leave the bag a money in the ladies' room at the station and take a train back to the city."

The ladies' room? Either the destination was remote or there was a broad involved.

"Okay. We gotta meet Ladd and get the dough. I'll call him now and ring ya back."

I hung up and dialed the hotel. When the clerk answered, I gave Ladd's room number. He answered quickly and I filled him in. I also made him swear again. No cops. No FBI.

We agreed to meet at Horn and Hardart at Forty-fifth and Fifth at one o'clock. I called Claire back and told her.

If I got there before the other two, I'd have time for a slice of apple pie and cheddar. Maybe two.

TWENTY-FIVE

*O*h, be still my heart. How I loved the Automat. For lotsa reasons. No waitresses to make me feel like a worm. Nice little rectangular windows so I could see the food I'd be eating. The style of the place, with its geometric designs repeating over and over. And the brightness that made it so much nicer than eating in a dark, stuffy dining room.

The tables were round, the chairs wooden. The floor was tile with all these intersecting circles. In the center of the big room a large column shot off in four sections when it reached the flashy ceiling.

The food was always fresh and cost practically nothing. But that wasn't the only thing you could say about the food. It was good. And no one made a better cup a joe.

Some people might not like that anyone could sit at any table at Horn and Hardart. This meant you might find yourself with strangers. That never bothered me. I'd met some pretty interesting characters that way. The elite *didn't* meet to eat here. H&H was a place meant for the hoi polloi.

I went over to the wall where the shiny little chrome-edged windows were lined up in their sections: SOUPS; SANDWICHES; HOT ENTRÉES; VEGETABLES; DESSERTS; CAKES AND PIES. I headed for the pies cause I wouldn't have time for a whole meal like macaroni and cheese, baked beans, or creamed spinach, some of my favorites.

With the war on, the dessert entries had been narrowed down, and the pie section had gotten pretty sparse. But they still had my favorite. I put in two coins, turned the handle, and listened for the click, which was the door unlocking so I could open it wide and take out my apple pie with the cheddar cheese on top. I got a cup a java, too, and carried it and the pie to an empty table near one of the big windows.

While I ate my pie, I looked around. The Automat was filled with soldiers, sailors, and marines. They were everywhere these days. And so young. That's how they looked to me anyway. Maybe the older fellas had families already and spent their leaves with them. Maybe New York City had a special pull for fledglings outta the nest for the first time. You could still see the fuzz on some of their faces. I knew we hadda fight this war, but why did kids hafta do it? On the other hand they were the most able.

I gazed out the window and saw more boys in uniform, lots of them with girls on their arms. It had become a world of instant love and heartbreak.

These kids would meet one night, marry the next day, and be off to war the day after that. Lots of em never came back. Their brides sometimes had babies, and those could be sad stories. It happened cause everybody was lonely, and lots of the tenderfeet shipping out were scared.

I'd volunteered at the USO center when I could, and those boys were homesick and in need of company, eager to yak and grateful for distraction.

News on the radio focused on where the bombs fell, what ground was taken. Same stuff in the papers, along with shining a spotlight on the brass handing out grand strategies. No one ever talked about the boys. Except Ernie Pyle.

It occurred to me that maybe this wasn't the best place to hold our meet. Any stranger could throw a monkey wrench into our plans by sitting with us. Had my desire for the pie clouded my judgment?

In fact, a guy was making a beeline for my table at that moment. I began making strange noises and talking to myself. I flapped my hands and made like I was deep in conversation as I faced an empty chair.

The mug took a sharp right turn and headed for another table. I looked at my wristwatch and saw that I'd better get going on my pie.

I hadda put on my loony act two more times to keep the table free of strangers until the others arrived. I finished my pie and a busboy came and took my empty plate. I breathed a sigh of relief. My pie eating would now be my little secret.

As I was lighting up, Claire came in.

"I'll be right with ya, Faye. I'm gonna get some coffee."

I watched her cross the room in her white dress and white pumps, the clack of her shoes on the tile floor sounding almost like tap dancing.

William Ladd came in carrying what coulda passed for a doctor's bag. He saw me right away, came directly to the table, sat, shed his panama hat, and parked it on an empty chair. He set the bag on the floor next to him.

"Why isn't she here?"

Hello to you, too. "She *is* here. She's gettin some coffee."

"How can she drink coffee at a time like this?"

I picked mine up and took a swallow. "Easy."

He drummed his fingers on the table.

"I hope I haven't made a mistake about meetin here. Anyone could sit with us."

"What do you mean?"

"Haven't ya ever been to an Automat before?"

"No. We don't have such places in Rhode Island."

You woulda thought it was a burlesque house. "The tables aren't reserved."

"That's uncivilized."

"That's the way it is."

He reached inside his jacket for a leather case, which I guess was for daytime, plucked out a cig, then lit it with a matching lighter.

When Claire arrived with her coffee, Mr. Ladd stood and they exchanged cold hellos.

I said, "We're doin one thing here, so let's do it and get out."

"But there are things to discuss, Miss Quick."

"Yeah? What things?"

"Well, exactly what Miss Turner is going to do?"

"We know what. She's told us."

"But what if something goes wrong?"

"What could go wrong?" Claire said.

"There's something about handing over that money and not getting Charles in exchange right away that I don't like."

"What choice do we have, Mr. Ladd?"

"Did they say when they'd release the boy?"

"After they got the money," Claire said.

"But how long after and where?"

"They didn't say that."

"You should have gotten a time and location." He banged the side of his fist on the table.

Claire looked like she might cry.

"Mr. Ladd, yer not bein fair. Claire did the best she

could. She wasn't the one in control of the chinfest they had. The kidnappers told her as much as they wanted and no more."

"I suppose."

"What *I* want to know is if ya kept to yer promise ya wouldn't get the law involved," I said.

"Of course. A promise is a promise."

"What about last time?" Claire asked.

"I didn't promise."

I felt like I was with two first-graders. "The bag with the money is on the floor between ya. When ya get up, Claire, take it. We'll leave one at a time. Someone mighta followed ya here."

"But when will we know if they've gotten the money?" Ladd said.

"When Claire gets back, she'll go right to her apartment, won't ya Claire."

"Sure."

"And she'll wait for the call that'll tell her where we can find Charlie," I said.

"I'll stay there until I hear. Ya wanna wait with me, Mr. Ladd?"

"That might be a very good idea. Why don't you call me at my hotel when you get back."

I guess Claire'd gone beyond caring if Mr. Ladd saw her apartment or what he'd think of it.

"You still have my number, don't you?"

"Natch."

"How do I know you won't just run off with the money?"

"This is too much," Claire said and stood up. "I don't need this kinda insult." Under her powder and rouge, spots of angry color were breaking through.

"Sit down," I said.

She did.

"Mr. Ladd, Claire wants Charlie back as much as you do."

Looking down at the table he said, "I'm sorry."

After a moment Claire put her hand on top of his. "Mr. Ladd, you have to understand that we're both on the same side."

He nodded.

"All I want is to get Charlie home."

"Home?"

"Let's not get goin on this now, okay?" I said. "Are you two gonna survive waitin together?"

"Would you come and wait with us, Miss Quick."

Oh, brother. "Yeah. I guess."

"I think that's a great idea," Claire said. "When I get back, I'll call you, too."

"Swell." I didn't feature a night like that, but she was my client. An evening with the two of them? "I might not be in my office when ya call but I'll be checkin in with my secretary. So let her know yer home."

"Will do."

"I think we'd better skedaddle now. Claire, pick up the case and walk out."

She did. We watched her go.

"You trust her, Miss Quick?"

"Why shouldn't I?"

"I don't know anything about the girl."

"Ya know as much as ya seemed to know about Barbara Swanson."

"What are you implying?"

"She's not engaged to yer son."

"How do you know?"

"I met her. Charlie hasn't written to her for months. If anyone's doin any lyin around here it's you."

"It's always been assumed they'd marry."

"Assumed by you and Mrs. Ladd, but not by Charlie. So why'd ya say that the other day?"

"I didn't want Claire . . . I wanted to . . . I don't know."

I knew. "Try to be nice to Claire when ya go to her place to wait, will ya?"

"Yes. Of course I will."

"Good. Ya can leave now."

He got up from the table. "Thank you for your help, Miss Quick."

"You're welcome. See ya later."

He tipped his hat.

I waited about ten minutes, thought about having another piece of pie, put it out of my mind, and left.

Outside in the Mojave Desert I looked for a phone booth. I knew I'd find one if I walked over to Grand Central, but I didn't want to take that route. One of the snatchers might be eyeballing me and think I was following Claire.

I beat a path down to Forty-second and crossed Fifth

Avenue. The library, with its guardian lions, was tempting. If anything could get the taste of that meeting outta my mouth, I'd find it in there. I was pretty soft on the place. Many a day I'd go to the research section, latch on to a book or a bunch of them about my current obsession, and read the afternoon away. Like last year when Montgomery's victory at El Alamein got me exploring northern Africa. By the end of the day I was Faye of Arabia.

No time now for indulging myself. I kept walking until I got to Times Square, where I found a telephone booth. I asked the operator for the number for St. Vincent's Hospital. When I was connected, I went through a rigmarole until I got somebody who could answer my question. Dolores could now have visitors for a brief time.

Then I rang my office.

"Claire's gonna call when she's home so I'll be checkin in with ya."

"Why?"

"Why what?"

"Why will Claire be callin to tell ya she's home?"

"Bird, it's too long to explain. If I don't get ya before ya leave, I'll give ya a jingle at home, if that's all right with you."

"It's hunky-dory. Where ya goin now?"

"I'm gonna see Dolores."

"Oh, that poor thing. Tell her I'm prayin for her."

"I didn't know ya prayed."

"I don't, but people like to hear that."

287

"That's the most hypocritical thing I've ever heard ya say."

"Then ya haven't been listenin. Talk to ya later."

I walked to the subway and took a train down to Fourteenth Street.

Dolores was on three. As hospital floors go it was pretty quiet. I went to the nurses' station.

"I'm here to see Dolores Sidney."

"Are you a member of the family?" She looked like she'd eaten a bar of Lux soap. I hadda be on my toes with this one.

"Daughter," I said.

She looked at a page in a file. "It only mentions sons here."

"There's a reason for that," I said.

"Yes?"

Oh, no. "I was adopted."

"What difference would that make?"

"Not *by* Mrs. Sidney, from her."

She frowned underneath her winged white cap. "Are you saying Mrs. Sidney gave you up for adoption?"

"Yes. That's right." Why hadn't I said *grand-daughter?*

"All right. Then why are you here?"

"I just found out she's my mother and I need to see her."

"That might frighten her. I think you'd better go."

"But . . ."

She narrowed the slits of her eyes further. "Don't

make me come out from behind this desk. You won't like it."

I believed her. And left. I went to the end of the hall and turned out of her sight. Then I waited. Eventually, the Warden would have to leave her post.

An hour later she hadn't. I hadda try something. So I crossed the hall, jammed myself against the wall, and crawled. As I passed under the nurses' station I was glad I had no more stockings cause they'd be ruined. I hadn't had stockings for a dog's age. I guess I was trying to count my blessings. When I got to the end of the station it was make-or-break time.

If the Witch had glanced to her left she woulda caught me. I slithered like an eel, hugging the wall and feeling like a character from *Freaks*. I'd seen the movie when I was fifteen and never quite gotten over it.

But she didn't see me and I was on my way. The trouble was I didn't know Dolores's room number. At the first open door I called in a hoarse whisper: "Dolores?"

Nothing. I called again. Nothing. It occurred to me I might not even be on the right side of the hall. Couldn't be helped. I snaked along to the next room and went through the same routine. The next and the next.

At the last door I was feeling skunked. Schneidered. I knew crossing the hall was probably gonna do me in. So I tried one last time.

"Dolores."

"I'm in here, bubele."

TWENTY-SIX

J took a peek and saw she was in a private room. No neighbors. But I stayed on my hands and knees until I got inside. Then I stood and went to her bedside. She was as white as a marshmallow and her eyes didn't have their usual sparkle. Tubes and wires were hooked up to her body, keeping her arms at her sides. And there was no wig. She had wispy white hair like a newborn chicken.

"I look meshuga, huh? Something out of a Saturday serial at the pictures."

"You look fine to me, Dolores. I'm in seventh heaven you're okay."

"It ain't under my belt yet, bubele. Faye, why were you crawling in here?"

"They wouldn't let me in cause I'm not family."

"Stupid. They shoulda asked. Yer family to me."

"Thanks. Can ya tell me what happened?"

"Why couldn't I tell ya? I don't have amnesia."

"I don't wanna tire ya out."

"I'll tell ya when I get tired."

"Promise?"

"Yeah. Sure. Ya want the whole megillah?"

"As much as ya can remember."

"What's this with memory? Sharp as a tack."

I smiled. "I know ya are, Dolores."

"Okay. So I was sweepin and this young man, with

a punim like a movie star, came in and was lookin around the lobby. He smiled at me and asked which was yer apartment."

"Like the last time?"

"But this time I was ready for him. At least I thought I was. He said he's an old friend of yers. I tell him he should call ya at yer office. He said he did, which was how he got the address, but no one told him which apartment."

"Did he say who he talked to?"

"I think we can agree he never called nobody. Would ya give me a little water, Faye?"

I poured a glass from her bedside pitcher. "Ya want me to hold it for ya?"

"You think I'm an octopus, I'm hiding other arms in the bed?"

She seemed to be her feisty self, which I thought was a good sign. I got one hand under the back of her head and lifted gently while I held the glass to her lips. She drank a small amount, then closed her eyes and moved back, pressing against my hand. When her head was on the pillow, she opened her eyes.

"Where was I?"

"He said he got the address from my office."

"I told him I couldn't help him. That he'd better call ya at home."

"What'd he say?"

"That he was already at home, your home. Why should he have to call when he was already there? I shrugged and went back to sweepin. Next thing I knew he was holding a gun to my back. He said we were going into my apartment and that's what we did."

"You let him into your place?"

"Faye, it's not like I asked him in to chat, have a glass a tea. I had a gun in my back. You'd have a better idea?"

"Sorry."

"So I opened my door and led him inside. He asked I'm alone. I told him yes. Then he asked me again which is yer apartment and when you'll be home. I told him I don't know either thing."

"You shoulda told him, Dolores."

"You think I'm a shnook? I could identify this putz. I knew he was gonna kill me, so I was making a little stall. He tells me to go into my bedroom. I asked him what he wanted with me."

I shook my head at the thought of the chances she took.

"Enough with the shaking."

"You were so brave."

"Brave shmave. I knew I was a goner, I might as well save your tushy. He told me he wanted to make sure nobody's in the bedroom. I swear there isn't. But he's not taking my word on this.

"He said he ain't gonna ask me again. I knew what that meant. He pushes the gun in my back and we go into the bedroom. My bed was made, thank God. He tells me turn around. I do. He looks under the bed and in the bathroom, but the gun is on me the whole time.

"Then outta nowhere he says, 'Yer a kike, aren't
ya?' My blood boils. I make believe I don't know
what that means."

"Did he . . ."

"What's going on in here?" The Warden.

"We're having a clambake, what else?" Dolores
said.

"And you. I thought I told you, you couldn't see
Mrs. Sidney."

What could I say?

"This girl is my daughter."

"You have two sons according to one of them. No
daughters."

"My son was here?"

"Yes. I can't remember his name now."

"Larry?"

I said, "No, Dolores. It was Morris."

"Morris. Yes. That was his name," the nurse said.

"Morris," Dolores said.

"At any rate, this young woman is not your
daughter."

"She is. I adopted her." Dolores's face was turning
red.

"Mrs. Sidney, please don't upset yourself."

The nurse came around the bed and bumped me out
of the way. She took Dolores's pulse.

"Pulse isn't good," she said. "Please try to calm
down."

"I was calm till ya came in here."

"If your . . . *daughter* hadn't come sneaking in here,

this would never have happened. I think she should go."

"She ain't goin. I'm tellin a story and I gotta finish."

"Go ahead then."

"Out," Dolores said.

"Mrs. Sidney, I . . ."

"Out."

"I'm calling your doctor," the nurse said.

"I guess I gave her what-for." Dolores smiled weakly.

"You did. Think ya can go on with what happened?"

"Why not? Where was I? Oh, yeah. The schlemiel asked me was I a kike. And I said, ya mean am I of the Jewish faith? And I guess he didn't like my question cause that was when he shot me. That's it."

"You poor thing."

"One thing I'm not, Faye, is a poor thing."

"You said he was good lookin. Can ya describe him in any more detail? What was he wearin?"

"A white, short-sleeve shirt and those blue pants. No tie. No jacket. No hat. I knew he was no gentleman in that getup."

"Blue pants? Ya mean plain blue trousers?"

"Nah. The ones ya see on cowboys in the movies."

"Dungarees?"

"I don't know what ya call them."

I knew that's what she meant. They were made of denim and sometimes sailors wore them, too.

"Ya know what, kid? I'm tired now."

"Oh, Dolores, why didn't ya tell me sooner?"

294

"Sooner I wasn't tired."

"Have the police been here?"

"Excuse me, miss. I demand to know what you think you're doing?" It was a man in a three-piece suit he musta gotten before the war. They didn't make vests anymore. They said it was cause of the war, which I didn't quite get. Did that extra bit of material make so much difference?

"Did you hear me, young lady?" he said.

"I did. And what I'm doin is leavin."

"Exactly."

"This is Dr. Hatfield," the nurse said. She looked up at him like he was Adonis. He reminded me of a giraffe.

I kissed Dolores, who was already asleep, on the cheek. Then I made my way past the two who stood like guards at the end of her bed.

"And don't come back," the doctor said.

I didn't say anything to that cause it was so stupid. When she was better, it was up to Dolores who came to visit. I was glad I didn't have to crawl to get out of there.

Even though it was still hot and humid, I was happy to be on the street and in the neighborhood I loved.

I walked down Seventh Avenue to Grove and turned right at my street. There was a knot of neighbors on my stoop. Byington, Jory, and Kilbride.

"There she is," Bruce Jory said.

I felt like it was a lynch mob waiting for me. When

I got right in front of them, they all started to talk at once.

"Wait, wait. One at a time."

"Have you seen Dolores?"

"Is she okay?"

"Who did it?"

"Quiet," I yelled. "I did see her and she's awake and full of . . . she's snappy as ever."

"When will she be home?"

"Not for a while, I'd guess."

"Did the police catch whoever did this?"

"Not yet."

"Will you find out, Faye?"

"I'm gonna do my best." And I would, cause now I knew for sure the shooting was linked to my case. I didn't know when I'd get over that one. "I gotta go in now."

"Will you keep us informed?"

"I will. I promise."

That seemed to calm them down some.

"Faye?" Jerome Byington said.

"Yeah?"

"Do you have any idea why someone would shoot Dolores? We heard robbery wasn't involved. Would it be, by any stretch of the imagination, mistaken identity?"

"I don't get ya?"

"Jerome thinks the bad man might've been after *you*, Faye," Ethel Kilbride said.

I stalled. "You mean ya think the shooter might've

mistaken Dolores for me?"

"I told him that was absurd," Ethel said.

"I don't think anyone would get us confused." I wasn't lying. But I wasn't about to tell them the particulars.

"That's what I said. You and Dolores?" Bruce Jory.

"We'll find out. Don't worry. At least Dolores is on the mend."

"You mean," Ethel said, "we don't have to be afraid?"

Ah. So that's what this was really about. Not that they didn't love Dolores, cause I knew they did. But they were scared. They thought there was a killer in the neighborhood. "I don't know. But I'd lock yer doors when yer inside. I'm sure gonna lock mine."

They all agreed and I headlined how much I needed to go inside to make an important phone call. I ran up the steps and into my apartment.

Zach was sleeping on his pillow on the large windowsill. I hadn't even noticed him when I was outside. He hadn't noticed me, either. Didn't notice me now. I turned on the fan, for all the good it did, and went right to the phone.

"Did ya hear anything, Birdie?"

"Not a peep."

"I guess it's too early. Who knows how far she had to go."

"Don't pretend I'm supposed to know what yer talkin about, Faye."

"Claire had to take a train somewhere to deliver the

money to get Charlie back."

"See how simple that was?"

"Yeah. Yer right."

"How long's she been gone?"

"About two hours."

"Give it some time."

"Yer right again. Okay, I'm home. She'll probably call me before you."

"You stayin put, Faye?"

"Far as I know."

After I hung up, I sat there thinking about Dolores's recollections. A man in dungarees. Whoever he was, he hadda be connected to my case. Was he planning to kill me? Why? Would he come back? I lit a smoke, blew out the match.

Maybe when they got the money, the button man would lay off. I didn't know anything anyway. Was Charlie alive? If they gave Charlie back, my job would be done. If Mr. Ladd wanted his money or the kidnappers caught, that was up to him, the police, and the FBI.

Would Claire and Charlie get married? Tune in tomorrow when . . .

The phone rang and I jumped. I grabbed the receiver.

"Claire?"

"I gather you haven't heard from her," Ladd said.

"No. But it's only been a couple a hours since she got to Grand Central. We don't know when she left or how far she had to go."

"That's very true. Were you planning to call me?"

"No. Claire's gonna call ya, but we had no arrangement."

"I suppose we didn't. I wish I could wait in the cocktail lounge. I don't like sitting here in my room."

"I can call the lounge, Mr. Ladd. They'll page ya."

"That's right. Of course. I think I'll go downstairs now."

"Don't worry. I'll ring ya the minute Claire calls me."

He thanked me and we hung up. If Charlie didn't come back, my job wouldn't be over. I wouldn't begin to know where to start. On the other hand, if the worst happened, the cops would most likely be in on it.

The afternoon was creeping toward five and the idea of a drink seemed aces. I went to my cabinet, but before I had a chance to mix a drink the phone rang again.

It was Johnny. He asked me about Dolores and the case and all I wanted to do was get him off the phone in case Claire was trying to get through.

When I said I was waiting for her call, he said, "I better hang up then."

"I'm afraid so."

"I guess we shouldn't make any plans for tonight."

"Can we wait and see?"

"Sure, why not?"

"You're all wool and a yard wide, Johnny."

"Call me when you know what's what."

I said I would and we hung up.

By ten o'clock that night nobody'd heard from Claire.

TWENTY-SEVEN

J found Marty at Smitty's bar. I couldn't figure when he had time for his extracurricular stuff.

Marty picked up the phone. "Yeah?"

"It's me. Faye."

"How ya doin?"

"Not good. I got a situation."

I told him what had happened. "Whaddaya think?"

"I think either they knocked her off or she's in on it."

"Yeah. That's what I was thinkin. I was hopin you'd come up with somethin else."

"There's nothin else."

"I don't like the choices."

"Not good."

"Mr. Ladd's blowin his stack. Can't say I blame him."

"Did ya tell him yer ideas?"

"No. Not yet. We just exchanged words about our fears for both of the kids. It's hard to believe Claire would help kidnap Charlie. She's one damn good actress if she did."

"It happens, Faye."

"I better go. I just wanted to check it out with you."

"How come ya didn't call yer boyfriend?"

"I don't like to involve him in my cases."

300

"Yeah. I can see that."

I knew he couldn't see it at all. It wasn't like Johnny was a civilian.

"Thanks, Marty."

"Keep me posted."

"I have a feelin ya won't need me to keep ya posted. If Claire doesn't turn up by mornin, this is gonna turn into a major case."

"I think yer right."

When we hung up, I lit a Camel and sat there staring into my living room again. The empty space waiting for the piano seemed bigger than ever. Had I blown this case? Did I get Claire Turner killed? She woulda done anything to get her soldier back. She knew it was risky but she didn't care. Or was that the sucker story? The one I'd bought.

I was some lousy PI if this was a scam. Nah. She was just a kid. A kid in love.

I tried to put myself in her shoes and think what I woulda done if it'd been Johnny. I wanted to believe I woulda done the same as Claire, but I wasn't sure. Was it that I didn't care for him enough? Or was I too smart to go out on a limb like that? And if I was too smart to put my neck in a noose, how could I let Claire do it?

Did my need to solve this case, get Charlie Ladd back, overshadow my smarts? And what if Claire was alive and well and she was in on this swindle all along? Shouldn't I have sniffed that out? Back to that again.

If she was involved in this scam, why did she come to me in the first place? To make it look legit? She knew I'd hafta get the Ladds involved, and that they'd more than likely go to the police. We only had Claire's word that kidnappers had called her. Maybe there weren't any kidnappers. And what did all this have to do with David Cooper, the dead guy in Charlie's hotel room? *Somebody* knocked him off.

The kidnappers. Hold everything. What was I thinking? The kidnappers iced Cooper and took Charlie. Cooper musta been in Charlie's room when they came to snatch Charlie. They couldn't leave a witness.

If Claire was dead, it wasn't my fault. I'd warned her. But thinking about Claire being dead didn't sit too well with me. I felt sick, and stubbed out my butt.

I hadda call Ladd and lay out the two possible scenarios. I dialed his hotel. And when I got him it was no surprise he was even drunker than he'd been earlier.

"Dishe call?"

"No. I wanna talk to ya about some possibilities."

"Wha kind?"

"What I think mighta happened." Considering his condition this didn't seem like such a hot idea.

"Wha?"

"Maybe we should talk tomorrow."

"I'm callpolice."

"Mr. Ladd, I think we should wait till mornin. If Claire's not back by then, we'll call em."

"Howdya know she's back?"

"I said we'll wait till mornin and . . ."

"Sicka waining. Lookmyself."

If this wasn't the caterpillar's kimono, I didn't know what was. "Go to bed, Mr. Ladd. We can work on this tomorrow. I'm gonna say g'night now."

I didn't know if this was the right thing to do, but I hung up and called Marty again. I gave him the lay of the land and asked if he could put a man on the hotel to make sure Ladd stayed put. And if that didn't work, then put a tail on Ladd to make sure he didn't hurt himself. Marty said he'd get right on it.

Now what? Wait for Claire's call, which could still come. I knew I wouldn't really sleep so I decided to stay on the sofa, closer to the phone. In the bedroom I took off my dress and got a summer nightgown from my chest of drawers. I slipped it over my head. Then I went to the bathroom and brushed my teeth.

I wished I coulda had the phone in my makeshift bed. I was afraid I wouldn't hear it if I did fall asleep. Worried that the radio might put me to sleep, I turned on the light behind the sofa and picked up *The New Yorker*. I didn't think I could concentrate on a story or an article so I turned to the reviews by Constant Reader, who was really Dorothy Parker.

The next thing I knew I was waking up with the magazine on my face. And when I pulled it off I saw the light outside. If the phone had rung, I hadn't heard it. I looked at the time. Five minutes past six. A rotten time to be awake. I almost went back to sleep, but knew I shouldn't. Besides, Zach was howling from where he'd planted himself on my stomach. Even if I'd left the magazine on my face and raised one eyelid, he'd have known I was awake and started yawping for his breakfast.

I shook him off and got up. I felt like jeeps and tanks had ridden over me all night. While I put Zach's breakfast into his dish, I started to face the fact that Claire was another missing person. If she'd vamoosed, I hoped she was in on the scheme. If not, she was dead. It'd be pretty awful for me if Claire had been in on it all along. But better to have her alive.

It was too early to call anyone. I put down Zach's food then spooned coffee into my pot, added the water, turned on the gas, and lit it. At least I could call Claire. If she was there and asleep, she couldn't get mad that I'd awakened her.

I dialed her number and let it ring twelve times. This had been a last-ditch effort so I wasn't surprised that she didn't answer. I'd have to call Lucille before this broke in the papers. Who cared that it was early? Even though the sisters were on the outs, I was sure Lucille would wanna know.

I got my pocketbook and scrounged around for the address book with her number in it. Before making the call I poured myself a cup a joe. This was nothing to tell a gal without a morning jolt. Best coffee in the Village.

I let Lucille's phone ring fifteen times. Maybe she was in the shower. Maybe she had a boyfriend and she was at his place. Maybe she'd gone in to work early. Nah. The work idea was dumb. Maybe she didn't wanna answer her phone so early in the morning. Ya couldn't blame a girl if she didn't wanna answer her own phone.

I lit a cig and dialed her again.

This time I gave it thirty rings. If she was there and didn't realize this was pretty important, something was wrong with the broad. I went through all the possibilities again. None of them washed except the possible boyfriend story. I'd have to wait until nine and call her at the bookstore.

So what could I do right then? I could have another cup of coffee and the éclair I had in the fridge. I didn't mind eating it cold. I took down one of the plates Jeanne Darnell'd given me when I'd moved in. I put the éclair on it and carried it to the telephone table. I decided that when I finished the éclair and coffee, I'd call Ladd. I ate as slowly as I could.

"Do you know it's seven in the morning?" A loud groan. "Oh, wait. Charles. Is he back?" Another groan.

It wasn't hard to tell he had a doozy of a hangover.

"No. He's not back. And neither is Claire, far as I know. She doesn't answer at her apartment."

"What do you think happened to her?"

The moment of truth was upon me. "I can only think of two things. One, she's in on it and . . ."

"In on what?"

"In on the scheme. The kidnappin."

"How is that possible?" He groaned again. "Can you hold on a minute."

He put down the phone, and after a minute or two he came back. The ice in his glass made a tinkling sound.

"All right. Now you're saying that that girl is a kidnapper? I knew she was trash."

"I'm sayin it's possible she's involved and this whole thing—her hirin me, gettin you to put up the dough—was part of the plan."

"What about Charles?"

"He could be part of it, Mr. Ladd."

"How dare you."

Good thing we had the phone lines between us cause I woulda slapped him. "We have to look at every angle now."

Silence. Broken only by the clink of ice against glass.

"Mr. Ladd? Are ya there?"

"I'm here. You said you could think of two things. What's the second one?"

"Claire's dead."

"Which means what about Charles?"

"He's probably dead, too." I didn't feel like softening these words for him.

"But not necessarily?"

"Yeah, that's right."

"I think it's time for me to go back to the police and FBI."

"Will ya be tellin them about this last foray?"

"I'll have to."

"I guess. Ya gonna do that now?"

"As soon as I'm dressed. I think it's best I go to the precinct rather than do this on the phone."

"Yer probably right."

"Are you going to continue to look into this?"

"I haven't been fired," I said.

I tried Lucille again and there was still no answer. My plate had bits of icing and custard stuck to it. I put it in the sink. Then I poured another cup of coffee and took it with me into the bathroom where I ran the water in my tub.

I dressed for the office in a blue skirt and a lighter blue short-sleeve jacket with big dark blue buttons. It was ten after nine when I picked up the phone and dialed Mostel's Bookstore. It rang a few times before a man answered and identified the store.

I asked for Lucille.

"Ve don't know Lucille, vere she is."

I told him who I was and reminded him I'd been in the store a few days before. He remembered me.

"Lucille's not here since. Ve don't know vat happened. She vas always here ven she vas supposed."

"Mr. Mostel, are ya sayin that she hasn't come in to work since Friday?"

"Vell, ve're not open on Saturday or Sunday, but she didn't come in Monday. Ve called her yesterday all day, but no."

"And today she's not there?"

"Not here today."

"What time is she supposed to come in?"

"Nine A.M."

"It's only quarter after nine now." It didn't sound like she was running late but I had to make sure.

"Lucille is never late."

"Mr. Mostel, if she does come in, will ya have her call me?"

"Certainly."

I gave him my number and we hung up. Lucille's disappearance, if it really was that, didn't hafta be connected to my case. Maybe she just quit her job. But she didn't seem like a girl who'd walk out without a word. Maybe she'd been hit by a car and landed in the hospital. Anything coulda happened. But it was a coincidence that two sisters were missing at the same time, and I hated coincidences.

Still, for all I knew, Lucille could be lying sick or dead at home. I'd hafta get Marty to ask the local police in Newark to look in at Lucille's apartment.

But first I wanted to check on Dolores. She was stable. Marty's precinct sergeant told me he was out on a case. There was nothing more I could do from home.

I grabbed my pocketbook and started out. But when I was about to lock the door, my phone started ringing so I rushed back in. It was Birdie.

"Well, you've been some blabbermouth," she said.

"Good morning to you, too."

"Listen, Faye, I got a message for ya from Marty so don't be so fresh."

"Why didn't he call me himself?"

"That was my point. Yer line's been busy, busy, busy for hours."

Birdie exaggerated a lot. "What's the message?"

"He said to tell ya they found the body of a girl on West Seventy-second Street behind Schwartz's Candy Shop. He said he thought you'd wanna know."

"Yeah, thanks." I could feel myself sinking.

"Ya goin there?"

"Yeah." The éclair was heavy in my stomach.

"See ya later."

There was only one reason Marty'd call me about a dead girl.

He hadda think it was Claire.

TWENTY-EIGHT

*T*here were lotsa police cars with their lights flashing, uniforms on foot, and the usual gawkers. Also the ambulance to take the body to the morgue. I was glad it was still there so I could see the corpse. I needed to get behind Schwartz's but flashing my PI license to any of these mugs wasn't gonna do the trick. I needed Marty. I went up to a beefy cop.

"Excuse me. I need to see Detective Mitchum."

"Look, girlie, everybody needs somethin, but I can't always give it to them. Now step back."

Wrong cop.

I made my way around the cops looking at their

faces. I finally chose one because he reminded me of my uncle Dan, except for a nose that looked like it could light up a room. Very scientific process. I went through the same routine with him.

"And whaddaya want to see the detective for, honey?"

"He's expectin me."

"Is that right? What for?"

I decided I might as well try it so I took out my license and showed it to him.

He looked at it, then back at me. I watched while his mouth turned up and into a smile and I knew before the bottomless laugh that I'd played the wrong card.

I snatched my license from his mitts and he stopped laughing.

"Sorry. I just never knew a twist who was a dick."

"Now ya do."

"Who'd ya say ya wanted to see?"

I told him.

"Ya sure he's here?"

"He called me to come up."

"Maybe he just wanted ya to have Out of This World chocolate-covered marshmallows." He pointed to Schwartz's shop.

"I need to get through to the yard."

"Ya seen a dead body before?"

"What's yer name, Officer?"

"Why?"

"I like to know who I'm talkin to."

"Officer Lundigan."

I took out a pad and pencil and wrote it down.

"Whatcha writin it in that for?"

"Reference."

"Huh?"

"Look. There he is."

Marty stepped through the doorway of Schwartz's, held a hand under his brow, and eyeballed the crowd.

"Marty," I yelled. "Over here."

He heard and gestured for me to join him.

"See that, Lundigan?"

"Get outta my sight."

I pushed through the crowd feeling hot and angry, smelling stale breath and BO, and finally got to Marty.

"Faye. I've been holdin things up here waitin for ya."

"Came as fast as I could and then no cops would let me past them."

"Numbskulls. C'mon."

"Why'd ya call me, Marty?"

He stopped. "I got a gut feelin. Never met yer Claire Turner, but somethin tells me . . . well, let's go and see."

He led me through the store where the smell was overwhelmingly sweet. Not that it bothered me. Two salesgirls huddled together behind a counter. We went out a back door into what passed for a yard. A rusted chain-link fence surrounded it except for one side, which was pushed down.

Detectives were standing around, smoking. I wanted a cig myself, but I thought I should wait. Glenn

Madison was there and gave me a nod. He'd met Claire. This gave me hope. Wouldn't he have identified her if it was Claire? In a space between two guys I saw a body lying on the ground.

Marty took my hand and moved me past some detectives.

"This is Faye Quick, fellas. I think she might ID the victim."

Suddenly I felt queasy and my knees were like pudding. I didn't like being on this stage. What if I couldn't ID her? But when I got closer I saw right away that it was Claire.

She was wearing the same dress she'd had on when we met the day before. She was on her back, her arms above her head and her legs bent at the knees. A rope was tight around her neck and her face had a purple cast to it. Eyes open, she looked like she'd never been so surprised.

"Yes," I said.

"No doubt?" Glenn asked.

"None."

"Thanks."

"Didn't ya recognize her, Glenn? It was only last week that ya met her."

"She looked familiar but I couldn't put a name to the face." His usual deadpan crumpled a little.

"How long d'ya think she's been dead?"

He cleared his throat. "Approximately ten to twelve hours. She's been moved. She died somewhere else."

"Why was she dumped here?" Marty asked.

He shrugged. "That's for you guys to find out."

"You got any more questions, Faye?" Marty said.

"No."

He put a hand on my back and guided me through the door as though I couldn't see it myself. In a way it was true. My eyes were blurred from the tears they were holding and trying not to let go. But the battle was lost and they streamed down my face. I quickly wiped them away even though it was only the Schwartz's staff looking at me. But it wouldn't help my rep if any detectives saw me. Not even Marty.

When we got out front, he said, "Sorry to put ya through that."

"It's okay."

"Ya gonna call her parents?"

I turned to look at him. "Her parents?"

"Yeah."

"I don't know who they are or where they are. They only came up once, when Claire told me they didn't speak to her sister anymore. Claire's a grown girl, I didn't think to ask anything about them."

Another hole in my procedure. Had I forgotten I was pretty new at this and let early success go to my noggin?

"What's the sister's name?"

"Lucille. And she's not answerin her phone and hasn't shown up at work for a few days. In fact, I was gonna ask ya to use yer clout with some cops in Newark to check out her house."

"What're ya sayin, Faye? Ya think somebody's after this family?"

"I don't know. I don't know what I think."

"I'll get on the horn to Captain Novack over in Jersey. You gonna be all right? You seem a little shaky."

"I need a smoke, is all." I pulled one from my pack and he lit it.

"You look like ya haven't slept in days."

"I feel like I haven't. How am I gonna find the parents?"

"I'll ask Novack to look into it when his men go over to Lucille's place. Oh, better give me that address and phone."

I did.

"I guess you're officially off this case now that Claire's not pickin up the tab."

I hadn't thought about that. "I guess."

"You wanna tell the parents if we find em?"

I knew I'd never be off this case until I found out who'd killed Claire. "I think I should."

"It's better comin from a girl," Marty said.

I agreed. "I'm goin to my office. See ya."

Birdie said, "Who was it?"

"Claire Turner."

"Ah, no. That poor little gal. So the nappers iced her. And Charlie Ladd?"

"Don't know. Before they find out from the daily rags, I hafta to tell Claire's parents."

"Yeah, I guess ya do."

"One problem with that. I don't know where they live."

"Ya want me to start searchin, huh?"

Birdie's eyes looked like they were gonna roll right outta their sockets.

"I don't even have the father's name."

"Ya want me to dig up a Turner with no first name?"

"No. I never said ya should search. I know ya don't have a Chinaman's chance of findin em. I was just tellin ya what's what. If only I could get ahold of Lucille."

"The sister. So how come ya can't?"

I explained.

"So yer off this case now, right?"

"Officially."

"What's that mean?"

"It means I gotta find out who killed Claire."

"Ah, Faye, ya can't keep doin these cases for nothin."

"Have I missed one week of your salary?"

"Don't insult me. You know I'm not thinkin of myself."

"Yeah, I do. I'm sorry."

"Apology accepted. I'm thinkin about you. How're ya gonna put food on the table, ya keep doin stuff for free."

"It wasn't for free when it started."

"You got a retainer from her, dincha?"

"I got a week's pay. She was savin up for her trousseau."

"Hell's bells."

"Yeah."

"So Thursday will be a week. Whaddaya gonna do after that?"

I shrugged.

"Yeah. Right. You need a business manager."

"I thought that's what you were."

"Me?"

"Oh, no. How could I make such a mistake? Yer my naggin secretary."

"A real thigh slapper, Faye. So what's next?"

I snapped my fingers. "I just thought of a guy who might know where Claire's from. Was from."

"I could never do that," she said.

"Do what?"

"Snap my fingers."

"Go back to readin yer magazine. I see it on yer lap."

"Jeez, Louise, ya put all our other cases on hold so what else do I have to do?" She brought the magazine up to her desk.

Love Fiction, it was called. The magazines always had a broad on the cover lookin like she never even heard the word *sex*.

"I know ya don't approve of my readin habits."

"No, ya don't. Just cause I don't want to read em doesn't mean I think *you* shouldn't read em."

"On the level?"

"Sure. I gotta make a call now."

I went into my office and was surprised to see the

scraps and shreds of paper all over the top of my desk, like I'd never seen it like this. I felt like crying out *Who did this?* but I knew who.

I sat down, lit a cig, and tried to make some order outta the chaos. Well, no, that wasn't what I was doing. I'd do that later or tomorrow. Now I was looking for a phone number. It took me about ten minutes. I dialed and his secretary answered.

"May I say who's calling, please?"

"Faye Quick."

"Quick?"

"Yes. Quick."

"Is he expecting your call?"

"No."

"Are you a client?"

"Listen, miss, I'm losin my patience here. Tell him who's on the phone."

"You needn't get so vicious. I'll ring him now."

That girl didn't know the meaning of *vicious*.

Finally George Cummings came on. "Faye. How are you? Did you find Charlie?"

I thought of saying something about Miss Priss, but I restrained myself. "No. Charlie's still missin. But Claire Turner's been murdered."

Silence.

"George? Ya there?"

"Yes. Claire murdered? Why?"

That was an odd question. Most people said how or when. "I don't know. Thing is, George, I gotta tell her parents and I haven't the vaguest where they live. I thought ya might know."

"Yes. Yes, I do."

I waited. "George? Ya there?"

"I'm just so shocked. About Claire. I can't believe that happened."

"Whaddaya mean?"

"Well, another murder. And a girl. Claire was so nice."

"Nice doesn't cut it when somebody wants someone outta the way."

"But why?"

Why again.

"Why would someone want *that* girl out of the way. And out of the way of what?"

"I don't have any of those answers. You were gonna tell me where the Turners live."

"Charlie mentioned it. They live on Twenty-sixth Street. Charlie said at least they didn't live on the Lower East Side."

"You mean here? In Manhattan?"

"Yes. Over between Eighth and Ninth avenues."

"That's a pretty tough area."

"I think Mr. Turner's a longshoreman."

"How'd Charlie feel about that?"

"Charlie didn't care but he was worried that his parents wouldn't like it. Still, he said he wasn't marrying her parents, after all. And he planned to marry Claire before they met her."

I was thinking Charlie sounded like a nice guy until I remembered what he'd done to Lucille.

"So can ya give me the exact address?"

"No. Sorry."

"What's Mr. Turner's first name?"

"When Charlie's found, he's going to be devastated."

If he's found, I thought. "First name, George?"

"Oh, yes. I don't know it. No reason for me to."

"Guess not."

I thanked him and when I got off the horn I shouted for Birdie. I heard her chair scrape and then her heels clicking across the floor. She opened the door.

"Were you screamin for me, boss?"

"We have to get one of those thingamajigs," I said for probably the hundredth time.

"I told ya I'd shop for one."

"We don't have time now. Find me a Turner on West Twenty-sixth Street."

"Still no first name?"

"No. It shouldn't be that hard, though."

"Phone number, too?"

I told her yes, and she went back into the other room. Everything about George's response to the news of Claire's death seemed cockeyed to me.

The phone rang and Birdie picked it up. Then she screamed for me. It was George, calling me back.

"I've been thinking," he said. "You have no one to pay your bills now, do you? I mean now that Claire's gone."

I wasn't surprised that he knew Claire was my client. It was never much of a secret. "That's right," I said.

"Are you calling it quits after you talk to her parents, or are you planning to stay on this case?"

"I wanna find Charlie and I wanna find out who killed Claire," I said.

"I had a feeling you would. Let me pay you."

"I couldn't do that."

"Yes, you could and you will. I'll put a check in the mail this afternoon."

"But you don't even know what I charge."

"Doesn't matter. We'll work out the details later. Have to run now."

He hung up, leaving me kinda stunned.

Birdie came in. "The father's name is Burt."

"Ya sure ya got the right one?"

"Only one on Twenty-sixth. Take it or leave it."

I took it.

TWENTY-NINE

*E*ven though the sun was spotless and bigger than a basketball, I decided to walk downtown. My heels were two inches high and I imagined a time in the future when women wouldn't have to wear these uncomfortable shoes. Men had it good.

I liked to walk. After six years in the city I still saw things I'd never seen before. Sometimes I'd be drawn into a store, but I didn't have time for that now. And I liked eyeballing people as they passed me. I couldn't understand why some people walked with their heads down, looking at the sidewalk.

Almost nobody made eye contact. It just wasn't done and I couldn't get used to it. If I caught someone's eye I often smiled and they either looked at me like I was bats or they seemed scared silly.

I came even with a big window poster of Uncle Sam—I WANT YOU FOR THE U.S. ARMY!—and I stopped and faced it head-on. With his tall white hat that had a blue band and stars cut into it, his blue jacket and pointing finger, I felt a quiver of fear whenever I saw him. Maybe it was his stern expression, maybe the piercing eyes that seemed to single me out.

And now I wondered if Jeanne was right. Should I join the Wacs? But who'd run the agency? I'd made a promise to Woody and I couldn't go back on it. I whispered, "You can't have me," and wheeled away from the poster.

I turned at Thirty-fourth and headed toward Herald Square. The two biggest department stores were there. Gimbel's and Macy's. They were archrivals but I shopped in both if I hadda shop, which was something that left me cold. Other girls found that odd. And I guess it was if all girls were supposed to be alike. I didn't think they were so it struck me odd that it struck them odd. One good thing about those stores was that they were air-conditioned.

When I got to the square, I was tempted to go into Macy's to cool off. But not tempted enough, so I kept walking till I came to Eighth Avenue and then went south.

As I made my way downtown things started to get a little seedy. Lots of tenements with years of grime rubbed into their faces, people sitting on the stoops and yelling to each other, kids playing in the fire hydrant water, underwear their only clothes. I hated being a snob, but I could see how different life was here from the life in Greenwich Village a dozen blocks away.

I passed some sailors looking stunned, over-whelmed I figured by the city that never slept. It musta been something to see Manhattan for the first time. It was for me when I was a little girl and came with my aunt and uncle. But it was love at first sight and even then I knew I'd live here someday. Something got under my skin and it wasn't dirt.

At Twenty-sixth I took a right. The Turners lived halfway down the block. Per usual, I hadn't called ahead. There was always the chance that nobody would be home, but it was worth it for the element of surprise. Not that I wanted to surprise them about the death of their daughter. But there were other things I wanted to ask. And that was a dilemma. Which did I do first?

Was it unethical to ask them questions before I told them Claire was dead? I knew if I did it the other way around, chances of them answering any questions were slim. I'd have to play it by ear.

I found the address and went up the steps, where I said hello to the woman sitting at the top in a house-dress and open-toed slippers. A strap from her slip hung below her short sleeve. Smoke curled from the butt that hung from her mouth, and in her fist was a bottle of Rheingold. I could honestly say she didn't resemble Miss Rheingold of any month.

She didn't say hello back. I passed her and went into the small dirty hall. Numbers but no names on the bells. Names on the mailboxes but no numbers. I came outside.

"Excuse me?"

"Who ya want?" she said.

"I'm looking for the Turners' apartment."

"Oh, yeah? What d'ya want with em?" She blew out smoke while the cig clung to her bottom lip.

"Can ya tell me their apartment number?"

"No." She took the cigarette out of her mouth, had a healthy swig of beer, then smacked her lips together and let out a meaty sigh.

"Ya mean they don't live here?"

"Did I say that? Huh? Did I?"

"This is the address I have for them." I showed her the piece of paper I'd written on.

She batted it away. "I don't wanna see that."

It dawned on me that maybe she couldn't read. "The address I have on the paper matches this one."

"La di da."

I was losing patience. "What's la di da about it?"

She looked at me with eyes whose whites were speckled with red veins. "You ain't got no business with Burt and Marj."

"But I do."

"Jus look at ya." She swept a hand in my direction.

I glanced down at myself as if I didn't know what I'd see. "What about me?"

"Nobody looks like you comes here."

It was worth a try. "What if I told ya I'm a detective?"

She stared for a few seconds and then whooped with a slash of laughter so loud it stopped people on the sidewalk.

"What is it, Binnie?"

"Ya wouldn't believe it," she said, and took another swig from her bottle, finishing it.

"C'mon, Bin, give."

Binnie started laughing again and the beer came whooshing out of her nostrils. She wiped it away with her sleeve.

"Now see whatcha made me do, ya stupid moron."

That was me. I waited.

"You botherin Binnie?" the man on the sidewalk said.

"I just want an apartment number for some people I need to see."

"Yeah, that's right, Connery. She's a lady detective." This sent her into another spiral of laughter.

"De-*tec*-tive? Never heard a that. No women I know would be such a thing. Yer a detective with the coppers?"

"No. I didn't say that. I'm a private detective. And I need to see the Turners. Ya know em?"

"Burt and Marj? Sure," the other guy said.

"You just shut him up, Connery," Binnie said.

I hated doing it but I had no choice. "Look, I have a client who left em some money."

They all went silent.

Binnie gave me a cocked head once-over and the two mugs came up a couple of steps.

"What kinda money?" Connery said.

"I can't tell ya that. After they get it, ask them."

"They don't tell nothin," Binnic said. "Like clams."

"That ain't fair, Bin. Burt tole us bout his daughter bein real successful at Wanamaker's."

"Yeah, that's right."

Binnic said, "And what about Lucille? They ever tell ya bout that one?"

"Nope."

"There ya go. Just what I'm sayin."

"What about her?"

Binnie glanced at me then back at the two guys. "Another time, fellas."

"You'll forget. Why don I go get us some beers," he said.

"Good idea."

"Before ya go, can ya tell me which apartment is the Turners so I don't hafta ring all the bells, bother everybody?"

"Fourth floor. Two B."

"You bigmouth, Connery."

"Why shouldn't they get money if it's due em, Bin?"

"Yeah," the other one said.

"Ah, what's the dif. Go on up, girlie. Girlie detective."

I heard them all laughing as I made my way up the stairs. I couldn't remember the last time I'd given people such a good time.

Two B was down a long dark corridor. I didn't feel scared but I did feel a cloak of depression come over me like a bleak, cloudy day. I knocked. It'd been a timid sound, so I did it again with more beef. Nothing happened. I tried again, four loud ones instead of three. I heard a stirring, then a sound like someone mopping the floor. As it got closer it became a shuffle.

"Who is it?" A deep male voice.

"Detective Quick?"

"Who?"

I repeated it for him.

"There ain't no girl detectives."

"I'm private."

"Yeah? Well, I'm public and I'm sleepin."

I could hear that he was turning away.

"Wait. Mr. Turner, I have somethin to tell ya about Claire."

"Claire?"

"Yeah."

"Somethin wrong?"

"Mr. Turner, could ya let me come in?"

He turned a lock and opened the door about two inches. All I could see was his nose and one blue eye, an accordion of bags beneath it.

"What about her?"

"I'm not talkin about this in the hall."

"Okay." He opened the door wider and let me

through. "I was sleepin," he said and looked down at the proof, his striped pajama pants. He wore a grubby undershirt on top. His full head of black hair was sticking up at odd angles. From what I could see in the dim light his features were square, like boxes.

"Should I get my wife? We both work nights."

"I think it would be good to get her."

Suddenly he didn't want to know why I'd come. He'd rather get his wife.

It was a railroad apartment, one room after another off the narrow hallway. Mr. Turner walked down it like he was navigating a plank.

The living room was dark; the one window had a blackout shade pulled down, its green color chipped. A sagging couch was against one wall, while a three-legged chair and another one with four legs were across from it. Small tables were staggered around the room.

Mr. Turner came back with his wife. He'd changed into a pair of work pants.

"Let's get some light on the subject," she said. Her voice was cheerful, as if she was about to kick off a party. When she raised the shade, it didn't make that much difference, cause outside the window was another brick building. She went around the room snapping on lights. It felt like it was three in the morning.

"There. That's better."

Mrs. Turner was a short scrawny woman. The back and sides of her fading blond hair were rolled up, while bobby pins kept the curls above her forehead in a straight line, and all of it was held in place with a hairnet. She was wearing a quilted bathrobe that was tattered and frayed at the cuffs. Her blue eyes looked lavender like her daughter's.

"So what's this about Claire?" he asked.

"Could we sit down?"

"You keep beatin around the bush. I don't like that."

"Now, Burt," she said, putting a hand on his arm. He shook it off.

I sat in the chair that had all of its legs. But no springs. I felt like I was on the floor.

They stared at me, then took seats on the couch, which I could now see had a pattern of big faded flowers. He looked angry and she tried to look sunny. They both looked tired. I didn't know how I was gonna tell em. Why hadn't I left it up to the police? They'd probably be here soon. Did I always have to be first?

Mr. Turner tapped a cigarette out of the package on the table in front of him. He opened a box of wooden matches and lit one by scraping his thumbnail across the top. "Whatcha got to say about Claire?"

"There's been an accident." Why had I put it like that. It was only a delaying tactic. I lit a butt to delay a little longer.

Mrs. Turner grabbed the lapels of her robe and brought them together like she needed to get warmer. He stared at me.

"Is she in the hospital?" she said.

"No."

"She's dead, ain't she?" he said.

"Yes."

"Dead?" She moved her hand from the lapels to her mouth.

He said, "Who killed her?"

I wanted to know why he'd asked that, but I couldn't put the questions then, I had to answer them.

"I don't know." I told them the rest of what I knew, leaving out details they didn't hafta know.

They sat in front of me as though I'd punched them both in the gut. And I had. A long time passed before anyone spoke again.

Finally I broke the silence. "Why'd ya think someone had killed her, Mr. Turner?"

"I could tell she was goin down the road her sister went. Girls like that get killed. With Lucille it was somethin else, but I knew Claire would come to a bad end. I don't get it. She was a real nice kid once." He blew out a last spat of smoke and crushed his cig in the ashtray.

"Mr. Turner, I don't think it was Claire's fault."

"Shut up."

He startled me. I hadn't expected that.

"Just shut up. You don't know nothin about em, my girls."

I had to admit he was right. I knew very little about either of them, as it turned out.

"Can I ask ya somethin?"

"Of course, dear," Mrs. Turner said.

"Has Lucille called ya recently?"

"She wouldn't dare," he said.

"Well, she did," Mrs. T. said.

He looked at her, shock in his eyes. "When was this?"

"All the time."

"Whatcha sayin, Marj?"

"I'm sayin that I never agreed with how ya handled everything with Lucille. I talked to her and I saw her every week. She's my daughter and I love her, no matter what. Same with Claire."

"Had ya cut off Claire, too, Mr. Turner?"

"No reason for her to leave home. She thought she was too good for us, so she had to get her own place. That's what whores do."

I felt angry for Claire. "She wasn't a whore, Mr. Turner."

"She made up like one, runnin around with sailors and soldiers and who knew what else."

"One soldier," Marj said.

"Ya don't know that," he said.

"I do."

"How?"

"She told me about him."

His mouth pulled back into something that he intended as a grin. "And ya believed her? You've always been a dimwit."

"I don't wanna argue, Burt. I just wanna see my girl. I wanna see both my girls. Does Lucille know?"

"No." Now I was gonna have to tell these people

that their other daughter was AWOL. "When's the last time ya talked to Lucille, Mrs. Turner?"

"Let's see. About a week ago. Last Wednesday to be exact. She'll be heartbroken about this. They were such good friends. I should tell her. Should I phone her or should I go over there? Oh, I don't know what to do." She began to cry.

"But they hadn't been friends for a long time, had they? I mean since Lucille . . ."

"Had a baby. Say it. She had a baby without bein married," he said.

"And you forbid Claire to see her, didn't ya?"

"You bet."

Through her tears Mrs. Turner said, "Well, she didn't listen to ya, Burt. That girl had a mind of her own. They saw each other all the time."

"Are ya sure of that, Mrs. Turner?"

"Sometimes I met with em. We'd go to real nice restaurants. The girls would take me."

"You went against me, Marj?"

"Yes. I did and I'd . . ."

There was a knock at the door. We all stopped short as if we were guilty of something. I was pretty sure I knew who it was.

"Police," a man called.

"I'll get it," I said. "And I'll leave then, too. I'm sorry about everything."

I went to the door and unlocked it. Detective Powell and two cops stood there.

"Just leavin," I said.

Powell's eyes got smaller than they already were. I hurried past them and hightailed it down the hall. "You're a menace," Powell yelled after me. "Thanks," I said.

THIRTY

J walked back toward my office. It was hotter than ever. I was bathed in sweat right away. I smiled. My mother, when she was somewhat sane, used to say to me, *Girls don't sweat, Faye. Men sweat. Girls glow.*

Sure as the devil, I didn't feel like I was glowing. I felt wet and sweaty. And confused. Why would both Claire and Lucille lie to me about their friendship? If they were still friends, what was the point of telling me they never saw each other? They had to have gained something from the lie, but what? Why would that make any difference to the investigation? In fact, it made it harder.

Now I could never ask Claire, and who knew if Lucille was ever gonna turn up. Why would she disappear? Had *she* been kidnapped? I didn't believe that one for a second. So where was she and why?

The Newark police woulda been to Lucille's place by now. Maybe they'd found something. I picked up my pace, hot as it was.

Before I went upstairs I stopped at Stork's. I needed a Royal Crown like I'd been marooned on the desert for weeks.

Stork was behind the counter reading a magazine, and the Ink Spots, singing "Don't Get Around Much Anymore," were coming from the radio.

"Whatcha readin?"

"A real good story, Faye." He lifted up the magazine so I could see the cover. It was the July issue of *Doc Savage*. A blond guy with a can of gasoline was pouring it on something I couldn't make out.

"This one's called 'Murder Up the Line.'"

"I didn't know ya read stuff like that, Stork. I mean mysteries and such."

"Sure, I read em. What can I do for ya?"

"I'm dyin of thirst."

"One RC comin up."

"Thanks. Where are the boys?"

"Don't know. Out doin somethin stupid probably."

Stork pulled on his earlobe when he said this so I knew he was fibbing. The earlobe pull was his tell. Everybody has one. Sometimes it tips off lying, sometimes it's a giveaway in poker games. And speaking of poker games, I knew they were in the back room playing. I never understood why Stork and the boys felt they had to lie to me about this. It wasn't really a lie, I guessed. More an omission. I figured even though I was private and not gonna rat on them, I was still a stand-in for law in their eyes, so I didn't push it.

He set down the glass with ice and the open bottle of RC on the marble counter. I thanked him and gave him my five cents, then took a deep swallow and though it was cold and tasted great, when I put it back down I was still thirsty.

"I gotta question for ya, Stork."

"Shoot."

"Why would two sisters say they weren't friends when they really were?"

"Is this a riddle?"

"A question."

Stork tapped a cig from his Luckies pack, lit it, and blew out a puff of smoke. Now he could think.

He mumbled my question to himself and ran a hand through his black hair. Then he took off his glasses with the thick black frames and put them back on. "They say this to you?"

"Yeah."

"They knew ya were investigatin?"

"Yeah."

"I guess they didn't wantcha to know they *were* friends."

I gave him a look.

"Yeah, well. That's the obvious part. You want me to get to the bottom of the reason they'd wantcha to think that, right?"

"Right." I took a swallow of my drink. Then I lit a butt. I wondered why I was doing this, putting Stork through the wringer.

"They said it together or separately?"

I almost told him to forget it but I could see he was taking this challenge seriously. "Separately. On different days. In different abodes. In different states, even."

He whistled and shook his head. "This is a toughie, Faye."

"You don't have to go on with it, Stork."

"No, no. I'll get it. Gimme a minute."

"Sure." I wandered over to the magazine rack and picked up a copy of *Modern Screen* that had an article in it about Judy Garland. She was one of my favorites. I flipped to the page and read:

Every spare second of Judy's life for the last two years has been tied up with a red, white and blue ribbon and handed to the lads in uniform!

That was as far as I got. Stork gave a little yelp and I turned around.

"I got one more question so I can be sure."

I put the magazine back and walked over to the counter. "What?"

"Was one of em your client?"

"Yeah."

He snapped his fingers. "I knew it."

"What did ya know?"

"If one was yer client, then they said they weren't friends cause they wanted to give ya a bum steer."

"But why?"

"They were pullin a one–two play."

"Ya mean they were in on somethin together?"

"That's just what I mean."

I stared at him. Of course. He was right. It was so simple I couldn't see it.

"Stork, yer a genius." I leaned across the counter

and planted one on his cheek. "I owe ya," I said, picked up my stuff, and practically flew out the door.

I'd never run up the stairs to my office so fast. I pulled open the door and rushed in.

"Marty call me?"

"Yeah, he did," Birdie said.

"He say where he was?"

"Smitty's. Yer all in a dither, ain'tcha?"

"I'll tell ya about it in a minute."

"Okay. I don't mind bein last to know."

I didn't have time to play the game. In my office I dialed Smitty's. Lupino answered and called for Marty, who came on almost right away.

"Faye?"

"Yeah. What's up?"

"I heard back from Newark. Lucille Turner's place was empty. No clothes, no nothin. Looks like she did a ghost."

"That fits. Sorta." I told him Stork's theory.

"Why'd ya say sorta?"

"If they were doin somethin together, why'd Claire turn up dead?"

"Why does anybody turn up dead?"

"Love or money."

"Right."

"Well, I don't think Lucille killed her sister for love. So it musta been money."

"Maybe. But who says Lucille killed Claire?"

"Ya got a point."

"The only one left is Charlie Ladd," he said.

"Who says he's alive? And I can't see Lucille doin *anything* with that guy after what he did to her."

"Faye, ya only got her word what he did."

Everything in this case was based on just one person's word. A bunch of storytellers. David Cooper's body was the one piece of concrete evidence.

"And if she was in on some scam, she'd want me to think she hated Charlie. Or maybe Claire and Lucille kidnapped him cause of what he did, bumped him off, and sat back to collect the dough."

"Yeah, that sounds right."

"Then Lucille musta killed her own sister. That's hard to swallow."

"Strange things happen when big bucks is involved."

"So the money's gone. Claire's dead. Lucille is missin, and we don't know about Charlie Ladd. And let's not forget the murder of David Cooper. Who did that and why?"

"It's gotta be connected since they found the kid in Ladd's room."

"Oh, it's connected all right. I just can't figure out *how*."

"Anything else I can do, Faye?"

"You can find Lucille and maybe Charlie."

"Swell."

"Powell must be on to all this by now."

"If he's not, he's got a demotion comin."

"Maybe ya can get a bead on what Powell and his boys know."

"I'll give it a hundred percent."

"Thanks."

After I hung up I sat there, trying to make the pieces fall into place. I'd add it up one way and then add it up another and it still didn't come out right.

There was a knock on my door.

"Yeah?"

Birdie opened it and said, "Do I have to beg to be let in the secret club? You want me to prick my finger to get blood?"

"What are ya talkin about?"

"You been off the horn for ten minutes. I wanna know what's goin on?"

"Pull up a chair."

When I finished telling her the whole story, the new theories, the ins and outs, she looked at me with crazy eyes.

"That beats all," she said. "To think Stork solved the case. This is one for the books."

"Wait a sec. He didn't solve it. It's not solved. Stork gave me an idea, is all."

"Whatever ya say. Hand me a cig, will ya?"

I did even though she was getting my goat. Stork solved it. Phooey. We both lit up.

"So what's next, Faye?"

"Lunch."

"You want I should call the deli or are ya goin out?"

"Deli. Pastrami on rye, lotsa mustard, lotsa pickles on the side."

"You think I don't know what ya want?"

"I don't know what I think."

"What's that supposed to mean?"

"Nothin. Call the deli."

"Don't gimme *nothin*. I know better. Somethin's got your dander up."

"Stork did *not* solve the case, Birdie."

"Okay, okay. I misspoke."

I knew I was being childish, but now I didn't know how to get outta it. "Just so ya know."

"I know."

"What? Whaddaya know?"

"This is nuts." She stood up.

"Where ya goin?"

"I'm callin the deli."

I grunted.

"Real attenuate."

I knew she meant *articulate*. "Thanks." I wanted this to stop now. She started for the door. "Bird?"

"Yeah?"

"I'm sorry."

She eyeballed me good, trying to see if I was on the up-and-up. "I'm sorry, too. Stork couldn't solve a hangnail."

I smiled.

"He couldn't solve what statue's in the Lincoln Memorial."

I laughed and then Birdie laughed and before we knew it we were howling and holding our stomachs cause the laughing hurt and I knew we were both trying not to go over that edge when the laughs turn into sobs. She was cackling as she went out to make the call to the deli. I was still chuckling some when I heard her give a big whoop of laughter, then suddenly stop. It didn't sound right so I got up and ran to the outer office.

At first I didn't recognize the man pointing a gun at Birdie and then I did. It was Raymond Cooper, David's father.

"Mr. Cooper, what's goin on?"

His mustache twitched. "The police won't do anything. So now you have to."

I remembered then he'd never called me about the letter David had written with the room arrangements he and Charlie'd made for New York.

"Mr. Cooper, can ya put down the gun?"

"No. Not until you promise to find out who killed David."

"Can my secretary put down her hands?"

Birdie was holding her arms straight up high above her head. I thought they must be tired.

"Put them in front of you on the desk." To me he said, "I never asked her to put them up. She just did it."

Sounded right. "Put your arms down, Birdie."

She did.

"Whew," she said.

"Now how about the gun, Mr. Cooper? You don't need it. We can talk about this. I mean, I could promise ya anything to get ya to put it down and then what?"

340

"You mean you'd lie?"

You bet. "Let's just talk this over like two grown-ups, okay?"

Slowly he lowered the gun and stood there with it at his side looking like a drooping scarecrow.

"I was just gonna call for some lunch. Ya want somethin, Mr. Cooper?" Birdie asked.

"Something to drink. A Dr. Pepper. It's so hot out there."

"Go ahead, Bird. Put in the order. Mr. Cooper, you come in my office, okay?"

He nodded and followed me in, still carrying the gun. I had him sit down and asked him if he'd put the peashooter on the edge of my desk. He did.

"I'm sorry about that," he said. "But I feel desperate. They won't release David's body and I don't think they're doing anything to find his killer."

The family and friends of victims often felt that way. "I'm sure they're doin somethin."

"They won't tell me anything. That's why I want you to deal with this case. I'm willing to pay you twice what you usually get."

"Mr. Cooper, I don't know if ya know this or not, but Charlie Ladd was kidnapped. And I'm workin on that case. I think they're connected, the kidnappin and your son's murder. So I'm already workin on it."

"But it's not your focus, is it?"

He had me there. "No. But I believe that when we find Ladd we'll know what happened to David."

"And what if you never find him?"

"I can't go into detail, but I'm close to findin him."

"I never heard anything about a kidnapping. Was it in the papers?"

"No. We kept that part out. Just said he was missin."

"Was there a note? A phone call? How do you know he was kidnapped?"

"There was a call."

"Why should I trust you?"

"Why'd ya come here?"

"Desperation."

"Then ya have to trust me. I'm all ya got."

"It's true. You're all I've got."

THIRTY-ONE

*D*o you think Private Ladd killed my son, Miss Quick?"

"I think it's possible. But I don't know why?"

"Will you let me hire you?"

"Mr. Cooper, someone else is already payin my bills."

"Can't you have two clients at once?"

"Not for the same case."

"But it's not for the same case, is it?"

"They're connected," I said.

"You're sure?"

"Nobody can ever be sure about anything."

"Hogwash. My son is dead and I'm sure about that."

"You're right. As for the case, well, I'm sure as I can

be that they're connected somehow."

"But you don't know, you aren't positive, are you?"

"No."

"Well, then, I want to hire you to find my son's killer."

"But Mr. Cooper . . ."

"You said you were all I have and that's true. Where can I turn, Miss Quick?"

"I can send ya to a good PI I know."

"I don't want anyone else. I want you."

"Mr. Cooper, ya don't even know me. Ya don't know if I'm any good."

"I know you're honest. When we met the first time, you said nothing would ever be the same for Thelma and me. No one else has said anything like that. They say time will help. Turn to God. Things like that. But no one ever says the truth. And you did. You're the person I want to help me."

"Okay. But ya don't have to pay me."

"I do. Please. I won't feel that I'm hiring you unless I do."

"Yeah, I can see that." I told him my rates and he wrote out a check.

"Thank you, Miss Quick."

"Please call me Faye."

"All right. Call me Raymond."

We exchanged sappy smiles. I said, "Did ya ever get one of yer daughters to read that letter about David's plans?"

"I did. There was nothing to indicate that there was

343

any rift between David or Private Ladd or that they were planning on separate rooms in New York."

Birdie knocked on the door and came in with the delivery of my lunch and Cooper's Dr. Pepper. Birdie'd already opened his soda bottle and he poured it into the glass she'd brought. I unwrapped my sandwich. We drank and ate in silence.

When he'd gone, I took out the picture of Charlie Ladd that Claire had given me. It wasn't the same one that had been in the papers. I tucked it into my pocketbook and left my office.

Birdie said, "Poor guy."

"Mr. Cooper?"

"Yeah. Course I wasn't crazy about him when he was ready to kill me."

"You know he wouldna."

"*Now* I know."

"I'll ring ya later for messages."

"Where ya goin?"

"Downtown."

"So don't tell me."

"I'm goin to see Dolores."

"Oh. I hope she's better."

"Knowing Dolores, she will be."

This time I had no trouble getting in to see Mrs. Sidney. She was propped up in bed, wearing her red wig, not quite in place, but if it had been I wouldna known who she was. There were flowers everywhere and Dolores was playing solitaire on her bed table. And she had a roommate I couldn't really see cause the curtain was pulled.

"Ah, bubele, just the person I wanted to see."

I gave her a peck on the cheek. "How come?"

"Cause I'm goin meshuga with . . ." She tilted her head toward the other patient.

I nodded that I got her drift.

"Groaning. Yelling. In the night. I want out. And I want you to take me."

"I can't do that."

"Why not? I'll get better faster in my own bed."

That was probably on the money. Still. "Who'll take care of ya?"

"Everybody."

Another bull's-eye. "I'm on a case."

"So? You think yer the only pal I got?"

"I know ya got lotsa friends, but who says they'll be able to help out?"

"I do. Look at all these flowers."

"I have. I know. But sendin flowers and takin care are two different animals."

"Ach. You got no spirit. No sense of adventure."

"You don't believe that for a minute, Dolores. Me of all people?"

"Don't make me use my ace in the hole." She pressed her lips together as if nothing, nobody could pry this info from her. I knew better.

"After all," she said. "I'm in here cause a you."

Ace in the hole. "So I should take ya away from

345

proper treatment cause of that? *Au contraire.*"

"What's this now? Yer speakin foreign languages at me?"

"Since I'm the reason yer in here, I think it's my responsibility to make sure ya get well. Get the best treatment."

"Faye. Bubee. Don'tcha know that hospitals make ya sick? It's a well-known fact. I'm surprised ya don't know this."

"I can't just take ya outta here."

"Why not?"

"Nurrrrrrse." From the other bed. "Hurtin."

"Ya see what I mean? All day and all night. How can I get better here?"

She had a point. "I suppose ya got it all figured out how to do it."

Dolores smiled. "It's not hard. You get my clothes from the closet and I go in the bathroom and put them on. Could it be any easier?"

"But then what?"

"We walk out together."

"We'll have to go by the nurses' station."

She pointed to her wig.

"You'll take it off?"

She nodded.

"They might recognize ya anyway."

"Never. Get my shmatas now."

"If we get caught, I'm sure I won't be able to visit ya."

"I'll survive."

"Nice." I went over to the metal locker and took out her shoes, skirt, girdle, brassiere—and nothing else. "There's no blouse."

"I guess it was too bloody."

"Ya can't walk outta here in a brassiere and nothin else."

"Nurrrrrrse. Hurtin."

"I have an idea," she said. "Go in her locker. Maybe there's somethin I can wear."

"Now ya want me to steal?"

"Borrow." She pointed to the locker on the other side of the curtain.

"She'll see me."

"So what?"

"I think Morris should do this for ya."

"Ecch. Morris is a shmendrik. He'd get it all wrong. You're the only one I trust. Go. Her locker. Now."

I don't know why I did what I was told, but I did. I tried to make myself invisible by hunching up and tiptoeing over to the other patient's locker. I didn't look at her and hoped she had her eyes closed. I opened the door and peered in. There was a dress and it looked huge. I grabbed it.

"Nurrrrrrse. Hurtin."

I jumped about a foot. I ran back to Dolores. "What if a nurse comes for that woman."

"They never come. What's that thing ya got there?"

"A dress." I held it up.

"Is she an elephant?"

"This is it. Ya wanna put it on or not?"

"I don't but I do." She threw her legs over the side of the bed. "Gimme it, bubee."

I turned my back while she got dressed. I was terrified someone would walk in and I also didn't know how we could get away with this.

"Okay, now ya can feast yer eyes."

Dolores was barely visible in the dress. She'd taken off her wig, and once again I saw the gray sprouts of hair. And her face. But that was all. The dress completely covered the rest of her except the tips of her shoes.

"Ya can't go out in that."

"I'm goin."

"Ya think ya won't attract attention?"

"I'm gonna bunch it up and you'll walk on my right side so they don't see."

"And in the lobby? On the street?"

"We'll take a taxi."

"If any'll stop for us."

"Do I have a handbag here?"

"No. How d'ya feel?"

"Like a diamond as big as the Ritz."

"Your wound. How does *it* feel?"

"Perfect."

"If ya start to feel weak, lemme know."

"I will. So let's go."

This was worse than going into an apartment you didn't know, wondering if there was a bullet waiting for you. They were the good old days.

"Lemme check the hall first."

"Good idea."

Oddly enough it was empty. I gestured to Dolores. I took her arm and we walked out of the room. She was holding up the dress with her other hand, and when we got to the nurses' station we walked on by without a hitch. The elevators were gonna be another story.

"Maybe we should walk down the stairs," I said.

"I don't think I can manage that, Faye."

"Are ya okay?"

"Hunky-dory, but walkin down steps ain't on my dance card."

"Okay."

When we got to the elevators, I pushed the button and we waited. I couldn't imagine how we were gonna get away with this. The door opened and we got on. Nobody, including the operator, noticed or said a word. Had I forgotten that this was New York City— and the Village to boot?

The rest of our escape went the same. Through the lobby and out the door to Seventh Avenue, where I hailed a hack. No one batted an eye. My kinda town.

The trip was rough on Dolores. I got her into bed as soon as I could after we got home. Then I went around to all the neighbors, some in the building, some on the block. Everyone agreed to help out with her care.

Ethel Kilbride elected herself captain of the care team. She was a good organizer so I felt okay about that. I had six keys cut for Dolores's apartment. No leaving the door unlocked. If the shooter got wind of her being at home, he might try to finish the job he'd started.

Bruce Jory offered to sit in the hallway and guard the apartment all night, but I didn't think that was necessary. Besides, it was time Morris did something.

After I looked in on Dolores, who was asleep, I went into my own crib and found the number Morris had given me.

Zachary twirled nonstop around my legs as I sat at the phone table. I leaned down and scratched behind his ears. I felt bad cause I'd been neglecting him. He got his food and water, but we hadn't chewed the fat lately.

I dialed Morris. And when he answered, I said immediately that he shouldn't be frightened, Dolores was okay.

"Thanks for saying that."

I heard him light a cigarette, which made me get one of my own.

"She's home now. She . . ."

"Home?"

I explained what had happened and how all the neighbors were gonna take care of her.

"It must be something to be loved like that," he said.

I felt a twinge of sorrow for him. "Look, the reason I'm callin is cause she'll need somebody there nights."

There was a silence on the other end.

"Morris?"

"I'm here. So you want me to spend my nights there, is that it?"

"She might be in danger."

"Okay. When do I start?"

"How's tonight sound."

"Lousy, but I'll be there. Will you?"

"I'm not sure where I'll be. But somebody will be there until ya get here."

"I guess I'll sleep on the sofa, right?"

"Can't think a where else." The sofa was dilapidated to say the least. And sitting on it was like having some kinda brutal massage.

"Yeah. That's okay. Maybe I'll sleep on the floor."

"Whatever ya wanna do."

"Okay. I'll be there in about an hour."

After I hung up I went across the hall. Jerome Byington was on duty. *Natty* was the word you'd use to describe Jerome.

"How's she doin?"

"She's asleep."

"No, I ain't," Dolores yelled.

"Bat ears," he said.

"I'd like to go in."

"Suit yourself." He picked up his copy of *Esquire*.

I walked back through the hall into her bedroom.

"So what's cookin?" she said.

"Yer not gonna like this but here's what's gonna happen."

I told her the schedule.

"Morris is gonna sleep here?"

"Now, don't get nasty, we need . . ."

"I wasn't gettin nasty, Faye. I'm just surprised he'd bother."

"He loves ya, Dolores."

She didn't say anything, which was unusual, and I thought I mighta seen a glistening of her eyes. I didn't mention it. And then I remembered why I'd gone to see her at the hospital in the first place.

I opened my bag and took out the picture of Charlie Ladd. "Dolores, have you ever seen this guy?" I handed her the picture.

"Don't kid a kidder, Faye."

"Whaddaya mean?"

"This is the guy that shot me."

THIRTY-TWO

*M*arty and I sat in the White Horse Tavern having a stein of beer. We had our order in for a burger. The bar had been around a long time and was a watering hole for longshoremen cause it was close to the docks and warehouses on Hudson. But a few regular people braved the place and ate and drank there on the early side before it became rowdy and the fights broke out.

It had a series of small rooms, and we sat in the back. The beams were painted black; everything else was plain tortured wood. People said it was the second oldest bar in New York. I never did learn which one was the first.

I wished that I could be talking things over with Johnny, but I didn't want him to think I was some girl who didn't know what she was doing. I didn't care what Marty thought.

I'd told him that Dolores had identified the picture of Charlie Ladd, now lying on the table between us, as the guy who shot her.

"You're sure we can trust the old gal to know what she's sayin'?"

"Marty, she's sharp as a tiger's tooth. If she says this is the guy, then he's the guy."

The waiter came and plunked down our burgers.

"Can we have some ketchup?" Marty said.

"Get it yourself. It's on the bar." He walked away.

"I don't remember that happenin before," Marty said.

"Before what?"

"You want ketchup or not?"

"Sure."

"I'll get it then."

I took a drag of my butt and stared at the photo of Charlie Ladd. He was a good-looking guy, no doubt. He almost had what they called a baby face. Innocent. I could understand why Dolores woulda talked to him.

But it was hard to see him as a scammer, a rapist, an extortionist, or a murderer—and he might be all four. Had he really raped Lucille? Had he set up the kidnap caper with Claire, then killed her once he got the money?

Marty was back with the ketchup. "Never heard of a burger without ketchup. You?"

"No."

"So it seems to me they should bring it or leave a bottle on the table like other joints do."

"Can we stop talkin about the ketchup and get back to Dolores and Charlie Ladd?"

"Yeah. Sorry. Stuff like that burns me up." He took a long swallow of his beer.

"The thing is where's Charlie Ladd now? And is Lucille with him? Or is she dead, too?"

"Why would Lucille be with him after what he did to her? Ya think he kidnapped her?"

"You said yourself I only had Lucille's word for it. I'm more of a mind she made up that story."

"Why now?"

"I'm not sure."

"Well, ya know from that Widmark fella that she was raped."

"Do I?" I squashed my cig.

"She told . . . ya never checked it out with him, did ya?"

"I got egg on my face with this one. I didn't check."

"Don't work yerself into a lather. We all make *huge* mistakes."

I looked at him and he was grinning.

"No kiddin, Faye. These things happen. Maybe when we finish, we should pay Widmark a visit."

"The doorman'll have to let us in when ya flash yer shield, won't he?"

"Yeah. He'll tremble before me."

The doorman didn't exactly tremble, but he paid attention and called Widmark on the phone, explained that the police were there, and up we went. Widmark didn't give us any trouble, either. We sat in his living room.

"So, what do you want?" Widmark's eyes were red, as if he'd been crying.

"I guess ya know about Claire Turner."

"Of course." He looked down at his lap. I figured he *had* been crying.

"I'm sorry, Mr. Widmark. I know ya cared for her."

"Cared for her? I loved her." He took a swipe at his eyes. "She was such a lovely girl, I don't know why anyone would kill her."

The particulars about what Claire'd been involved in hadn't been released to the papers.

"Do you know why she was killed?" he asked.

Marty said, "We can't really talk about that, Mr. Widmark."

He nodded. "I understand."

"Did ya know Lucille was missin?" I said.

"What do you mean she's missing?"

"Vanished."

"Into thin air," Marty said.

"Wanna tell me about her?"

"I have no idea where she is. This is outrageous."

"Calm down. I'm not sayin ya know where she is. I'm talkin about when she used to come visit ya."

"What makes you think . . ."

"Let's not get on this merry-go-round, Widmark," Marty said. "We know ya knew her and that she used to visit. And we know she suddenly stopped. What we don't know is why."

"And don't give me any malarkey about it bein for her sake," I said.

"It was, in a way."

"Ya mean she started showin she was pregnant?"

"How do you know about that?"

"Lucille told me," I said.

"What else did she tell you?"

"Why'd she stop coming here to see ya?"

"I thought it'd be too hard on her. Making that trip in from New Jersey."

"I want ya to tell me what else ya know."

"Will it help you find her?"

"It might."

He ran a hand over his red crew cut. "I don't know why I'm protecting that bastard."

"What bastard?" Marty asked.

"Ladd. He raped Lucille."

"She told ya that?"

"Yes. When she got pregnant, her parents threw her out and even Claire wouldn't speak to her. I wouldn't have expected that from Claire." He drifted to someplace we couldn't go.

"Mr. Widmark," I said.

"Sorry. Lucille was beside herself. She didn't want to have the baby, but she didn't want to have an abortion. I wanted her to tell Claire, warn her about Ladd, but she wouldn't. She said Claire wouldn't believe her. That she'd think Lucille was trying to ruin her happiness."

"Why didn't *you* warn Claire?" I said.

"Why do you think?"

"Yeah. I see."

"I offered to marry Lucille but we both knew that wasn't the answer. Wouldn't solve anything."

"Did she say that she'd told Ladd she was pregnant?"

"She hadn't and she wasn't going to. There was no point, she said. So she had the baby and gave him up for adoption."

"Ya mean to an orphanage?"

"Yes."

"Would ya know the name of the place?"

"As a matter of fact, I do. It's near a spot Lucille loves."

"And where's that?" Marty said.

"The orphanage is in Asbury Park at the New Jersey shore."

New Jersey again.

"And Asbury Park's the place she loves?"

"No. She likes a town on the shore nearby. Point Pleasant."

"Did she ever say she was gonna move there?"

"Someday, she said. When she was married. But that was in the future."

Marty said, "Some futures are shorter than others."

"So she didn't have a house there?"

"She rented every summer for a week. When she and Claire were little their parents once took them there."

"Do ya know if Lucille's baby was ever adopted?"

"She didn't know. The place isn't allowed to give out that information."

"Was Lucille plannin to take the baby back once she got married?"

"Yes. But she knew by then he might not be available."

"What's the name of the orphanage?"

"St. Mary's."

"Catholic?"

"Yes. She didn't leave him there for religious reasons."

I stood up. "Mr. Widmark, you've been very helpful."

"Good. I'm glad. Could you let me know if you find Lucille?"

"Sure." Marty shook hands with him.

As we got near the door, Widmark called out to me. I turned.

"You don't need a nickel this time?"

"No, thanks."

While we waited for the elevator, Marty said, "What was that nickel thing about?"

I hadn't told him I'd been a mark like any ordinary person. So I told him now.

"Got any idea who did it?"

"I think it was this big guy who was sittin next to me."

Marty nodded like it had to be a big guy. I changed the subject.

"You think Lucille's in Point Pleasant?"

"I'd bet my bottom dollar on it," he said.

"What's next? Should I tell the whole story to the cops?"

"What story?"

The elevator came and the gal running it was the same one who was there on my first visit.

"Ya have a nice visit with Mr. Widmark?"

"Swell," I said.

"He's a sweetheart, isn't he?"

If there wasn't a war on, this tomato wouldn't last a day running this elevator with her Nosy Parker ways. On the other hand, if it wasn't wartime she wouldn't have the job at all.

When we left the building, the soggy heat hit us like we'd been dropped into a vat of warm tea.

"About that story for the cops. What's it gonna be? That Lucille Turner quit her job and left her rented house to go somewhere else?"

"Somethin like that."

"Where's the crime?"

"She's a missin person."

"Is she? Who's lookin for her besides you? Anyway, isn't this about Charlie Ladd, who we now know is alive and well and runnin around shootin old ladies?"

"Don't forget David Cooper."

"I'm not, but what's that gotta do with Lucille? And don't you forget Claire."

"I don't forget her for a second."

"Listen, Faye. I think Ladd and Claire cooked up the kidnappin to get some money out of his old man but then Charlie Boy decided he'd like it better if he didn't have to share the dough. It's him we gotta find, not Lucille."

"So why'd we question Widmark about Lucille?"

"That had to do with Ladd, in case ya forgot. We wanted to know if Widmark knew about the rape. Now we know."

"What we know, Marty, is that Lucille was pregnant. It's still her word on who made her that way."

"Why would she tell Widmark that Ladd did it, if he didn't? Nothin to gain there."

"Yeah. Yer right," I said.

"The cops on this case are lookin for Claire's killer now. We don't know where to look so let em handle it."

"Marty, I have two clients I gotta satisfy. One wants to know who killed his son, and the other wants me to find Charlie Ladd."

"So work those cases. But there's nothing right now ya gotta share with Powell and the rest."

"Yeah. Yer right again. I'm gonna concentrate on David Cooper. But that brings me right back to Ladd."

"Give that gal a cigar. Where ya gonna start?"

"With Lucille Turner. Wanna come? I know ya got a couple a days off."

"Where?"

"First Asbury Park, and then Point Pleasant."

"Ya wanna go to that orphanage?"

"I do. But I need a car again. Ya think yer friend'll lend ya his if he knows yer drivin?"

"Who said I was comin?"

"Aren't ya?"

"See that cab up the street, Faye? Take it and I'll pick ya up tomorrow."

When I got back to Grove Street, Johnny was sitting on the stoop. My heart did a sleigh ride.

"I thought I'd catch you eventually," he said. "And this was the best way to have that happen. Do you mind?"

"Course not."

I sat on the step next to him. He gave me a peck on the cheek and took my hand in his.

"How are you, Faye? I know it's not true, but it seems like a month since I saw you."

It felt that way to me, too. "I'm okay. You?"

"I'm okay, too. Sorry about Claire Turner."

"Yeah. Thanks. She was only twenty-two years old."

"Got any idea who killed her?"

"I think it was Charlie Ladd."

"Yeah. I was thinking that, too."

It surprised me that he'd thought about my case at all.

"So you're out of a job now, huh?"

"Well, no." I told him that I had two clients on the case.

"Two to keep you twice as busy?"

"You mad at me, Johnny?"

He looked down at the stoop and let go of my hand. Uh-oh.

"No, I'm not mad. It's just that I never get to see you."

"But ya knew how things were gonna be. Same thing when you have a big case."

"I guess I didn't know how it was *really* going to be. How I'd feel about it." He looked up and into my eyes.

"What're ya sayin, Johnny?"

"I wish I knew."

I didn't like this cat-and-mouse game. "Ya breakin up with me?"

"You don't mess around, do you?"

"I thought that was one a the things ya liked about me."

"I did. I mean, I do. I guess when it comes at me, it's different."

"You didn't answer my question about breakin up?"

"I'm just telling you what's bothering me."

Whew!

He said, "I got the day off tomorrow and I thought we could see a movie in the afternoon, get cool, and then go out to dinner. How about it?"

What was I gonna do? He had to understand, he just had to. "Sounds nice, Johnny, but . . ."

"But you can't."

I nodded.

"The case?"

"Yeah."

He stood up. "I think I'll go now."

My heart did a nosedive. I didn't know what to say. A first.

"Good night, Faye." He pecked my cheek again.

When he got to the bottom of the stoop, I called out to him.

"When will I see ya, Johnny?"

"I'll call you."

"Okay."

I watched him till he got to Grove and Bleecker where he turned left. Then he was out of my sight.

Gone.

THIRTY-THREE

*M*arty honked the horn at eight-thirty. I was dressed and ready to go but I felt down in the mouth. Sleep wasn't my pal the night before. I kept waking up thinking of Johnny, feeling confused, sad, angry. I'd lost him, but I had to remind myself that if he wanted a gal who'd stick to tending the home fires, he wasn't for me. I didn't want him. Where'd I get the impression he liked me being a PI? What a dope I'd been.

I shook Johnny from my mind. I had to. It was so

strange leaving my place not to see Dolores sweeping. I'd stop by when I got back from the shore.

Outside, Marty was sitting at the wheel of a beat-up gray two-door. It was a far cry from Jim's LaSalle. But it would get us where we wanted to go.

When I got in he said, "Ya look too pooped to pop. What happened to ya?"

"Couldn't sleep."

"You really think yer on to somethin, don'tcha?"

I let him think that was the reason I was so wrung out. "You bet. Any trouble gettin the car?"

"Nope. Good thing it's got an X sticker so I could fill her up."

"No limit on that one?"

"Nope. Believe it or not, this baby comes under the emergency vehicle list."

"Why?"

"Beats me."

"What's yer friend do?"

He shrugged, and I knew I oughta drop that subject.

"What is this car, anyway?"

"A 1940 Chevy coupe. Lotsa mileage on her but she runs good. Ya ready?"

"Sure."

We took off.

It was a long ride and I was ready for lunch by the time we got to Asbury Park. But I knew that had to wait. Marty had directions for St. Mary's orphanage and headed there. I didn't hold out a lotta hope they'd cough up much of anything, but I hadda give it a try.

As we approached, the place loomed up, looking like the orphanages of my imagination and maybe ones I'd seen in movies. The building, made of gray brick, had half a dozen towers, and the windows were covered with a tight-knit wire.

"Homey," Marty said.

I couldn't laugh cause all I could think about were the kids who were inside.

"Park over there," I said.

We got out of the car and stood staring at the grim façade for a few seconds.

"Let's go," I said.

The gravel path had no flowers along its edges. And the brownish grass grew right up to the building, no shrubs or bushes laid out in a border. The big double doors were dark oak and I suddenly felt I wouldn't be able to open them. But Marty did it for me.

The moment we stepped inside I smelled disinfectant. It was dark and cold. Straight in front of us was a counter with a nun behind it.

"May I help you?"

I had no history of nuns in my life, but the face that looked out at us from the black-and-white head garb gave me the creeps. Close up I saw that she was kinda pretty and I was mad at myself for feeling afraid. Maybe I should stop going to the pictures.

Marty had taken off his hat and held it with both hands in front of him.

"Good mornin, Sister."

She nodded.

"My name is Faye Quick and this is Detective Marty Mitchum from the NYPD."

"Oh, you're detectives?"

"Yes, Sister."

"How exciting. Do you have some identification?"

We each handed over our IDs and she pored over em like they were scriptures. Finally she gave them back.

"What's your name, Sister?" Marty asked.

"Sister Margaret Agnes."

"Well, Sister, we'd like some help. We're lookin for a child that mighta been left here by mistake."

"Oh?"

"Terrible thing," Marty said.

"That would be terrible if a child were left here by mistake. But I've never known it to happen." She sugar-smiled and cocked her head to one side.

This nun was no sitting duck. It wasn't gonna be easy. "There's always a first time," I said. And smiled back at her.

"Tell me the tale," she said.

So I told her what I'd cooked up.

"Sometime in the last year a girl had a baby boy out of wedlock. A few days later her sister kidnapped the child and we're pretty sure she brought him here. Then the mother died." I tried to work up some tears. "Now the father wants him back. And Detective Mitchum and I have been hired to find the boy."

"I hope you know I can't show you any records."

"Of course. See, the sister knows the father is tryin

to get the boy back. We think she may've been here in the last week and tried to take the boy."

"If she did, I can't tell you that, either. But it's doubtful because we don't hand over babies to just anyone."

"No. I didn't think ya did. What we really wanna know is if anyone *tried* to get a child back in the past week."

Marty said, "That wouldn't be breakin any rules, would it, Sister Margaret Agnes?"

"Are you a Catholic, Detective Mitchum?"

Marty's face started flushing. "I was raised a Catholic, Sister."

"But you're not a practicing Catholic now. Is that it?"

"Yes, Sister." He looked like a little boy who'd been caught stealing.

"And you, Miss Quick? Are you a Catholic?"

"No, Sister, I'm not."

"I see."

I had no idea what that *I see* meant. "So can ya tell us if a girl was askin about a little boy in the last week?"

She closed her eyes and kept them closed. I looked at Marty. He put his hands in the prayer position to let me know what the sister was doing. Finally her eyes opened.

"I don't see what harm it will do to tell you. Yes. There was a girl here asking for a boy. Now, that's all I'm going to tell you so don't try to get more information from me."

"No, we won't," Marty said.

"That's a real big help, Sister Margaret Agnes. We can't thank ya enough."

"Oh, you probably can." The smile again.

"How?"

She shifted her eyes to look past my shoulder. I turned around. But since I didn't know what I was looking for I was in the dark.

Marty said, "Yes, sure, Sister. We'd be glad to. Thanks for everything."

"Thank you, Sister," I said.

Marty put his hand on my arm as we turned to leave and guided me to the left. On the wall was a locked box. A slot in the center had DONATIONS painted on it in white.

I dug in my purse and came up with the loot. Marty took his from his pant pocket. We slipped our donations into the box and left the orphanage.

We didn't say a word to each other until we were back in the car.

"Do ya think the girl was Lucille?" Marty said.

"I'd bet anything on it."

"She mighta gotten the kid, but maybe not. I don't think it'd be a cinch."

"Kid or no kid I think she'll be in Point Pleasant."

"Me, too."

Marty started the car.

"Can we look for a place to eat along the way?" I said.

"I'm already lookin."

The summer was in full swing. We passed lots of people in bathing suits and kids carrying rubber rafts. All of them had tans. I got a load of the beach and water in flashes and wished I'd brought my suit.

Asbury Park hadda be the big city around here cause after it the towns got smaller. When we hit one named Belmar, we spotted a little restaurant across the road from the beach.

Marty slowed down. "Whaddaya think?"

"I think I'm hungry and it looks fine."

He parked in front. Loy's Lobster looked like a buncha other joints I'd eaten in, but inside it was decorated with fishnets, lifesavers, and big stuffed fish hanging on the walls. We didn't look like we belonged cause everyone else was in beach clothes. I'd dressed to be cool and Marty was wearing a short-sleeve shirt. Still, we were pasty next to the other customers.

We took a table near the big plate-glass window; across the street between two houses I could see a strip of beach and patch of water. A waitress brought us menus.

"Anything to drink?"

"Ya got beer?"

"Why wouldn't we have beer?"

He shrugged. "I'll take a Rheingold. How about you, Faye?"

"If ya got lemonade, I'll have that."

"Rheingold and lemonade comin up," she said.

We both fired up cigs before we looked at the

menus. I saw what I wanted right away. Fried clams. I'd never had them, but I'd read about them in books more than once. They came with fries, which was fine by me.

When the waitress came back with our drinks, she took out her pad and pencil. I gave her my order.

"Burger," Marty said. "Well done."

She looked at him and shook her head in disgust. "Loy's is famous for its seafood, ya know."

"Burger," he said again.

"Okay, but ya don't know what yer missin."

"I'm missin a pain in my gut."

"Fried bother ya?" she said.

He nodded.

"It don't have to be fried."

"Thanks, but I don't like fish."

"Sometimes," she said, and walked off.

Marty took a swig of his beer. "So how're we gonna find her?"

"Real estate agents."

"Faye, she coulda rented a place from anywhere and she coulda rented it under a different name."

"I know it's not gonna be easy, but ya got a better idea?"

"Nope."

"So then that's what we try first. And as for her rentin from an agent in another town besides Point Pleasant, I don't think so. Why would she?"

"Why wouldn't she?"

"If ya wanted to live in Point Pleasant, wouldn't ya

start by goin to a real estate place in that town?"

"Yer right. At least that's where we should start. But here's what I don't get, Faye. Say we find her, what then? I mean, what's she done besides move?"

"Maybe nothin. But why move at this time? Why ditch yer place, leave yer job, and take a powder at the exact same time yer sister is killed after deliverin a ransom for the kidnappin of the mug that maybc raped ya?"

"She left before Claire was killed."

"Don't pick nits with me, Marty. I'm makin a point here. It's all too much of a coincidence and it doesn't stack up with me."

The waitress was back with my clams and Marty's pathetic-looking burger.

I forked one of the fried clams, dipped it into a tartar sauce, and popped it into my mouth. Delicious. How could I have missed these little darlings? While I ate my lunch, all my problems seemed to vanish.

Back in the car we headed for Point Pleasant. I liked how everything looked. Maybe someday I'd settle down in a beach house. On the other hand, I'd miss the beat of New York. But when I was old, without Johnny, it might be nice to get away from the noise. At a town called Brielle we went over a little bridge across the Manasquan River—so said a sign—and then we were in Point Pleasant.

"So now we start lookin for real estate agencies?"

"Right."

Wc saw one almost immediately, but it was no help.

By the time we were on our third I had a ghost of an idea cooking, but I didn't say anything to Marty. I thought I'd wait to see what happened.

Inside the agency, a man too old for the war sat behind a desk. He wasn't old old, maybe in his fifties. The nameplate on his desk said MR. CLARK ANDREWS. His hair was receding and his chin had already doubled. His brown eyes were wide apart and unmemorable.

"May I help you nice people?"

Now how in Hades did he know if we were nice or not?

"We're lookin fer a person, not a place, Mr. Andrews. Well, that's not quite right. We're lookin fer a place somebody mighta rented in the last few weeks."

"I don't follow," he said.

"We're from the New York Police Department," Marty said.

Andrews backed his chair into the wall as if one of us had given him a big push. "What do you mean? Why are you here? If something's wrong, why aren't the New Jersey police here?"

Marty and I exchanged a fast glance and I knew we were thinking the same thing. Mr. Andrews had something to hide. I didn't care what it was cause it was gonna be helpful to us.

"The New Jersey police have turned it over to us."

"Omigod."

"Just relax," Marty said.

"Relax?"

"Have a smoke." I offered him one of mine, which he took. Marty lit it for him. Mr. Andrews took a huge drag and released it in a trickle like he could put off whatever was coming as long as there was smoke in his lungs.

"We'd like to know if you've rented any bungalows to a woman alone, or with a young child?"

"I have to . . . I have to look at my records. Is that all you want to know?"

"That depends," Marty said.

"On what?"

"Let's stick to my question," I said.

Andrews looked like he might faint. He opened a large journal and ran his finger down the page. "Yes. Yes, I thought I remembered this. A woman did rent a bungalow on the beach but not with a child."

"That's okay. What's the address?"

"Well, there's no real address. There's a sign outside that says Lion in the Sun. L-i-o-n."

"Cute."

"Everyone names their place. I don't make up the names."

"Didn't think ya did."

"You just keep going on this road and you'll find it." His fingers were going so fast on his desk he coulda been beating out the story of his life in Morse code.

"What's the woman's name?"

"She was very lovely. Her name was Lana Tierney."

THIRTY-FOUR

*M*arty and I knew that runaways or criminals often kept their own initials when they gave themselves a new name. Lana Tierney. Lucille Turner.

"It's her," I said.

"Yeah."

"Let's go get her."

Marty started the car and I began looking on the beach side of the road for Lion in the Sun. It was hot and humid with a fog cover coming in over the water. We didn't see a lotta people walking along cause they were probably on the beach. Mr. Andrews had been right. Everybody named their cottages: Paradise Found; Hook Line and Sinker; Coffey Grounds. I wondered what it was that made people name their houses and their cars.

There was plenty of space around each house for privacy. It did look appealing. What would it feel like to wake up and look out at the ocean? But what would you do after a few days of lying on the beach and swimming? It was quiet and peaceful and I knew I'd grow to hate it.

"There it is," I said.

"Lion in the Sun."

There was a sandy driveway so Marty turned in but parked the car close to the road. The cottage looked more like a regular house to me. It had dark brown shingles, two stories, and a small screened-in porch. The front, which we couldn't see, faced the ocean.

We walked up the driveway along the side of the house to the front. She was sitting on the porch like she was waiting for us, but I knew she wasn't.

"Lucille," I said.

She glanced up from the book she was reading then almost knocked over her drink when she recognized me and jumped to her feet. Her book dangled from her hand. She was wearing blue shorts and a white blouse, with gym shoes on her feet and the beginnings of a tan.

"What're you doing here?" she said.

"Looking for you."

"Why?"

We walked around the porch to the three steps up.

"Can we?" I asked.

"Can I stop you?"

She gestured to two white wooden chairs. We took them. Even though it was shady it was still hot. Even the wind coming off the ocean didn't help much.

I introduced Lucille to Marty.

"Can I get you something to drink?" Lucille asked. "I'm having a Tom Collins."

As thirsty as I was, I didn't want her to leave my sight. "No, thanks."

"Not right now," Marty said.

"It's no trouble," she said.

I remembered the back door and as she kept asking I thought that might be what was on her mind.

I said, "Lucille, what're ya doin here?"

"I'm on vacation," she said.

"Ya didn't let Mr. Mostel know ya were takin one. How come?"

"Is that what he said?"

"Yeah. He did. Said ya didn't show up."

"He's getting senile, I think. He must've forgotten."

"And how come yer house's been cleaned out?"

"I don't know what you mean."

I tapped a Camel from my pack and lit it. "Do we have to play this game? We know ya took a powder from yer job and yer house, okay?"

She bit her lower lip and her eyes got misty.

"Why don'tcha tell us about it," Marty said.

"There's nothing to tell. I got tired of working and tired of that place. That's all there is to it." She lit up with her Zippo.

"Did ya get tired of yer sister, too?"

"What's that supposed to mean?"

"Why'd ya kill her, Lucille?"

Her mouth fell open and her shock looked genuine.

"Claire? Claire's dead?"

Marty and I kept our traps shut. I listened to the sound of the waves hitting the shore. It had a soothing effect on me.

"Tell me. Is Claire dead?"

"I think ya know the answer to that question, Lucille," I said. "But yeah, she's dead. Murdered."

"Murdered? You're sure?"

"Absolutely sure."

"But . . . I don't understand. Why?"

"What is it ya don't understand?"

"Why anyone would kill Claire. Do you think it had something to do with Charlie Ladd's kidnapping?" She killed her cigarette in a small tin can on the table next to her. The hiss told me there was liquid in it.

"First off, Ladd was never kidnapped. Second, Claire went off to make the money drop and was never seen again until she turned up dead."

"What do you mean, Charlie was never kidnapped?"

"Why don't *you* tell *us,*" Marty said.

"I don't know what you're talking about. Miss Quick, when you came to see me last week, you told me Charlie'd been kidnapped."

"That's what we thought then."

"What changed your minds?"

"Charlie takin a potshot at one of my neighbors."

"Now I *really* don't know what you're talking about."

"Ya might not. It all depends."

"On what?"

"How much ya were let in on the whole deal."

"What deal?" She lit another cig.

"Let's put it this way, Lucille. If you didn't kill Claire, who did?"

"I don't know." Her eyes told me she *did* know. "I can't believe Claire's dead. I don't mean I don't believe you, I mean, she's my baby sister."

"Yer baby sister ya no longer talked to?"

"I, I lied about that."

"Why?"

"I can't tell you."

"Listen, Lucille, Detective Mitchum can take ya back to New York and book ya for yer sister's murder, ya don't start comin clean with us."

"I don't know anything about Claire's murder. I don't."

"Why'd ya say ya hadn't talked to her?"

"I told you. I can't tell you that." She took a quick glance at her wristwatch, trying to seem casual. It didn't work. "I think you'd better go now."

"Is that right?" Marty said. "Suppose I tell ya we ain't goin until we're good and ready. Unless ya wanna come with us."

"All right," she said. "I'll come with you."

I was caught off base by this one and I couldn't imagine that Marty wasn't, too.

"You'll come with us?" I asked.

"Yes. You want to arrest me for Claire's murder. Let's do it now." She stood.

I got it. Someone was about to show that Lucille didn't want us to see. "But ya said ya didn't kill her."

"I lied. I lie about everything. Haven't you caught on to that yet, Miss Quick?"

"No."

"Then you're pretty slow on the uptake."

Marty said, "Are ya tellin us now that ya killed yer sister?"

"Yes."

"How?" I asked.

378

"How?"

"Yeah. A simple enough question. Ya can even lie about it if ya like. But if ya want us to believe ya, ya'd better tell us the truth. So how'd ya kill her, Lucille?"

She stared at us, then at the floorboards. Finally she raised her head. "I stabbed her."

"Where?"

"In her heart."

"Ya sure of that?"

"Well, that was the most serious place. I stabbed her everywhere. I was in a frenzy. I didn't know what I was doing."

"Temporary insanity?" I asked.

"Yes."

"So ya just kept stabbin her all over, huh?"

She brought her hands up to her face and I heard her starting to cry. I didn't say anything for a while. Neither did Marty.

Finally she dropped her hands. Her face was a mess of mascara. Tears kept running down her cheeks. They were real.

"Nice try," I said. "Claire was strangled."

"I told you I lie."

"Don't even bother with that one. Ya didn't kill yer sister. Charlie Ladd did."

"Oh, he wouldn't." She sounded panicked.

"No? Why not?"

"They were engaged."

I almost laughed. "That hasn't always been a crime stopper, Lucille."

Marty said, "You mean he loved her too much to kill her?"

"Something like that."

"How come yer defendin this guy who raped ya, Lucille? Or did ya lie about that, too?"

"Yes, I lied."

"Well, I don't lie. Claire's dead after deliverin a lotta money to the so-called kidnapper, who I think was Charlie himself. Then Charlie tried to kill me, but I wasn't home. So he shot my neighbor instead." I took a flier: "And now yer waitin here for Charlie Ladd to show up."

Her eyes widened. She twisted around like she was literally looking for a way out. But there wasn't any. She knew she couldn't get past Marty to the shore, and she couldn't get past me to go inside the house. But then she fooled us both and made a run for the part of the porch behind her and jumped the railing.

We stalled for a second out of surprise, then we both hurled ourselves over the railing and made tracks after her. She had a pretty good lead, but I was faster than Marty and caught up with her first. I grabbed her arm but she slipped easily out of my grip and took off again. I didn't have a choice. I tackled her. We both went down with a thump. I was glad it was in the sand of an empty lot.

Marty appeared next to us. He was breathing hard. I got off her but held on to her collar. Marty cuffed her.

"Okay, that's it," he said. "Yer comin back to New York with us."

"You can't do this," she said.

"Watch me."

We helped her to her feet, then walked toward her house one on each side. She complained the whole way there. We went onto the porch.

"Ya got anything interestin to say?" Marty asked.

"I didn't kill my sister."

"That's not interestin cause ya keep changin yer mind. So which is it, lady? First no, then yes, now no."

"I think Lucille wanted to get us away from here," I said.

"Please take these things off me. I'm not going any- where. Where would I go?"

I gave the nod to Marty.

He shook his head. "She's a suspect, Faye."

"But she didn't kill Claire."

"Why? Because she says so?"

"Because I don't think she's capable of that. Charlie Ladd killed Claire. What was the deal the three of ya had, Lucille?"

"Please take these handcuffs off. They hurt."

"Yer worried, Marty, cuff her to the chair."

He unlocked the cuffs but left one on and let her sit down. Then he snapped the other cuff around a slat in the arm of the chair.

"I need a cigarette," she said.

Her pack was lying on the table next to the arm she was cuffed to. I got one out for her and she took it with her left hand, put it in her mouth. I picked up her Zippo and lit it.

"Where'd ya get this lighter?"

"I don't remember."

"Sure ya do. A soldier gave it to ya. Charlie?"

"No."

"I thought ya didn't remember." I didn't wait for another lie. "Why don't we move the table to her left side," I said. I didn't feature being her servant.

Marty moved it.

"Now ya can be self-sufficient," I said. She didn't thank me.

"Whose idea was it, Lucille?" Marty asked.

She laid her glims on him like he was dirt. I hadn't seen this look on her before.

"Answer him," I said.

"Why should I?"

"Because he asked."

"You people make me sick."

"The feelin is mutual," I said. "Even so, we wanna know who was the big brain behind it all."

"What difference does it make?"

"Look, ya don't get to decide what questions make a difference."

"Says who?"

"Says us who got ya handcuffed to a chair. I guess ya could say we're in the driver's seat," Marty said.

"Lucille, ya gonna get yer little boy back?" I said.

Her head snapped up like I'd pulled her hair hard. "Who told you that?"

"Never mind who," Marty said. "Stop askin questions. We're askin the questions."

"So ya gettin the boy back?" I said.

"I don't know."

"If she was, she ain't now. Murderesses don't get to have their kids."

"I didn't murder anybody."

"Yeah, you and Bonnie Parker," Marty said. "Two peas in a pod."

"But I didn't. I couldn't. Especially Claire."

"Then we're back to square one, Lucille."

"What's that?"

"Charlie Ladd killed yer sister."

"I can't believe that. He wouldn't hurt her."

"You of all people know how violent he can get," I said.

"I told you. I lied about that, too."

"I don't believe ya."

She shrugged.

"But ya were pregnant."

"Yes, I was."

"So who was the father?"

"My husband."

THIRTY-FIVE

*W*ho's your husband?"

"I'd rather not say."

"Lady, you're behind the eight ball," Marty said. "Ya better start spillin."

"Is your husband Charlie Ladd?" I said.

383

"My husband is dead."

Everyone was silent. I looked out at the sea. I could hear tiny yelps from kids on the beach, others in the water, heads bobbing, parents yelling for their kids not to go out so far. It all looked idyllic, but here I sat with a girl who was a liar and who was telling me her husband was dead.

Lucille reached toward the pocket in her shorts.

"Hey," Marty said and pointed his gun at her.

"I want a Kleenex."

"Bring it out slow," he said.

"Marty, she couldn't have a gun in there."

"Ya never know."

"I don't own a gun, Detective." She pulled out a crumpled tissue and wiped the corners of her mouth.

I didn't know why that was necessary.

"Your husband die in the war?"

"No."

"That lighter his?"

"Yes."

"So he was a soldier?"

"Yes."

"How long's he been dead?"

"Not long."

I felt a chill cause I knew.

"Was your husband Private David Cooper?" I said. She didn't even blink. "Yes."

"Holy mackerel," Marty said.

"I guess things got kinda bungled, didn't they?" I said.

"Is that how you see murder, Miss Quick? Something bungled."

"It's how I see a deal like this one. Who're ya expectin today, Charlie?"

"Yes."

"Aren't ya a little annoyed with him for bumpin off Cooper?"

"I don't believe he did that. He'd have no reason."

"You were gonna split the ransom in half, weren't ya? Half to Charlie and Claire and half to you and David," I said.

"Yes."

"Half to you and half to Charlie's even better."

"Depends how you look at it."

"Maybe Charlie's lookin to keep it all himself."

"What do you mean?" she said.

"I mean when he gets here, maybe he's plannin to kill ya."

I could see her face grow paler even though it was lightly tanned.

"You think that, Miss Quick, because you're assuming Charlie killed Claire and David. I don't think he did."

"Then who did?"

"I don't know. But Charlie's a decent guy."

"Very decent," I said. "If nothin else, he's swindled his own father."

"William Ladd can afford it."

"So that makes it okay?"

"It helps." She dropped her cig in the can and it did

its hissing routine again.

"You're some hard-boiled dame, ain't ya," Marty said.

She said nothing.

"Let's get back to Charlie. What time's he comin here?"

She looked at her ticker. "Soon. Half an hour, maybe less."

"Marty, we hafta hide the car."

"I'll find a place." He stirred his stumps, tore down the steps and around the house.

I looked at Lucille. Funny how things could change. When I first met her, I saw her as innocent and pretty. Now she looked evil and kinda ugly to me.

"You're the boss of this whole thing, aren't ya?"

A smile came and went so fast I almost missed it.

"How'd ya let things get so outta hand?"

"I don't know what you're talking about," she said.

"I think ya do."

She shrugged. "I'd like another Tom Collins."

"Too bad," I said. "And don't try anything, Lucille, cause you may not have a gun, but I do." This time *I* was lying. I hadn't brought my gun with me. I hated the thing and kept it in a box on a shelf in my closet. Now I wished I had it. Yeah, Woody, I know.

"When Marty comes back, I want ya to show us a place for us to hide."

"Sure," she said.

"Don't tip Charlie to us bein wherever we're hidin cause I don't think ya know who yer dealin with."

"You?" Her mouth worked itself into a sneer.

"Charlie."

"You're so off base it's funny."

"Keep laughin."

"Oh, I will."

"I guess we'll hafta be somewhere we can keep ya in our sights. I think we'd all better go inside."

"Should I drag the chair with me?" She held up the palm of her cuffed wrist.

"Marty'll be back any second. He's got the keys."

"Miss Quick? What made you think you could be a private detective?"

The question kinda threw me. I knew people laughed and said mean things when I told them my profession, but nobody'd ever asked me that right out.

"Same as you with Charlie."

"I don't see the similarity."

"Your instincts tell ya that he's innocent of any crime, right?"

"Yes."

"I followed my instincts about bein a PI."

"It's hardly the same. Charlie loves me and I love him."

That knocked me into the next week.

Marty clipped up the stairs. "Got it stashed."

"Unlock the cuff. We need to go inside and find a hidin place."

He did and we did. Marty kept his gun on Lucille the whole time. I looked around. The front windows faced the beach. It was furnished in white wicker with colorful pillows. There was a filled bookcase behind the sofa. Another time I'd be looking through the titles.

"What's this?" Marty asked.

"A closet," Lucille said.

He opened it and we could see that there was plenty of room for us.

"Okay. Yer gonna sit right there on the sofa and we're gonna be in the closet. We'll be able to hear and see everything."

"What if he wants a drink?"

"Get him one."

"I don't see why you have to hide."

"Cause maybe he'll tell ya what he's done. Don't try to stop him, Lucille. It'll go easier for ya if ya cooperate."

"You've seen too many movies," she said.

I wondered if that was true.

We all heard it at the same time. A car was pulling up the sandy drive; it stopped next to the porch. Marty and I scrambled to the closet and pulled the door almost closed. I whispered, "Lucille told me she's in love with Charlie." His eyes got big.

I put my finger from the bottom of my nose to my chin across my lips.

"Hey, Lucille. Anyone home?"

"In here."

We heard him bound up the steps, open and close the screen door.

"That's a nice welcome," he said. "Can't even bother to get up and come greet me."

He was wearing civilian clothes and carrying the bag that William Ladd had used for the money. The one Claire carried to Charlie.

"I stubbed my toe," she said.

"Poor baby. Let me see it." He put the bag on the floor.

"Later," she said. "Give me a kiss."

He sat down next to her and they kissed. Long and passionate. She pulled away. "Charlie, I want to ask you something?"

"Sure."

"What happened to Claire?"

"Ah, that was tragic."

"What do you mean?"

"She was all jumpy when she met me with the money, which was understandable. Then she said she wanted to take a walk. I could kick myself, but I was tired and didn't want to go. So she went alone."

Lucille was looking at him with an expression of disbelief. But Charlie was so wrapped up in his story he didn't seem to notice.

"And she didn't come back, and she didn't come back. I was frantic, but I couldn't call the police. I didn't sleep all night. The next day I heard what'd happened. I couldn't believe it. I hate to say it, but it's made things a lot easier for us."

"You *should* hate to say it. Claire was my sister."

"I know, baby. But you didn't seem to have any qualms about telling her about us."

"How do you know? I never got the chance."

"You were willing. I guess it never occurred to you that she might give us trouble, threaten to turn us in."

"And if she did?"

"I thought we'd play it by ear."

"No, seriously, Charlie. What if she'd done that? What would we have done?"

"I don't know. Why're you asking me all these questions? I need a drink."

She started to get up, then stopped. "Oh, my toe."

"I'll get it. Where's the makings?"

"In the kitchen through there."

It was clear he'd never been in this house before. He got up and headed where she'd pointed. Lucille looked strange, still on the fence. She didn't know whether to believe him or not. Good.

When he came back, he said, "Thought any more about where we should go?" He took a long swallow of his drink, then put it on the coffee table. "Got any smokes? I ran out."

"In that," she said.

There was a bamboo box on the table. Charlie took a cigarette from it and lit it with his Zippo. "So have you thought about where to go?"

"Let's talk about David," she said.

"David? Why?"

"He *was* my husband."

"And he never should've been."

"I thought you liked David."

"I thought I did, too. Then I found out he was a kike."

"What?"

"A heeb. You didn't know, did you? Cooper wasn't his real name. It was Kupfermann. The guy was a Jew, Lucille."

"So?"

"A Jew. Didn't you hear me?"

"I heard you. He was a Jew and you killed him because of it?"

"It was an accident. He let slip that he was a Jew bastard and we got into some name-calling. Then he pushed me and I pushed him back and you know how those things go."

"No. I don't know how those things go. Tell me."

"One thing led to another. I didn't mean to kill him, but I have to tell you the truth. I'm not sorry. One less sheeny in the world doesn't break my heart."

"And Claire?"

"I told ya what happened to Claire. You're getting me mad, Lucille. Hey, let me show you the money."

He reached down, lifted the bag, and put it on the coffee table. Then he stood. Before he undid the clasps I told Marty to get ready.

As Charlie reached into the bag and pulled out a gun, we crashed into the room and Marty yelled, "Freeze."

Charlie swiveled around and put his hands in the air, the gun pointing toward the ceiling. "What's this?"

"This is Detective Mitchum from the New York Police Department and Faye Quick, a private detective. Say hello, Charlie."

"Put the gun on the floor and kick it over to me," Marty said. "And do it slow."

He lowered his gun arm slowly and kept going till the piece was on the floor. Then he kicked it over near us. I picked it up.

"You bitch," he said to Lucille.

"You killer," she said. "This was supposed to be about money."

"And how did you think we were going to work things out with Claire and David? Claire was in love with me and that hymie was married to you. You oughta be thanking me for resolving this thing, not siccing the cops on me."

"He's right, Lucille. Ya should be thankin the guy. At least he brought the money. Let's see how much he's still got. Kick the bag over, Charlie."

"What if I don't?"

"Ya don't hafta," I said.

Marty gave me a quick, confused look.

"Get up and go over to the window."

"Ya heard her, bub."

"Why?"

"Just do it," Marty said.

Charlie sighed and walked around the coffee table. When he got even with me, he reached out and grabbed me by the throat, dragging me backward and holding me like a shield between him and Marty. His arm stayed tight around my throat.

"Give me the gun or I'll crush her windpipe."

Marty held the gun on him. "Don't be a jerk, Ladd.

This place is surrounded."

I couldn't see Charlie's face so I didn't know whether he believed Marty or not.

"Sure it is."

"It is," Lucille said.

"I don't believe it."

Lucille said, "Then believe this." And she shot him in the back.

His arm slipped from my neck and slid down me as he started his fall. I turned and watched him crumple to the floor.

He wasn't quite dead. He managed a last sentence. "We could've had it all, Lucille." And followed that with a whoosh which turned out to be his last breath.

Lucille sat on the couch, the gun in her lap. I walked over and picked up Charlie's bag. I turned it upside down and nothing fell out. No surprise to me, but I could see it was to Lucille.

"Just in case you had any second thoughts about killin this guy. And by the way, I thought ya didn't have a gun."

"I lied," she said.

THIRTY-SIX

*L*ucille was charged with aiding and abetting a conspiracy. The murder charge against her was dropped cause I said she saved my life. Which she did. Besides, she was gonna be in jail a long time until the case came to trial since she had no money for bail.

After the money in Charlie's car was returned to William Ladd, he went home to Jennifer and God knows what they told each other about their golden boy, Charles Ladd.

Raymond and Thelma Cooper tried to make do with the knowledge that their son's killer had been identified and killed. I don't think it did a thing for them.

The Turners had lost both of their daughters, in a way. I'm not sure the father cared. The mother was another story. Still, she'd stay with him, listen for the rest of her life to her husband calling both her girls whores and worse.

Van Widmark missed both Claire and Lucille. But nothing much changed for him. I promised myself I'd visit him if he'd let me, but I wondered if I would.

Marty got a commendation for breaking the case. Detectives Powell and Stevens tried for the glory, but it didn't work.

Stork got a bottle of Johnnie Walker from me, which I knew was his favorite, cause he'd pointed me in the right direction.

Birdie still had Pete. And I gave her a small raise just for being Birdie Ritter.

Dolores was back sweeping the hall floor in front of her apartment and trying out new wigs. She'd changed her tune about Morris since he'd tended her every night. He was her favorite now cause the other one, Larry in California, had sent her a bouquet of flowers but was always too busy to call or visit.

George Cummings and Mr. Cooper each gave me a bunch of money for solving the case. Cummings had the blues over the whole thing but went back to his life.

And me? I put a down payment on a Weber upright piano. I'd pictured a baby grand taking up residence on that spot in my place, but it would take me a lot longer to pay it off. I was high as a kite about almost owning it. Once again, I'd been reminded that life can be unexpectedly short. I'd make the upright work in the space I had.

But I wasn't walking on air every minute cause I was alone, except for Zachary who was growing bigger every day and eating me outta house and home. I missed Johnny like crazy. I thought about giving him a ring but what would I say? I hadda be my own person and that meant doing my job. The thing he didn't like most. So I didn't pick up the phone.

A few days later, as I left my apartment, I wondered when a new case would come my way and what it'd be like.

Dolores was there doing her best to make it to the Clean Hall Hall of Fame.

"Hello, Faye. My bubele who got the man who almost killed me."

I smiled at her. She said this now every time I saw her. She also kept the neighborhood entertained with her near-death story. Each time new details were added, like Dolores almost wrestling Charlie Ladd to the floor before he shot her.

Today she was wearing a yellow sunsuit, a purple

checked blouse underneath it, and a blond wig, reasonably straight, in a pageboy style.

"Why so glum, chum? I learned that from Morris. Speaking of Morris, have you ever known a better boy? He's workin on his art. Paintin great big pictures. Soon he's gonna bring me to his studio to see."

I wondered what Dolores would think of them. Maybe she had a mother's blindness and would love anything he did even if she didn't understand it.

"That's great, Dolores."

"So back to you. You just solved a big case and whaddaya look, down in the dumps."

"I'm fine," I said.

"Okay, if you say so. But ya don't look so fine to me."

"Trust me."

"With my life." She gave me a big smile.

I said again that I was fine, left the building, and got the shock of my life. Detective Johnny Lake was sitting on the bottom step, smoking a butt. When he heard the door close behind me he turned, saw me, and stood up. He tipped his hat.

"Hello, Faye."

"Johnny. What're ya doin here?"

"I came to see you. You going to work?"

"Yeah." To say my heart was doing backflips was soft-pedaling it.

"Mind if I walk you to the subway?"

I came down the stairs. "No. I don't mind."

We started walking toward Seventh Avenue. In the

396

middle of Bleecker I was a step ahead of him when I realized he'd stopped dead. I turned around.

"Faye."

"What?"

"I'm not good with words."

"Sure ya are. Ya didn't have any trouble sayin goodbye." I couldn't help myself.

He looked like I'd given him a kidney punch. "Guess I deserved that."

I shrugged.

"Faye, have you got a new boyfriend?"

"It hasn't been that long, Johnny. You think I'm the kinda girl goes from one to the other?"

"No. No, I didn't mean it that way. I just needed to be sure."

"Sure?"

"Faye, I've been miserable ever since we split."

I thought of saying nothing but I didn't wanna play games. "I haven't been feelin so hot myself."

"So why aren't we together?" he said.

"You know why, Johnny."

"I was being stupid."

"I can agree with that, but it doesn't mean ya changed yer feelings about me and my job."

"I'd rather live with that than live without you."

I didn't know what to say so I stayed buttoned up.

"I'm not pretending that it won't peeve me now and then, but we can nail that down. Can't we?"

"It's you who's gotta nail it down, or not. I do fine with it."

"I heard how you broke that big case."

"I figured most people thought Marty broke it."

He smiled and his eyes played a samba. "I know better. See, I've come to realize you're good at this game. And if you're good, why shouldn't you do it?"

"You on the level, Johnny?"

"Give me another chance and you'll see."

"Why not?" I said. In my head I was clicking my heels. On the one hand, I didn't wanna play games, but on the other, I didn't wanna be too easy.

"You mean it?" he said.

"Sure."

"I'll make it up to you, Faye."

There was nothing more to say right then. He reached out and took my hand in his. We walked silently to the subway, holding hands.

It felt swell.

Center Point Publishing

600 Brooks Road • PO Box 1
Thorndike ME 04986-0001 USA

(207) 568-3717

US & Canada:
1 800 929-9108